5511

W9-AAC-771

Over the Line

WITHDRAWN
BEAVERTON CITY LIBRARY
BEAVERTON, OR 97005
MEMBER OF WASHINGTON COUNTY
COOPERATIVE LIBRARY SERVICES

Also by Emmy Curtis

Dangerous Territory: An Alpha Ops Novella

Over the Line

An Alpha Ops Novel

EMMY CURTIS

New York Boston

This book is a work of fiction. Names, characters, places, and incidents are the product of the author's imagination or are used fictitiously. Any resemblance to actual events, locales, or persons, living or dead, is coincidental.

Copyright © 2014 by Emmy Curtis
Excerpt from *Pushing the Limit* copyright © 2014 by Emmy Curtis
Cover design by Elizabeth Turner
Cover copyright © 2014 by Hachette Book Group, Inc.

All rights reserved. In accordance with the U.S. Copyright Act of 1976, the scanning, uploading, and electronic sharing of any part of this book without the permission of the publisher constitute unlawful piracy and theft of the author's intellectual property. If you would like to use material from the book (other than for review purposes), prior written permission must be obtained by contacting the publisher at permissions@hbgusa.com. Thank you for your support of the author's rights.

Forever Yours
Hachette Book Group
1290 Avenue of the Americas
New York, NY 10104
hachettebookgroup.com
twitter.com/foreverromance

First published as an ebook and as a print on demand: October 2014

Forever Yours is an imprint of Grand Central Publishing.
The Forever Yours name and logo are trademarks of Hachette Book Group, Inc.

The publisher is not responsible for websites (or their content) that are not owned by the publisher.

The Hachette Speakers Bureau provides a wide range of authors for speaking events. To find out more, go to www.hachettespeakersbureau.com or call (866) 376-6591.

ISBN: 978-1-4555-3076-2 (ebook edition)
ISBN: 978-1-4555-3094-6 (print on demand edition)

With love to the Chief, as always.

Acknowledgments

As always, this book is for my husband who has supported my dream to write for many, many years. All my heroes have aspects of him in them, but only he knows which parts…

I'd like to thank Heather for giving me some breathing space at work, and Tahra and Mary for their support and crazy willingness to stay up all night reading for me.

Thank you to Leah, who never panics when I e-mail her asking her to remind me when my deadline is, and to the whole team at Grand Central Publishing's Forever Yours imprint for giving me awesome covers, and awesome support.

And lastly, to the beautiful little girl (and her mum) who lent me my name: Thank you, Emmy.

If you enjoy reading about Senior Master Sergeant James Walker and are interested in supporting the USAF community of TACPs, please go here to see the good work the TACP Association does for the families of their fallen American heroes: usaftacp.org.

"The strong will stand, the weak will fall by the wayside."

—The Tactical Air Control Party's motto

Over the Line

Chapter 1

Khost Province, Afghanistan

Alone at last," Walker whispered as he crouched next to Beth. Dust flew up as the crack of a bullet hitting the ground ricocheted around the valley. He flattened himself next to her.

"You are *shit* at taking orders," she hissed back.

He ignored her as he tried to figure out where the shots were coming from. If he could just neutralize the immediate threat, he could patch her up and get her to safety. His blood had flashed ice-cold when she radioed that she'd been hit. And she'd still been laying down covering fire for the guys when he'd found her. If she was the first taste of females in combat, bring it on.

A pool of dark blood glistened in the hazy moonlight, expanding and trickling across the sand as he watched.

Crap.

Their simple mission of relieving another patrol group had gone to hell in a handbasket. Another shot echoed around them, and this time Walker was ready to identify the telltale muzzle flash. As soon as he saw it, he swung his gun and sent a shot downrange toward the insurgent.

Silence. He took that as a good sign.

"Okay, Sergeant. Turn over so I can look at that leg."

Beth grunted but complied, biting back a moan as she did.

Walker's heart dropped when he saw that her BDU pants were completely soaked with blood. A lot of it. *Shit.* Maybe the bullet had nicked an artery. He grabbed his knife and cut away the pant leg to expose the wound. It was about two inches below her panty line. And blood was still pumping out in rhythm with her heartbeat.

He undid her belt and pulled it off. No way was he going to let her die in this crappy valley, in the middle of Shithole City, Bumfuck. No fucking way.

As he slid the belt around the top of her thigh, trying not to touch anything that could get him court-martialed, one of the Strike Eagles he had called for screamed overhead. He threw himself over Beth, and waited for the bombs to drop.

They exploded with precision, of course. Walker had been the one to give them the coordinates. That was his job. The only air force guy on the team, he was the one who communicated with the aircraft patrolling the skies above the war zone. The only one who could give the bombers precise targets. The valley lit up with orange fire as they detonated. Rocks and scree sprinkled them, sounding like heavy rain, feeling like stones.

That should keep the Taliban out of his hair for a bit. He made to get up and realized how close to Beth's face his was. He hesitated for a split second. A bad, bad second. He'd been deployed with her unit for a couple of months and had spent most of the time dreaming about her at night, and trying to ignore those dreams by day.

He swallowed, and went back to business. "I have to tourniquet your leg. It's going to hurt like a fucker," he said as he fastened the belt as high on her thigh as he could manage. "Just think, all this time I wanted to see your panties, and finally…"

Beth opened her mouth, probably to give him hell, and he used the distraction to pull the belt tight.

"You bastard," she ground out between gritted teeth.

The wound stopped pumping blood and he silently thanked whoever was looking out for them upstairs. He grabbed the first-aid kit from his pack and took out gauze and dark green bandages. A shot sounded again, and sand flew up just inches away from his foot.

Shit.

Walker threw himself down again, this time lying between her legs, face about five inches from her wound. Which meant it was seven inches from her…

"Well, this is awkward," he murmured. It worked, and in relief he heard her gasp a laugh.

"Next time…buy me dinner…first, all right?" she said between pants of Lamaze-type breathing.

He laughed quietly. "I've got to get you out of here first. Then I promise I will." He loosened the tourniquet, and watched to see if the blood flow had stopped. It hadn't, but it wasn't pumping out as it had been before. He tightened it and vowed not to check again.

"Walker," she ground out. "I have a letter. It's in my pants pocket." She groaned as if she was trying to get control over the pain. "Take it out before it gets soaked in blood. Make sure my sister gets it if I…don't make it."

He didn't waste time placating her; he stuffed his hand into her thigh pocket and grabbed the papers in there. He found the letter and stuffed it in his own pocket, before replacing the note-book and loose papers back in hers. "Got it. I'll look after it. But I'm going to do everything I can to get you home to her, okay?"

"Look!" Beth grimaced as she propped herself up on one elbow and pointed up the valley where they had left their truck. A huge cloud of sand was making its way toward them, seem-ingly in slow motion. She made as if to get up, but fell back down with a moan as soon as she tried her leg.

The impending sandstorm made up his mind. They couldn't get stuck in it—Beth would die in all likelihood. If they didn't move now, the storm would be on them, and no rescue would be able to get to them until it dissipated. No time for second-guessing.

A cloud passed in front of the moon, and Walker instinctively jumped up. "Put your weight on your good leg." He held her opposite hand as if they were about to shake hands, and he pulled her up. "Come on, Garcia. Walk it off."

She breathed a laugh as he bent his knees and gently slid her over his shoulder in a fireman's carry, so her good leg bore the brunt of pressure against his shoulder. She wriggled pretty weakly in protest.

"What the fuck? Put me down. I can walk," she said, her words not reflected by the strain in her voice.

Yeah, not so much. "Sure you can, sweetheart…I mean Ser-geant. But we need to run. Are you going to stay with me?"

"I've got your six," she whispered.

He launched his pack on his other shoulder and took off, away from the sandstorm. He knew he could outrun it—it was slow-moving—but the quicker he could get her to a reasonable land-ing zone, the quicker the helicopters would land and get her to a hospital.

The cloud passed the moon and in the sudden light they were sitting ducks. Another shot rang out, whizzing past so close he could feel it rip the air next to his face. Beth's stomach tensed muscles against his shoulder and she pulled herself up. One hell of a soldier. One hell of a woman.

She let off three shots as he ran, and then she flopped back down. "Got him," she said. And then there was silence except for his own breathing that filled his head. Blood pounded in his ears as he ran. Blood pumping, and breath puffing.

In out, in out, nearly there, nearly there.

His muscles strained under her weight, and the eighty pounds of their combined body armor, but he'd trained for this, and frankly, it wasn't his first rodeo. It was his eighth. His legs kept pumping toward safety.

He hoped.

The familiar *whop whop* of a helicopter penetrated his thoughts, as well as the more constant gunshots as he neared the last of their vehicles. Five soldiers were on the ground, firing their weapons into the hills opposite them.

He skidded to a halt and laid Beth down. He dropped alongside her and asked for a sit rep from the guys.

"Marks took one to the face. We lost him. There seem to be about eight TBs left in the hillside, but they're not giving up. Only small arms fired, so I figured the helo can land over there to the right of the valley entrance." The soldier pointed to the only real possible landing zone for the choppers.

"I have to go clear the LZ, Beth. I'll be back." He looked at her but she didn't look back. Eyes closed and barely breathing, she looked like she had already checked out. His heart clenched.

No. Fucking. Way. He pulled the tourniquet tight again, and started CPR. "Hey, you." He slapped the nearest soldier on his helmet. "I need you to do CPR while I clear the landing zone, okay? Keep the tourniquet tight."

The soldier took over without question. And then realized who it was. "Shit, is this Garcia? Oh man, my wife will kill me if I let her die," he said.

"So will I. Keep that thought in the very front of your mind. I'll be back in a few." He hesitated for a second. Could he trust the soldier with her? Everything in him wanted to stay and breathe life into her himself, but he was the only one who could talk the pararescuers in, and the only one who could clear a landing zone to the pilots' satisfaction.

Walker grabbed his radio and one of the soldiers' flashlights, and ran to the potential LZ. He walked the square, checking for IEDs or anything suspicious. He didn't think there would be, because the convoy had passed over this area on their way into the valley. He could still see their tire tracks. But it was better to be safe than sorry. As he paced, he couldn't stop thinking about Beth. How pale and lifeless she looked in the moonlight, how shallow her breathing, and how totally opposite that was to how she normally was: vibrant, prickly, beautiful, and strong.

The gentle *whop whop* of the helicopters became much louder as he finalized checking the LZ. He took out his radio.

"This is Playboy. PJs come in."

There were a few seconds of silence, during which he checked his radio for loose wires. Then, "This is PJ one, Playboy. How're we looking?"

"We have five able soldiers, one KIA, and one seriously injured. I've set up the landing zone at these coordinates." He rattled off a series of numbers.

"Can you light it up?"

"Roger that." Walker snapped some green chem lights from

his pocket, and threw them to the corners of the cleared landing zone. He would normally use flares, but he didn't want to give the Taliban an invitation to pick the PJs as their new target. Once it was clear the helo was good to land, he sprinted back to Beth. *Please, God. I'll do anything if you just let me get her to the hospital alive.*

The second trail helicopter opened fire into the hills, backing up the guys on the ground. Two Combat Rescue Officers ran from the helicopter toward them, weapons drawn. They took one look at Beth and started work on her. They secured her tourniquet and put an oxygen mask over her face.

Walker stood back and let them run with her back to the helo. His heart rate finally normalized, but the clenched fist in his stomach did not fade. Following the others to safety, all he could see was Beth's white face, and he wondered if she would live to have the promised dinner with him. As he unclenched his fists to climb into the Pave Hawk helo, he realized his fingers were crossed.

Chapter 2

Womack Hospital, Fort Bragg; nine months later

Army Sergeant Beth Garcia ran with determination. She imagined flying by the Washington Monument, the Lincoln Memorial, the reflecting pool, all places she'd never seen in real life... and she would have pulled off her fantasy if not for the constant chatter of the colonel running on the treadmill next to her. Bluetooth was the very devil.

Her reverie interrupted, she couldn't help feeling for her healed bullet wound. The puckered skin moved under her fingers as she ran, reminding her of that FUBAR night in Afghanistan.

Her leg was better. Had been for months, but the powers that be insisted on eight months of physical therapy before she could be cleared to go back on a deployable status. If she didn't complete another deployment, she wouldn't be competitive for her dream job: CIA Protection Officer. She didn't need another deployment, not really, but she knew it would be the one thing on paper that would negate her injury.

She didn't feel like herself when she was twisting in the wind, assigned to a desk and returning each night to her house and dog. She only felt like herself when adrenaline was coursing through her veins, and adrenaline had been hard to come by this past year.

She tried to focus on her leg and how it felt, sending repairing vibes to the wound that only gave her a small twinge every now and again.

Where the hell was her physical therapist? The sooner she could get signed off, the sooner she could flag her availability for deployment. There was only so far she could run. The odometer on the treadmill said she had already run six miles. She looked around for the person who had pushed the start button—she couldn't get off it without a therapist seeing that she could in fact run. For the love of God, where was she?

Sweat dripped down her face, throat, and back. She was going to need one hell of a shower before heading back to her unit. Just as she was losing the will to live, the therapist came back to her, hit "Stop" on the treadmill, and handed over her medical papers.

"You really mustn't overdo it, young lady," she said.

Are you freaking kidding me? I could have run for two miles if you hadn't effed off for a coffee break or torture training or wherever you went.

"Yes, ma'am," she said, all but snatching her medical certificate.

As soon as the torturer left to go on to another patient, Beth slumped over the handrail of the treadmill. Catching her breath, she gently stretched out her thigh, trying not to pull the wound in any way. She wondered if her leg would always feel as if it was a stretched-to-its-limit rubber band.

Her eyes closed, she visualized oxygen flowing through the skin and muscle of her leg, just as her therapist had taught her. As she took deep breaths, she couldn't believe the damned colonel from the next treadmill was still talking. Sweet Jesus. She snapped upright, ready to give him the stink-eye—she wouldn't dream of telling off a full-bird colonel—when she realized there was a uniformed man standing at attention in front of him.

"At ease, Walker. I'm in the freaking gym. I'm sweatin' like a pig."

"Yessir," he said.

Beth couldn't believe her eyes. She smiled, and watched James Walker do a double take when he saw her. Now what would he do? He was a sight for sore eyes. She swallowed. Still as handsome as ever—tall, broad-shouldered, with a self-assured attitude that she had secretly salivated over during their deployment together.

"Excuse me, sir," he said, not taking his incredible blue eyes off her.

The colonel followed his line of sight and raised his eyebrows at her, then frowned at Walker. She decided to do him a solid.

"Colonel. This man here risked his life to rescue me after I was shot in Afghanistan last year. I'm imagining that he's shocked to see me standing here." She wiped her sweaty hand on her shorts and stepped forward, offering it to James. "I heard you came to check on me at the hospital, and I know I wasn't really all that coherent, so in case I didn't thank you then, thank you. So much. I owe you big time."

He held her hand, even though it was still pretty sweaty, for a few seconds more than strictly necessary. Long enough for her to get a good look at him. Yup, he was definitely as good-looking as she remembered. Short dark hair, light blue eyes, and an expression of barely concealed admiration. She had figured the year before that he looked at everyone like that. But in this less formal situation she wondered about that, and liked the warmth flooding around her at the possibility that right now, that look was reserved just for her.

Probably a workout high.

"Absolutely my pleasure, Sergeant. I'm very happy to see you here. Not med-boarded out then?" he asked.

"No way." Beth laughed at the thought. This was her life. What the hell would she do in the real world, except for her dream job, of course?

The colonel cleared his throat. "Well, I'm happy to hear that you're on the mend, Sergeant, and I'm happy to hear my new Senior Master Sergeant here was in the right place at the right time. Walker? Sorry I dragged you in this close to the weekend. Go home, unpack, and report at oh-seven for PT on Monday."

"Yes, sir," he replied, before turning to Beth again. "Truly great seeing you looking so well." He stuck his hand out, and grabbed hers again.

"Thank you, again," she said, hoping he could tell how earnest she was. "I owe you."

He nodded, smiled, and turned away. She watched his broad shoulders as he left the physical therapy room. Well, maybe she watched his ass, too. Slinging her towel over her shoulder, and securing her papers in her pocket, she was going to say good-bye to the colonel, but he was already back on his phone.

Shower. Lots and lots of shower. And maybe thoughts of James.

* * *

It was fate. Kismet. It had to be. She looked just as gorgeous as she had last year, and his body had reacted to her in exactly the same way. He was glad that she had been working out, because as soon as he saw her, he was sure his hands had started sweating. Very smooth.

There was no way he was letting her out of his sight this time without asking her out. She did say that she owed him, although if he were being totally truthful, she'd kind of saved him from that shooter, too. Not that fulfilling a debt was a great basis for scoring a date. He paced up and down the corridor outside of the women's changing rooms, throwing his black TACP beret back and forth between his hands, and had a twinge of guilt at what he was considering.

He glanced at his watch. In less than twenty-four hours his older sister's wedding festivities were going to start without him. Beth would be a great distraction from the guilt that had been pin-pricking him all day. But there was no way he was attending that clusterfuck. Ex-girlfriends, parents, pomp and circumstance. He had left that part of the family years ago. And besides, every second he spent in his parents' presence was a risk to the career he loved. His father was powerful. And didn't like at all that James had elected to enlist in the air force instead of working on Capitol Hill.

Distance was best. And he knew his sister totally understood, applauded his independence, even. If his parents hadn't loved his ex's pedigree so much, if they weren't so obsessed with making him quit the air force and take up in the "family business," this would be a perfectly ordinary weekend. But add in a wedding, and the fact that he'd lied to them about his "no deployment" duties and told them he already had a girlfriend...it was a family IED waiting to explode. And his sister would never forgive him if it exploded all over her special day.

Beth Garcia had been his unattainable dream last year. One of the first females in a special forces role, and she'd fit in so well, been so squared away, she was mostly known for intimidating the male troops. A good thing, he guessed, when she was one of the only women doing the job. She was all work and duty and nothing else. It was so hot, it was insane. Drove *him* insane.

She emerged from the changing room with some papers in her teeth, trying to wrap her damp hair into some kind of regulation do. She stopped in her tracks when she saw him. Although her mouth was otherwise occupied, her eyes flashed with a smile as she finished pinning her hair.

When she snatched the papers from her mouth, she said, "Hello again, Senior. Congratulations on your promotion."

"Thanks, I just sewed on the new rank and moved. Got in yesterday."

"That's great." She nodded toward the exit, and he started to walk with her. "I've been here two years. I guess I have another year or so to go."

"Do you like it?" he asked, interested in her opinion, since he still had unpacking to do and had zero experience in North Carolina.

"It's okay. To be honest, this last year has been spent trying to get back on a deployment status. It's been hell, just sitting behind a desk. But"—she waved the papers with teeth marks on them—"I got them today. Maybe you're my good luck charm."

"So what are you doing to celebrate?" he asked, hoping the answer was "nothing."

"Not much. I guess I hadn't really thought about it." She put on her sunglasses when they rounded the corner to the parking lot. Inexplicably, his heart started beating faster, and he knew he had to get this right. He had a sneaking suspicion that a guy only ever had one chance with Garcia. If you fucked it up, you were over.

"Can I take you out for dinner tonight, or maybe tomorrow?"

She was silent for a few seconds, and he wished he could see her expression behind her glasses. Should he have been more casual? More subtle? Should he let her ask him out? *Oh please, let me have got this right.*

"Sure. The army has a long weekend. Friday's off, do you want to go tomorrow?"

He tried not to show his relief by shoving on his own aviators. "Sure. Sounds like a plan."

She stopped at a Mini Cooper convertible and pressed her key fob. It bleeped, and she opened the door. She grabbed something from the passenger seat and scribbled her address on it. "Pick me up at eight?"

As he reached to take her address, his phone bleeped. He held up a finger and read the message. It was a text from Sadie.

I have wicked cold feet or something. Please come. I need you. If you don't come, I'll send one of dad's guys to sit outside your house waiting for you. He will bring you at gunpoint if necessary!

Shit. He assumed that she was joking about the gunpoint, but he knew she was serious about sending someone for him. She'd done it before. And she knew why he wasn't attending her wedding, and until this text, she had seemed okay about it. Change of plans.

"Are you free the whole weekend?" His mind kicked into overdrive. Remembering the conversations from the Humvee when they'd been on patrol. "Would you like to go climbing? I hear there are some great places around the Appalachian Trail."

"The whole weekend?" She hesitated a second, then grinned. "Sure."

He took the address from her hand, his fingers brushing hers as he did. A jolt of awareness flashed through him, something he hadn't felt in…he didn't want to think about how long it had been. "Then I'll pick you up at eight a.m. tomorrow?"

She gave a very non-regulation salute, got in her car and slammed the door shut. A second later, the roof pulled back, revealing a very tidy interior. No surprise there. "Wait a minute. Climbing. Is this just a way to look at my ass for a weekend? 'Cause you know you'll be a pitch behind me all day, right?" She winked, grinned, and pulled out of her spot, wheels spinning.

All that was left was a grin on his face. *Boo-yah.*

Chapter 3

Beth flexed her fingers around the steering wheel, trying to ignore the stickiness. She blew on her sweaty hands and shook them out to try to get the feeling back in them.

Had he just asked her out? Shit. She should have stayed and talked about some rules of engagement. Now she was left hanging, not knowing if he was expecting a date, or a relationship, or just a climb. God, it had been so good to see him again. *So good.*

She should have said thanks but no thanks, but seeing him again after he'd hauled her out of a battleground...all chiseled jaw and impossibly light blue eyes, the dark hair that was cut short, but not army-short. She'd just...stumbled. Hadn't given a second thought, or even a first, about her cardinal rule: no attachments. No attachments until she had a job that would have her not deploying for a year at a time. James Walker. If she hadn't been so intent on her work performance in Afghanistan, she'd have swooned over him. All taciturn and calm and built like a...she shook her hands out again. Just sexy.

Shit, what have I done? Not even I have the required amount of willpower not to jump him.

She considered returning to the parking lot, but really, how lame would that be? She thumped her fist on the dashboard in frustration. It sucked being a woman. There was no easy way to have the 'I don't want a relationship, but I also don't do one-night-stands' conversation without sounding presumptuous. And then if you left it too late to have the conversation, you were a tease.

In all probability, it probably wasn't a date. He'd saved her life, maybe he just wanted to check that she wasn't screwing it up. She was fine with that. And climbing? A thoroughly wholesome pastime that didn't really lend itself to sexy times anyway. Fingers crossed.

She never went out on dates. She'd put an end to that after the last three totally disastrous ones. And that allowed her a one hundred percent focus on work and her career path. It was a good thing. A very good thing. She didn't want anyone knowing that she had relationships. She couldn't afford to show any weakness in her unit. It was completely okay for men to be miserable about a breakup, but if a woman was, she was branded weak. It sucked, but she didn't want anyone thinking about her as less than she was. She didn't want anyone to even think of her in a relationship. She just wanted the guys in her unit to think of her as a soldier.

Not just that, but she was a firm believer that her line of work did not lend itself easily to relationships. She saw the cheating and heartbreak that went on when husbands and wives, boyfriends and girlfriends, were out of sight and mind for a year or more at a time.

In fact, on more than one deployment, she'd seen men get news of infidelity or divorce while trying to focus on their mission. Seen how they reacted, how they lost their edge, and even, in the dirt and ugliness of war, lost their will to live, too.

She was pretty sure that was why Marks, the one soldier to be killed on her last patrol, had gone home in the cargo hold instead of a seat. He had just heard that his wife had been messing around with a neighbor, and had been devastated. Whether he got distracted, careless, or had realized he didn't have anything to go home to…well, she'd seen it happen too often. Had even benched soldiers who had seemed too distracted to leave the compound. She should have seen it in Marks. Should have benched him, too.

She shook off the feeling. She'd been through enough therapy to know it wasn't her fault. But that didn't stop the bubbling feeling of guilt whenever she thought about him.

Dragging her thoughts back to Walker, she figured she had all evening to think about how to broach the subject with him tomorrow. Dating: off the table. If, indeed, it felt like the weekend was anything other than a platonic climbing one.

A strange feeling turned in her stomach. She liked him. He'd saved her life, true. He was to-die-for gorgeous, true. Basically, he was a heartbreaker on legs. So add that into the equation and this was a non-starter. She was not a risk taker in any aspect of her life. She wasn't going to risk anything on this hot airman. No sir.

She sighed as she passed through the base's security point. She had gone so long without sex…at least, sex with another person. She didn't need a man messing with her heart and her… well, everything else. All she needed in life was work, getting deployed, and landing her dream job in the CIA.

What if he didn't find her attractive at all? Or worse, what if he was like her last dates years ago?

Yup, scarier than him not finding her attractive would be to discover that yet another man wanted to be spanked for being a "bad boy." Unfortunately, she seemed to have that vibe about her. She was very, very tough in uniform, which in turn made the last three guys who had asked her out expect to be punished after dessert.

Walker probably just wanted a climbing buddy. Nothing more. Hopefully.

She relaxed into her seat and realized just how tense the encounter with him had made her. Twenty minutes later, she pulled in her driveway, noticing her sister's car parked crookedly in front of the garage. There was no getting around it. Typical Tammer. Showed up when she wanted, disappeared when she wanted, parked her car exactly where it would be the most annoying.

She fumbled for the front door key, one she rarely used. "Tammer Garcia! Move your effing car!"

"Yeah. No, sorry. I'm on my second glass of wine," a voice answered from the kitchen. "It would be irresponsible of you to ask me to get in the car."

Casting a quick look at her watch she shrugged. Six o'clock. Fair enough. "Pour me one then," she said as she dumped the week's dirty PT gear by the laundry door. "What are you doing here?"

"I came over for the *Supernatural* marathon. I know you have tomorrow off, so I figured wine and those Winchester boys would smooth our way into yet another weekend here at the last-chance convent."

"Umm," Beth said, and took a slug from her wineglass. "I'm going away for the weekend. Climbing in the Appalachians." She took another gulp before she casually met her sister's eyes.

Tammer took a second. "By yourself?"

"With a friend." She busied herself sorting through the mail her sister had brought in with her.

Wild cackling laugher erupted from her sister, and stopped just as abruptly. "Seriously? You have a friend? A go-away-for-the-weekend friend? How is that even possible? You don't like people."

She had a point. Not that she didn't like people. She liked a lot of people. But she obviously never let anyone know she liked them. That way she could never be accused of giving some young stud climbing the ranks the wrong impression.

"It's complicated," she said, and plopped on the sofa. She pulled a thread from the fringe of a cushion and started twisting it.

"*Dios mio*," Tammer breathed. "Tell me everything. It's a guy, right?"

"It's the TACP. You know, the one who saved me last year. Sergeant Walker. Er, James."

Tammer clasped her hands to her heart. "I love him already, you know that, right? I owe him, you know?"

Tears prickled Beth's eyes, thinking for the second time that day how close she had come to losing everything, and leaving her younger sister alone. She nodded. "Me too."

Tammer cleared her throat. "When are you leaving?"

Still twisting the fringe on the cushion, she told her when he was picking her up.

"Okay, so we still have a *Supernatural* night ahead of us. And the wine." She peered at Beth's face. "Are you okay with this? We can always watch *Buffy* instead."

"It's not a date," she blurted out in a hellish non sequitur before she could stop herself.

Great, Beth. Way to be a level-headed CIA officer candidate.

"That's not what I was talking about, but okay. Well of course it's not a date. If it was a date, that would make him one of those freaky nut-jobs you kept attracting, wouldn't it? And I refuse to let the guy who saved my sister's ass be bat-shit crazy like the others."

"I passed my PT test today."

"Wow, you are the queen of smooth conversation today. But that is awesome news." Tammer squeezed her arm. "Wanna tell me what's really bothering you?"

Nope. She didn't want to admit that she liked Walker, and that she dreaded having the no-dating conversation with him. If he didn't think of her that way, he'd just think she was a dick. Beth groaned and shoved her face into the cushion.

"Fair enough. Is it anything that a *Supernatural* marathon won't fix?"

She picked her head up and sighed. "No. Nothing it won't fix."

* * *

The next morning James gunned the throttle of his Audi and shifted down the gears as he approached the guard building of Beth's gated community. He hadn't known really what to expect, but this remote country club was still a surprise. He had no idea why he felt anxious. He didn't do anxious. Ever.

The whole time he'd known her downrange in Afghanistan, he'd thought about taking her out back in the States, But it had been a remote dream, one he never expected to have the opportunity to see through. And when he did, he couldn't even wine and dine her properly. It happened to be the one weekend he had to get the hell out of Dodge.

He should have just asked her out like a normal person. Hell, he didn't even know if she was dating anyone else. Hadn't even checked her fucking finger for a ring.

Shit, what a moron he was.

Well, he couldn't do anything now except enjoy the weekend with her, and forget about Sadie and her wedding. The whole situation was strange. He had made the decision to ask her in a split second, and that wasn't him at all. He was a plan guy, a consider-all-angles guy. But his brain just threw up the question. Why didn't he just ask for her number and then decide when and where to take her?

Climbing? Smooth, Walker.

A fucking great way to seduce someone when you spent the weekend a rope length apart from each other.

He checked his GPS against the number on the mailbox, and pulled in. Her Mini wasn't in the driveway, but a newish Camry was. Boyfriend? Something twitched in his chest.

He got out and rang the doorbell. He'd barely had time to turn around and step back off the step before the door flung open and a tiny dynamo flew out and wrapped herself around him.

What the . . . ?

It wasn't Beth. It was like—he pulled away slightly and looked down at whatever was attached around him—a mini-Beth.

"I love you. I love you. Thank you so much. Thank you."

Beth came into sight in the doorway, with a slight smile on her face and one hand on her hip. She pointed at him and his new appendage, and said, "Don't expect this from me, okay? I already said thank you once. That is positively all you're getting."

The dynamo pulled away and blew her hair back from her face. She was, he guessed, maybe five years younger than Beth, but the familial similarity was astounding.

"Thank you for saving my sister. That's all I wanted to say. I'm Tammer, and I'll be going now." She stepped away from them and unlocked her car door. A startlingly loud whistle came from her as she opened the rear door. A huge dog barreled out of the house, barely stopping to sniff James, and jumped into the Camry. Tammer slammed the door shut, and he watched, bemused, as they both stuck their heads out of the window as she reversed down the driveway.

"That was some welcome," he said, although he couldn't help but wish it was Beth who had plastered herself on him.

"She's some sister. She would have been twenty and completely alone, if I hadn't... if you hadn't... you know."

James grinned. "I do know. And we have about six hours in the car to tell me how much you owe me and how you'd love to pay me back... Ow!"

He rubbed his arm where she'd given him a half-hearted punch.

"Don't push your luck, Sergeant."

"Don't say 'Sergeant.' No, really, you can call me 'Senior.'" He gave her a fake superior smile, loving that he outranked her now.

She rolled her eyes at him and made a gagging face. "Why don't you make yourself useful and put my bag in the car while I lock up?"

"Yes ma'am." He grinned to himself as he turned away. She was as prickly as he remembered. Shit. He struggled momentarily with the idea of pulling her into him, so he could kiss her, just to see if she'd soften in his arms. He restrained himself, though, and picked up her bag.

She was wearing three-quarter length climbing tights, with a short skirt over the top. A tight athletic top that molded her breasts perfectly sealed the deal for him. Her hair wound around her head in a messy braid. He wanted to touch her so bad. So freaking bad. Maybe a six-hour drive, alone in close proximity to her, hadn't been the best idea.

As he turned the ignition, he thought, *don't blow this.* He mentally shrugged. What could go wrong?

"This is a really nice area," he said as they drove through the neighborhood. "It amazes me that it's so close to base." It was true. Usually half an hour in every direction from a military base was cheap housing and strip malls. Beth had found an oasis from all that.

"That's what I loved about it. Really, it was love at first sight. I hate living on base and having people know my business, you know?"

"I do. I'm in temporary housing right now, right next to the commissary."

"Ouch. I bet that's annoying," she said, pulling her leg up to adjust the cuff of her tights. "Yeah, living this side of base is definitely quieter. The downside is that there is no nightlife at all. A few restaurants downtown, but nowhere you can just go for a quick drink. But the trade-off is worth it."

James didn't answer. It was way too early to even suggest he was interested in her neighborhood. Way too early. "I've got to find somewhere to live soon. Base lodging is killing me." He looked sideways at her. "Especially now that the army has taken over the housing on the old air force base. More crime, more noise. Gangs. It's a nightmare."

"Nice. Air force is just so stuck up its own ass, it doesn't know how to have a good time." She slid her sunglasses down from her hair and elbowed him in the arm. "Don't piss me off or I'll drop your ass from the belaying rope."

"Oh talk it up, Garcia. We'll see who's king of the climb." He pointed at himself.

"Dream on, dude."

There was a lull in conversation as she seemed to be content watching the scenery go by. He felt very comfortable driving in silence with her; they'd done it many times in Afghanistan. But he really wanted to know more about her.

"So what happened to you after you left the hospital at Bagram?" he asked as they hit the I-95 northbound.

"A couple of days after it happened, they took me to Germany, and then back stateside to Walter Reed. Then from there back home."

"You look in such good shape now, I mean at the gym yesterday. It's like you were never shot. How come you didn't quit? You could have lived very nicely on a medical retirement."

"Yeah, but I wouldn't know what to do with myself. I want to get back in the field. It's what I trained for, you know. I worked effing hard to make the special forces cut. And besides, what are the odds of me being shot twice? Fairly remote, right? At least that's how I'm looking at it." She turned in her seat to sit more or less facing him.

If she only really knew the odds of being shot again. Wait until she saw his scars.

"How was the rest of your tour?" she asked.

He laughed, at first sarcastically, and then properly.

"What? What happened?" Beth leaned forward and poked his arm. "Tell me or I'll break your arm."

"You could try."

"I guess I'd only get into trouble now that you outrank me, right? Tell me anyway."

"Okay. Stop poking me!"

"Come on then! I love hearing other people's war stories."

"I was assigned to another unit after *our* fun night out. I only had a month or so to go, so I was looking for a slightly less exciting time. We had an interpreter with us to translate the radio chatter, who turned up to work in varying states of coherence."

"He was drunk?"

"Or something. The Taliban had been victimizing the local interpreters' families, so we basically had to take what we could get."

"Fair enough. What happened?"

"We were in a regular patrol—you know, a hearts and minds, blankets and cookies run at a village—and we came under fire. I kept trying to get us out of range but they kept shooting at us. I asked the interpreter what the chatter on the radio was, and he said nothing, that they weren't saying anything about us, or anything like that."

"Yeah? What happened?" She leaned forward even more.

He smiled to himself. War stories were the best. Everyone had them; they were always fun to reminisce about. Mostly.

"It had been about two hours of us driving into fire and rocket-propelled grenades. Let's just say, the last time I went out on patrol with you, was *not* the last time a vehicle I was in blew up."

"It was you," she said. "You were the jinx on us!"

"Very funny."

"What happened?"

"After two hours of being pummeled by the TB, I woke up the interpreter…"

"He was *asleep*?"

"Yeah. Air support was an hour away and we'd already taken some minor injuries, so I figured enough was enough. I kicked him awake and made him tell me exactly, word for word, what they were saying on the radio. He said "It's nothing, just numbers, like math…add a hundred, a hundred more, left a hundred…""

"Oh my God!" Beth shrieked with laughter. "All that time they were zeroing in on your location and he didn't realize?"

"I swear, I have never come so close to killing someone in cold blood. Never. Seriously. To this day I don't know if he realized or not." Walker's hands tightened around the steering wheel as he spoke. He was laughing, but he could still feel the tension just remembering.

Beth sat back in her seat and said, "Phew. That's just crazy. No one was seriously hurt?"

"Not as bad as you were, anyway."

Silence fell in the car, and James noticed the display on his dash was asking if he wanted to synch up an iPod. He pressed yes, knowing he didn't have his with him, and that the car must be picking up the signal from Beth's. A couple of seconds later South American jazz came over the speakers.

Beth sat up. "I feel like you just stole my music!"

"I guess I did. I have to say, this is a surprise. I had you down as a thrash rock kind of a person."

"Why is that, exactly?" she asked.

He paused to think. "Actually, I have no idea. It's just the vibe you give off."

She visibly tensed, as if she was waiting for something, but he had no idea what he'd said to cause the reaction, or what he could do to quell it.

"It's nice. Great driving music at least," he offered, almost in question, casting a look to see her reaction.

She seemed to slowly relax, and she started tapping her foot in time to the music. As she relaxed, so did he. His hands unclenched but there was still tightness in his stomach where his sister and her crazy wedding was. Guilt was a terrible thing. He didn't want it to ruin his weekend with Beth.

Chapter 4

When he'd made the comment about thrash rock and roll, the music her guys usually played while deployed, she was suddenly scared that he was segueing to a conversation about her being strong and in charge. For some reason, guys saw how strong and in control she was in uniform, and figured she was like that at home, or in bed. Amateurs.

Her last date had been particularly disturbing. When a guy from a neighboring unit kept telling her, over sushi, that he'd been a bad boy and needed to be punished, she had faked food poisoning and grabbed a taxi home. A hundred-dollar cab ride. Just no. That was not her scene.

She wanted a man who liked her strength, but wasn't intimidated by it. Not that she wanted a man right now. And even if she did, which she didn't, there was no way she was ever going to deploy leaving a boyfriend at home. Nope. No way.

Jeez. Who was she trying to convince anyway?

Now her favorite song washed over her and soothed those worries away. This was just a climbing weekend. Nothing more. Although, God knew, if Walker put the moves on her, she would struggle to say no. Crap, she hadn't been touched by a man in so long. Sometimes she just fantasized about it. Sometimes that was enough. As she listened to the music, she closed her eyes and pictured James's face between her legs as they were being shot at in Afghanistan. Then she stripped out the war scene and put them in bed.

He was strong himself. God, he had to have been to carry her, as well as his backpack and both their body armor, out of that hellhole of a valley. He was taller than her and had much, much more muscle. She opened her eyes and cast a glance sideways. He wore a t-shirt, and the mere suggestion of a tattoo peeked out from under the sleeve. Maybe she should suggest he show her his, and she show him hers.

Down girl.

"What are you smiling about?" he asked, glancing over at her as he overtook a semi.

"Just the music," she said, sitting forward again. "So what are we doing this weekend?" She figured she could do a search of the place they would be climbing and read some reviews on her phone from climbers that had been there before.

"I thought we could hit Whitetop Mountain if you're up for it. It's in Virginia. I climbed it once when I was young. My sister and I used to escape there," he said.

She laughed. "Escape from what?"

At that second, his phone bleeped again. He grabbed for the phone but fumbled it. It somersaulted over the console and dropped to the floor. "Eyes on the road, Senior. I didn't do a year of PT for you to kill me in a car crash." Beth reached down between his legs to grab the phone. Her finger swiped the screen as she picked it up.

Are you coming home?

"Uh...sorry, I didn't mean to." She showed him the screen, but in that second it went black.

"What did it say?" he asked.

"It just said, 'are you coming home?' Something like that." A trickle of coldness ran through her. "You're not married, are you?" The text had sounded worryingly like the kind of thing a wife might send.

"No. No. I'm not married, and I don't have a girlfriend. It's nothing like that."

Phew.

"What's going on, then? Whose home are you avoiding?"

"The family home. Can you see who sent that? It had remarkably little swearing in it to be Sadie." He glanced at Beth. "Sadie is my older sister. Can you see who it was from?"

Beth swiped the touch screen and went to the message. "Maisie?"

James was silent for a moment. "Really?" he asked eventually.

"Really." *Who the hell was Maisie?*

"My younger sister, before your brain starts kicking into gear," he said.

"My brain was in gear before I got in the car, trust me. So what's going on with your family today?"

"Sadie's getting married this weekend. There'll be hundreds of—"

"*What?* And you're going climbing with someone you barely even know? What's wrong with you?" She was sure there must be a good reason for him not to want to be there, but still.

"My family is super-complicated. The less time I spend with them, the more I can love them. From afar. From very afar."

Beth couldn't even get her head around that. Family was the most precious thing to her. She'd never known her father, but she, her mother, and Tammer had been an inseparable unit. And then when their mother died, it was just Tammer. Beth couldn't fathom him not wanting to see his sister get married.

"I probably would have gone if I had a significant other. But turning up without one as a buffer, I would have spent the whole weekend fending off my father's 'daughter-in-law' choices for me." He leveled a look at her. "He once tried to push his own ex-mistress on me. Thought she was a suitable addition to the family. Came with the right pedigree."

"He *what*? Do you live in a telenovela story? That's…awesome! I mean, I'm sorry, I know it's your life and all, but what a great story." She laughed, then pressed her hand over her mouth. "I'm sorry. I just can't imagine…"

"It's okay. I see how absurd it is." He laughed with her. It started out as a snort, then turned into a proper belly laugh. It was as if he'd only just seen the absurdity in it.

"Oh my God, I'd love to meet your family. They sound crazy. Tell me more stories." Beth settled back into her seat with an expression of anticipation.

The rest really wasn't as much fun. "My father runs this… business that he wants me to join, like my older sister did. I decided to join the air force, and he thinks I never see any front-line action."

"Um. You have one of the most dangerous jobs in the air force."

"I also lie to my father about almost everything to keep him from interfering in my life."

"Okaaay…"

"My parents also want me to marry my ex-girlfriend. They're really quite single-minded about it, so…" He stopped.

"So?" she said, feeling like she knew what was coming next.

"This is why I'm not going to the wedding. Every person my

father introduces me to, and there will be a bunch, I have to wonder if they want to marry into the family, or if they want to offer me a better job than the one I have. It's just too much pressure. Sadie understands. She's lived through it and always did what she could to protect Maisie and me from it." He shifted his attention from the road to his phone. "Or at least I thought she did. I'm going to call Maisie, see what's going on. They've both known for months that I wasn't coming; I can't imagine why this is suddenly an issue." He took his phone from her and placed it on the console. "Call Maisie."

* * *

He was wondering if he'd misjudged his sisters' texts. After a couple of rings, Maisie picked up.

"James?"

"Hey, munchkin. What's going on? You know I already had plans for this weekend." He glanced in Beth's direction to gauge her reaction to the out-and-out lie. She pulled a face at him.

"I know." She sounded miserable, and when she sniffed, his heart squeezed tight.

"What's wrong?"

"I keep getting weird e-mails. Sadie does too, but she told me not to tell."

James's blood ran cold. "Did you tell Dad?"

"Sadie told me not to."

He looked at Beth, who frowned at him. "What do they say, sweetie?"

He could hear her voice shaking through the phone. "The last one said that I looked nice in my bridesmaid dress. But no one's seen it except mom and Sadie. I think someone must have been watching us at the store." He could feel his heartbeat pumping faster than it had been moments earlier.

"Are you sure?" James checked his mirror and moved over to take the next exit.

"He described the dress," she said baldly.

"Maisie. You have to go tell Dad." He stopped at the top of the exit ramp and put on his hazard lights.

"Sadie won't let me." She was out and out sobbing now.

"All right, sweetie. Let me speak to Sadie. I'll call you back in a little while." He hung up and clenched his fists around the steering wheel. Hell in a hand basket. What the fuck was Sadie thinking?

"You should go. I should go. I mean. You should go to the wedding and make sure your sisters are okay, and I should just go home. You can drop me off and I'll rent a car; it's no problem. We can rain check this weekend," Beth said.

No. Way. As on edge as he was after Maisie's call, not being with Beth this weekend added a whole other layer to his tension. There was only one way to resolve this.

"We should both go to the wedding. That is, if you don't mind. I know it won't be as fun as climbing…" Suddenly, in his mind they were at the wedding, slow dancing, sharing a room…

Dragging his thoughts back, he changed his mind. His desire to be with her shouldn't override the reason to go to the wedding. She started to say something but he cut her off. "I've changed my mind. I don't think this is a good idea. I wanted to take you away for a weekend we could enjoy. Doing something we love doing." He hoped she couldn't read his mind. "Climbing, I mean." He definitely meant the other thing.

But Beth seemed to also have made up her mind. "Oh come

on. It'll be fun. I will try my hardest not to embarrass you... unless, you know, you want me to throw down with the phantom e-mailer. Then I'd be totally happy to."

"Aww, aren't you sweet. Offering to beat up people for me." He rolled his eyes at her.

"Hey, you never know. Or I could totally have to tear some scheming woman of your father's off you. Or stop a jewel thief, or..."

"I have a nasty suspicion you think going to the wedding is going to be more of an adventure than it will be. It's likely to be boring, embarrassing in one way or another, and filled with mildly to moderately annoying people. At best we'll just need to beat some sense into Sadie, and watch after Maisie." He turned to her, flicked off the hazard lights, and shifted into gear. But before he released the clutch, he asked, "Do you really want to do this?"

She stared through the windshield, but he could see the wheels turning in her head. "My only problem is that I don't have anything to wear," she said finally.

"Neither do I. We'll hit the mall before we get to my parents' house. It's on me. You can buy whatever you'll need."

She grinned. "All right then. Wedding it is." She rubbed her hands together as if she was a super-villain. "I can't wait. A weekend in a telenovela. It's like a dream. Tammer won't believe it! Oh. I can pretend to be your girlfriend. Will that keep away the predators?"

He laughed. "Hell, yeah. Dream come true."

A startled expression appeared on her face, so he covered. "I mean, having a girlfriend as a buffer zone." He shook his head at himself. He needed to rein himself in.

"I don't have a credit limit. So you can go telenovela-clothes mad." He smiled. He was psyched to see her so excited and up for anything. Swallowing, he put the car back on the road and shot back down to the interstate.

"So I'm your girlfriend for the weekend," she said in a breathy voice. "I kind of like that. It's fast, and unexpected, exciting… and blissfully short." She laughed out loud as she came to the end of her sentence.

He groaned. "You might not want short. You might end up wanting long. Like, really long."

"Keep dreaming, stud. I like everything short, even my drinks. And don't you forget it."

"Yes, ma'am."

"But if I'm going to be your girlfriend, *for the weekend*," she said meaningfully, "I need to know more about you."

He gave her the highlight reel of his previous girlfriends, the nightmare with his own father's ex, and what the family absolutely didn't need to know. At the end, he gave a sigh and relaxed back into his seat. "Are you sure you want to do this?"

"I won't let you down, Senior. I'm going to be the best girlfriend you never had."

He didn't doubt it for a second.

"Just so you know, Henrietta will be there. The ex who my parents adore? She's Sadie's maid of honor."

"Henrietta? Lovely name."

"Lovely girl. Just not for me," he said with a rueful smile.

"So what kind of girlfriend will pass muster, do you think? Who do I have to be? It doesn't sound like an army sergeant is going to be a suitable fiancée for your parents. I mean girlfriend. Sorry, I have no idea where that came from."

"You know what? This morning I wasn't even going; just the fact that we will be there is enough. You can be you, or anyone you want to be. I actually can't believe you're being so cool about this."

"Short of having me kill someone for you, I guess I kind of owe you, you know." Her fingers plucked at the tights over what he knew to be her inner thigh scar. "And I can't have you not see your sister get married."

"Don't say that. You don't owe me anything. I didn't do anything for you that I wouldn't have done for someone else. That I haven't done for someone before. You think you were my first near-death experience?" She hadn't been, but nearly losing her had done a number on him from which he still hadn't totally recovered.

She didn't say anything, and more, her eyes seemed to be welling up. So he tried to break the tension. "Although I will say that yours were positively the first lacy underwear I'd been that close to on deployment. I mean you were totally my first."

She laughed out loud. "I better have been." She stopped laughing and went back to tapping out the rhythm of the music on her leg again.

He could feel his blood pressure rising the nearer they got to D.C. He wanted to throttle Sadie for not letting their dad sort out the threat. If indeed it was a threat. Thank goodness Beth didn't mind riding in silence when there was nothing to say. A couple of hours later, he pulled off the I-495 to hit the mall. "We'll stop at Tysons Corner and I'll leave you to buy whatever you need. Three days and two nights. One day just hanging out, then the rehearsal dinner, the wedding, black tie evening reception, then on Sunday we'll head back to base. Does that sound doable?"

Even as the words came out of his mouth, he knew it sounded overwhelming. It had seemed that way to him. He'd played with the invitation for nearly two months, so he knew the wedding details better than he knew his rank and serial number.

"Are you one hundred percent sure you want to do this?" He chanced a quick glance at her, and she was staring out of the windshield, seemingly deep in thought.

"Sure." She turned to him and added, "Will we be even? You saved my life, and I'll save you from your father's women. My debt will be served, right?"

"Yes, ma'am. Whatever you say." He wondered what she was thinking, and just had no idea whatsoever. She was totally inscrutable. But she was there with him, which was half the battle.

"Just remember to ignore my parents, okay? You will not have met anyone like them before, so you'll just have to try to be unfazed by them."

"Explain?"

He wiped a hand over his face, as if that could wipe his parents away. If only it was that easy. "My parents are a force of nature. And a force of politics. And frankly, my father could ruin my career with one phone call. He's lived his whole life connected, and he's spent all of *my* life wishing I was more connected. If he made a call, my job would disappear and I'd be reassigned to a trash disposal plant, in the hopes I'd come home and join the family business. I only tell him what he absolutely needs to know. It keeps him off my back. It keeps me from hating him, and keeps him from ruining my life."

He thought she would give him shit for this, which would be well-deserved. But she didn't.

"It's okay. I understand. I spent my whole childhood in pink lacy dresses playing secretly with G.I. Joe. If my mother hadn't died—" She paused as if to collect herself. "If she hadn't died, I would never have been able to join the army. To do what I do.

"If she was still alive, I'd be married, pregnant, and barefoot in the kitchen. It's all she wanted for me. It's everything she never had, and always wanted."

She put a hand on his arm, briefly, obviously to make a point, and the heat of her skin on his almost made him stop listening to her. Almost. His mind wandered momentarily to a familiar place in his fantasies, where she was virtually naked, and reaching for him. He dragged his attention back to the here and now.

"I would never have wanted to disappoint her. It was unfortunate that it took her dying to give me my freedom." Her voice dropped to a whisper with the last comment.

Damn it. If they weren't driving, he'd grab her to him in a fierce hug. He hated hearing the pain in her voice.

"I'm sorry," he said with a degree of inadequacy that was embarrassing.

"It's all right," she said with a stronger voice. "It was a long time ago. A really long time ago. I just wanted to say that I understand the unreasonable expectations of parents. That's all."

"Thanks. I'm sorry our plans changed. Especially since we now have to brave the Hammer House of Horror. And I'm not really exaggerating. But maybe we'll find time to have a little fun, too." Was that too subtle? Should he just say he wanted to spend time with her and this seemed like a kill-two-birds-with-one-grenade option?

She grinned and settled back in the seat. "As long as there's an open bar, a band I can sing along to, and drunk uncles I can dance with, I'm golden."

Oh shit. He was totally owned.

So why was the biggest shit-eating grin spreading across his face?

Chapter 5

Walker dropped her off at Nordstrom with a freaking black, metal American Express card while he went off on an errand. If she hadn't really listened to him in the car, she might have thought he was up to no good. Arms dealing or something. But although he didn't say it, everything about his Audi, the need to smooth over relations with his parents, and his way of speaking suggested, quite strongly, that his family came from money.

Now here she was in a private dressing room which was only slightly smaller than her own bedroom, and much better furnished. She had given the wedding itinerary to the shopping assistant, and sat perched on a plush, dusty pink chaise longue. The windows and walls were covered in billowing silk drapes that rustled with the flow from the air conditioning vent, and the coffee table had bottles of water and cookies on it.

Who the hell ate cookies while trying on dresses?

A knock at the door preceded a waft of warm air as it swung open. A huge clothes rack on wheels made a bang as it entered the room. The assistant pushed the rail to the side of the room by the window and gestured to the clothes at the end of the rail nearest the door.

"Day dresses, casual evening wear, and then formal evening wear," she said as she walked the length of the rack. "Underwear for all of the above. I noticed you aren't wearing undergarments suitable for summer dresses."

She was right about that, but still it felt uncomfortable having another woman look at her so critically.

"On the rack below each outfit are appropriate shoes. Feel free to mix and match, and put those you would like to take home with you on the rack over there." She pointed toward a smaller rail attached to the wall. "If you need assistance, please use the call button on the wall. If you get stuck, use the red button."

"Stuck?"

The assistant gave her another appraising look. "I'm sure it won't happen to you, but a few extra cookies, some Spanx and a dress that's a size too small…let's just say that it's happened enough that we installed an alarm button." She drew a silk curtain across the room in front of the door, and left the room.

"Wow. Okay, thank you," Beth said to the empty space, feeling not just a little overwhelmed. Old Navy and Athleta were more her usual style. She felt way out of her league. Way out.

She rose, wiping her hands on her skirt. Why was she doing this again? Oh yes. She owed this man her life, and it would be *really* good experience for her potential new career as a CIA Protection Officer. She needed to know how to blend into any situation, deal with every type of person, and this was as good an opportunity as any to practice. And hello? Missing your own sister's wedding? Not on her watch. She refused to think about the logistics of them pretending to be girlfriend and boyfriend.

It wasn't until after she'd suggested it that she realized the implications. Hand-holding in front of people at the very least.

Not thinking about it.

She stripped, and replaced her sports bra and Hanes with a pink lace set the woman had put out for her. In the mirror she could see a different Beth. One she'd literally never been before. She undid her braid and let her long brown hair cascade over her shoulders. Wow. She felt…different. Looked… feminine.

Standing a little straighter, she started trying on dresses. They all looked peculiarly fantastic. The assistant really had a great eye. She moved two that fit the best to the "take home" rail and moved on to the evening dresses.

As she checked the fit of the first one, smoothing the black fabric down her hips, she began wondering how James would see her. Whether or not he would approve of the dresses. What his taste was like. If he would find her sexy in them.

She *wanted* to be sexy for him. She winced as the thought crossed her mind, but it was true. She liked him. She had, ever since he'd first started going on patrol with them. Quiet, determined, unflusterable, yet funny. Ready with exactly the right words. In any situation. He was just a few inches taller than her, and so strong. She remembered how he had effortlessly slung her over his shoulder and run with her. How he'd saved her life. Tears threatened to well up again and she fought them back. *Enough with the tears.* This was going to be a weekend of fun. And then she could move on. Concentrate on her work. This was a respite weekend.

It was a yes on this dress. A long black sheath, slightly shimmery with beautiful draping over just one shoulder. It left her other bare, and she figured with her hair up, she may just blend in to James's fancy family. The black strappy, sandal stilettos were a yes, too. She shimmied out of the dress and hung it at the end of the rail.

She took a deep red dress off the hanger and tried to undo the complicated clasp and a series of hooks and clasps. She dived into her bag for her reading glasses and put them on to see the mechanics of the dress a bit better.

As she examined it, she wondered how difficult James would find it to take it off her. She paused as she visualized that situation in a little more detail. Heat flooded her, pooling between her legs as she thought about the dress sliding down her body, as slowly as his hands were stroking her. *No, no, no.* They were just friends.

Oh God, she should have brought her vibrator with her.

* * *

It had to be a dream. A fantasy. James blinked once, and felt his pulse jump like he was running for cover in a firefight. It was real. It was really real. She was... Words, and coherent thought evaded him. She looked like a princess in a tower room, shiny drapes blowing around her as if she was in an old Aerosmith video. Pink lacy underwear, and high, high black heels.

Sweet Jesus.

He'd been directed into the room by the assistant, and had opened the door and been confused by the weird curtain in front of him. It was silent inside, and for a second he wondered if he'd been directed into the wrong room. Maybe it was empty, or worse, had the wrong person in it.

He'd decided to peek around the curtain, and had every intention of doing a fast, combat scope-out, so he wouldn't be seen.

But as soon as he peeked his head around the curtain he froze at the scene in front of him.

Blood rushed to his dick as he fought with himself. Continue to watch, or make a noise as if he was just coming into the room? He just couldn't look away.

She was frowning at the dress, peering through glasses that made her look like a crazy-sexy librarian. His hand pressed against his erection as he watched. *Down boy.* She wriggled her legs together as she played with the dress, and he imagined his hand between them, feeling her writhe against him. Her breasts were covered in a lacy bra that only just concealed her nipples. He ached. Ached for her. As he found himself reaching to stroke his dick through his pants, he decided he couldn't watch any more without drawing attention to himself.

He opened and shut the door noisily and said, "Beth?" as he pulled the curtain aside.

She looked up with a shocked expression and grabbed the dress to her body, trying to hide herself. "Really? You can't just barge in here..." Her voice trailed off, her eyes dipped down to the front of his pants, and a half smile appeared.

There was nothing he could do to prevent himself from covering the distance between them in a heartbeat. He stopped an inch short and watched the conflicting thoughts flicker across her face. She wanted him, he was sure of it. But some doubt remained still. Against every instinct he took a step back. He didn't want her to have any doubt about him.

Before he could take more than one step, her hand flashed out and grabbed his shirt, wrapping her hand in the material. She hesitated for a split second, and slowly pulled him toward her.

He was on fire. She was so strong and beautiful and her expression was sexy as hell. She bit her lower lip, but as she propelled him to her, she blinked, long and slow behind her glasses. Her lip pulled free of her teeth and as she opened her eyes, her gaze remained on his mouth. He wasted no time.

He slid his hand into her hair at the back of her head and virtually yanked her to his lips. Her mouth opened under his instantly, no chaste first kisses here. His tongue dominated hers, laying claim to her mouth.

She moaned under his assault and the sound seemed to pluck finely vibrating strings inside him, making his dick so hard he could feel his pants almost cutting off the blood flow to his lower body.

He backed her into the wall and she pulled his hips to hers. In a second his dick was pressed against her panties. Her breasts heaved against his chest as she gasped for air.

"More. I want to feel more of you," she said, rocking her hips against his.

He wanted to feel more of her, too. Taking a step back, he slowly drew his hand down her throat, kissing her in its wake. His hand grazed her breast and gently plucked her nipple, before dipping and stroking across her taut stomach. As his fingers stroked the front of her panties, his teeth found her nipple.

Beth whimpered, and he tightened everywhere at the sound. Her softness and hardness aroused him more than he ever remembered being aroused before. It felt as if his soul wouldn't be satisfied until he owned her. Totally. He needed to be the master of her body, to know it better than she knew it herself.

His dick surged at the thought, and as if she read his mind her hand reached down and pressed the hard ridge in his jeans. A low groan rumbled through the room and only abstractly he realized it was his own.

She ground herself against his hand, although he was teasing her with only light touches over her panties. "Please. Touch me," she whispered, her sweet hot breath fanning across his face.

"How bad do you want me right now?" he ground out, desperate to hear the words he'd longed to hear the year before.

He slid his hand under the elastic of her panties and hesitated, wanting to hear the words before he touched her, although at this stage, he was wildly uncertain which of them he was teasing.

"Bastard," she whispered as she bit the lobe of his ear. She touched his inner ear with her tongue and he nearly exploded. "You want to hear the words?"

"I do."

"Touch me and I'll tell you." As she said the words she pressed her hands against his dick again, making him feel as if the world was folding in on him, becoming only as big as them both, pressed against the wall.

"Ahem." The disapproving sound came from the door.

Fuuuuck.

"Oh my God." Beth said, coming out from behind him. "I'm so sorry. We're so sorry." She cast a look at him. "I'm nearly done." She gestured at the clothes.

The woman frowned and said, "Come out when you're ready." She raised her eyebrows at the pair of them and shut the door behind her.

"I feel like I'm back at Catholic School." She winced and looked away, a flush creeping up her face.

The room was suddenly filled with awkwardness. He wasn't going to leave it like that. No way.

Beth ducked her head and went to pick up the dress she'd dropped when he came in. He grabbed her arm gently and pulled her to him.

"I'm sorry. I didn't mean to put you in a position where you could be embarrassed."

"It's okay." She still wouldn't look at him, and there was no way he was going to let this moment pass into weirdness.

He put two fingers under her chin and made her eyes meet his. Then he leaned forward to kiss her gently on the lips, smoothing the hair off her face. "I'm sorry about that. But I saw you, and you looked so beautiful. I thought about doing that all the time we were downrange together. I want to see where this goes. You have to admit our chemistry is insane."

She looked into his eyes and he wondered what she saw there. "I don't know. I mean yes, of course we have chemistry. I just have no interest in a relationship, so I don't do…this." A small line furrowed her brow. "I don't want to deploy and leave someone at home. I don't want the stress, the wondering what he's doing, who he's with. I need a clean mind when I go. You should understand that."

Fuck. His heart shrunk in his chest as disappointment rushed through him as quickly as desire had. "Sure I do." He nearly choked on the words. What was up with her? Had someone done the dirty on her while she was deployed? He took her hand and kissed her cheek. "Whatever you need. And speaking of that…" He gestured with both hands toward her and the rail of clothes and the various bits of underwear that were draped over the chaise and the rail. "Just tell her we'll take everything, and we'll sort it all out later."

She nodded as he stepped away from her and moved toward the door. Every bone in his body ached for her again. He paused to look at her, sexy with her newly mussed hair. And then he remembered his recent errand and delved into his pocket.

"I nearly forgot. You gave me a great idea in the car." He tossed her a ring box in Tiffany's signature blue. "Marry me? I figured we may as well draw a line under our relationship. Show people, especially my parents, they can't mess with us this weekend."

She laughed uncertainly as she opened the box. Her hand flew to her throat in surprise, and then her expression turned wistful. "Oh, it's beautiful." She dragged her gaze from it and said with a frown, "For God's sake, don't lose the receipt!"

"I'll see you outside." And against every impulse in his body, he closed the door behind him, and on his every fantasy of actually being in a relationship with her.

Chapter 6

As the shopping assistant was scanning the labels on the clothes, they argued over who was paying. "I'm not letting you buy clothes for me—it's weird."

"Look. You're doing me this favor, so I'm paying. Also, I don't just have a Senior's salary. I have a trust fund, too."

She eyed him accusingly. "Wait a minute. You'll avoid your family, but still take money from your trust fund? That's kind of low."

"The trust fund is from my grandmother, who spent way more time with me than my parents did when I was a kid. And for your information, I absolutely only touch it when I'm trying to buy a lady's affection. Or buy an Audi." He shrugged fake-casually. "Mostly, those are the only times I use it anyway."

She didn't bat an eye. "Still, there's no way you're buying shit for me. Let it go."

"That comes to twelve thousand, three hundred and twenty-six dollars, fifteen cents. Will that be on your Nordstrom card?" the disapproving assistant said.

Beth froze.

"Still want to pay?" he asked fake-innocently.

"Not even slightly. You go ahead." Damn. Could she feel any more like Julia freaking Roberts right now?

He laughed at her. "As I thought."

She punched him on his arm as he turned to pass his black metal card across the counter. Holy hell. All those clothes. All those Jimmy Choos. She was going to hell.

At least she'd be well-dressed for the devil.

Her brand new ring flashed on her hand. She'd never thought she was the type to wear diamonds. Or maybe she never expected to inspire a man to want to give her diamonds. But this ring was the most incredible one she'd ever seen. Instead of a traditional diamond on a band, the ring was silver, or probably platinum, made into a spiral that wound around her finger three times, diamonds glittering all the way along it. The whole of her finger from the very base to the first knuckle sparkled like a strand of lights. It was delicate but made a bold statement. She'd never seen anything like it, but damn him, it was perfect. He'd ruined her for all other rings.

She gave herself a silent talking to. *It wasn't real.* Her main concern should be that it would dazzle someone and cause them to crash a car, or walk into a lamppost. Or that she'd lose it.

She shook herself. On their way back to North Carolina, they would stop at Tiffany's and take it back. It was a loaner. Not hers.

"Jamie!" A woman's voice came from very close behind them. Beth spun, dismayed at her lack of situational awareness. A tiny blonde held her arms out to James. She was utterly beautiful. Beth couldn't remember ever seeing anyone who looked so alive, and vibrant, and that petite. She made Beth feel like a giant.

"Henrietta!" James said, accepting her hug. "How are you?"

The woman pulled away from him a little, but still held him

in her arms. "Just fine now I know you're back. I've missed you. I hoped you'd be here for the wedding, but Sadie assured me she'd given you a pass for it. It's so good to see you again."

So which way was this going to go? Beth held her breath, wondering if Henrietta was going to be in on the game, or if it would stay between James and her.

James gently disengaged from her and snaked his arm around Beth's waist. She let out a quiet breath of relief.

"This is my fiancée, Beth. Beth, this is my good friend Henrietta."

Henrietta's smile brightened just a little as she slid a glance over Beth's frame, lingering for an instant at the ring. Beth couldn't resist placing her hand on James's chest and watching the diamonds dazzle his ex. That probably made her an awful person.

What was wrong with her? She'd gone from friend to lover, to jealous fake lover in the time it takes to reload an M-4. That is to say, no time at all. She dropped her hand. What kind of person was she?

"It's truly good to meet you," Beth said, trying internally to make amends. "James speaks very highly of you." She stuck out her hand and Henrietta gave it a firm shake.

"I had heard that you weren't coming at all. And now you show up with a glorious fiancée. I'm thrilled to be able to catch up with you both this weekend. This is going to be so much fun!"

Beth stepped away from James's embrace and touched her arm. "I'd love to have a drink with you to discuss his... foibles." She winked at Henrietta to underline some kind of unspoken girl code, and James laughed.

Henrietta's eyes sparkled. "Oh, I have a lot to tell you, honey. I'll look forward to seeing you later." She left them, swinging her own Nordstrom shopping bags.

They waved her off and took their excessively expensive bags to the car. "She seemed really nice," Beth said.

"She really is," he said, steering her toward the store's entrance to the parking garage.

"What happened between you?"

"Nothing really happened. She's a widow. She married as a teenager, became a widow in her early twenties and completely changed. Or maybe didn't change at all. I don't know. She's awesome—we just couldn't make it work between us. You'll like her." He grinned. "Just don't believe any of the shit she'll tell you about me."

"Ohh, now I'm dying to sit down with her!" she said. "And wow, a widow at such a young age." Beth couldn't fathom how someone could seem so light and vivacious after going through something like that.

"It was a long time ago," James said, as they reached the car. "Anyway, hopefully you'll be able to spend some time with her this weekend. She's definitely fun, and very interesting to talk to. Might give you some light relief from my family."

"Light relief? I'm going to get that from the open bar," she said with another wink.

He groaned, and she decided to make a peace offering. "I'm not going to take the tags off these things. We can take them back to the store on our way back to base."

"You do that? I mean, borrow clothes from a store?"

"I never have, but I suddenly understand why people do." Beth laughed. "I won't lie. Those are probably the most expensive anything I've ever worn. Outside of my uniform, I seem to only wear yoga pants and workout gear."

"On that note, I should warn you about my family," he said as he shifted into gear and headed out of the garage.

Uh-oh. "Warn me?"

"If you're going to do this, you're going to have to *really* do this. My parents are...set in their ways. They have spent the past ten years or so trying to set me up with very particular girls. From the right families, looking the right way. Pedigreed, they call it. And those women couldn't interest me less. The ones I've met, anyway. So don't be over-awed by anything. They have a big house, but it's only because they can't bear to spend too much time together. A big house gives them a big buffer zone. And my father's work is...well, let's just say that he works all hours, and he has a protection detail."

"He has a what?" Goosebumps erupted on Beth's arms. It was one thing to pull the wool over his parents' eyes for a weekend of fun, but to do so to a guy with a protection detail suddenly sounded like they were going to be lying to someone who had the resources to find them out.

"Don't worry, they only accompany him when he leaves the residence. They have a house in the grounds but they don't hang around the property much unless someone important is due to arrive."

"What exactly does he do?"

"He's the Director of the CIA." He rattled the title out as if he was saying "the manager of Wal-Mart."

"What?" But her subconscious mind was already processing the information. Her next job. He could prevent her from getting her dream job. Any wrong step and...oh my God...her very presence there was a wrong step. She gaped at him. But she couldn't tell him. The number one rule of applying for the job she had applied for was "do not tell anyone you are applying for this job."

Shit. Shit. Shit.

"What's wrong?" he asked, putting on his turn signal and pulling off into a side street. When they came to a halt, he turned to look at her. "Are you really freaked out that my dad's CIA? I promise it's all fairly low-key."

"What? How could it possibly be low-key? As soon as I set foot in your house, I'll probably be security checked. Won't they know instantly that we're not really together? And how does he not know about your job at the air force?" Beth was amazed at his lack of foresight. This wasn't the on-the-ball, ready-for-anything hero she had been thinking about for a year.

"Look, I don't want to burst your bubble, but he'll be far more interested in foreign terrorists and overseas missions than he will be about you. He's been director for a long time and as far as I know he hasn't ever checked up on his family. I mean, why would he? It'd not only be an abuse of power, but also…well, he'd never waste time on anything that wasn't important to the security of the country. Sure, he could look at my service record, but why would he? I promise you Al Qaeda is a lot more important to him than I am."

She needed time to think. She wanted to believe him, but she was so, so scared that this "fun" weekend in a telenovela would blow her chance for leaving the army and serving her country in the capacity she'd longed for. "Why don't you start from the beginning and tell me about your family?"

"Okay. Sadie is my older sister; she's the one who's getting married. She's five years older than me, and she's marrying Simon Phelps. He's in the military. CAG, I assume."

Beth was startled. In all the time she had been in the army, she didn't think she'd ever met a CAG guy. Not that she'd necessarily know. They were the elite, secret Delta Force.

Walker continued. "They haven't been together all that long.

They met somewhere out of the country." He laughed humorlessly. "You see how messed up my family is? I don't even know what they were doing when they met, or where they were." He slipped a look at her as he took to the road again. "Basically, inside the walls of my family house, it's always been better not to ask 'what do you do,' or 'what did you do today.' I learned that pretty early. You only get well-meaning lies in return, and that isn't a good way to have a familial relationship."

"So weather, vacations, and food. That's basically all I can talk about?" She pulled at a stray cuticle with her teeth.

He smiled. "That'd be a good start, anyway. You're not nervous, are you? I won't leave you to fend for yourself, I promise. Besides, I haven't gotten to Maisie yet."

"Oh yes, Maisie. Are you worried about what she said?"

"I am. Not as much as I would if we were a normal family, but yes. Of course neither of them have a protection detail and I honestly don't know what Sadie was thinking by not reporting it. We were drilled at a young age to flag anything strange that happens to us." He frowned at the thought. "But at least there is security at the house. The actual wedding is at the Washington Cathedral, but aside from that, all the rest of the activities should be done at home. I'll feel better when I talk to Sadie and see the e-mails."

Beth nodded. She wanted to see the e-mails, too. It wasn't really any of her business, but she'd received training on threat assessment, so maybe she could see something that he wouldn't. Maybe. "Tell me about Maisie."

"Younger sister, thirteen, rebel, goth, sharp as a tack. There is nothing you can do today that will overshadow whatever awful thing she has concocted to get attention. I promise. Short of a striptease as the vows are being taken, all attention will be on her.

Although, you know, if you have the irrepressible urge to actually do a striptease, just tip me a wink and I'll find somewhere private."

She punched him lightly in the arm. "Ha! A weekend of fake fiancée does not automatically give you the rights to a striptease, Senior."

"Damn it." He put a pissed expression on his face and she laughed.

"I have everyone you might expect to find in a family with a home in McLean, Virginia. Drunk uncle, terrorist younger sister, uptight mom, absent father..."

"I have no idea what to expect. Really. I just have my sister, and before that, it was just my mom and sister. So I guess this will be fun. Once we've ruled out the e-mail problem, at least." She smiled hopefully at him.

* * *

"Here we are," he said as he downshifted and turned a slow right-hand corner. He tried to see her expression as the huge black iron gates swung open. He'd never, ever brought someone here as a girlfriend, let alone a fiancée. *Fake fiancée. Must remember.* Henrietta had been Sadie's college friend, so she'd never come to the house as his guest, only Sadie's.

He hid a smile as Beth's eyes widened as big as a Manga princess's.

May as well give her time to absorb the clusterfuck she was getting into. He remained silent as he drifted in neutral to a security hut. He leaned out the window and addressed the older uniformed man, who had a clipboard and a gun on his arthritic hip. One thing James could say about his father, he never abandoned staff who had been with him for years. But then he knew that Chip would lay down his life for any one of the Walker family, CIA director or not. And that the house was protected by technology now, more than anything else.

"Hey, Chip. How's everything going?"

A huge crash echoed through the trees from the direction of the house, followed by angry shouts. "Oh, about as well as you can imagine," Chip replied, looking briefly toward the noise and infinitesimally raising his eyebrows.

James laughed and pulled a face back at him. "Loud and clear. I'll come see you tomorrow."

"I won't be here later. I've been relieved of my duties until Monday, sir."

James slid the car out of gear again. "What?"

"They have some different security people coming in, I think. I wasn't told. I was just told to take the time off and return on Monday." He placed his pen under the clasp of his clipboard and shrugged. "The wife's happy at least."

"That's so...strange," James said.

Chip nodded. "I thought so, too. But it's not my place to question."

James paused and stared out of the windshield for a second. "Okay. Well enjoy your time off. Your cell phone number still the same?"

Chip nodded once. "Yes." He returned to the hut and pressed the button that allowed the bollards halfway up the driveway to sink into the ground, allowing them to pass. "Have a good day, sir. Miss," he said.

As they drove off, James said, "Chip's been with us since before I was born. Sometimes he was more nanny than security guard."

"I bet he has some stories." Beth smiled. "Thank you for not introducing us. I expect it would have felt strange to lie to him about me."

James hadn't actually consciously thought that, but now that she mentioned it, that was why he hadn't introduced Beth to Chip. It was one thing to lie to his family, who had rarely been truthful with him, and another thing completely to lie to Chip. She was perceptive.

And she was perfect. And she wanted him, he was sure about that. He just needed to convince her how good they could be together...

The tree-lined driveway gave way to an open expanse of lawn, rolling down toward the thick trees in front of the twelve-foot-high walls surrounding the property.

The house itself rose on a mound in the center of the property. Three floors with a garret at the top. He looked at it as if for the first time, viewing it through Beth's eyes.

"How long has this been in your family?" she asked.

"It belonged to my father's grandfather. He had one son, who had my father, and my father has one son. So, I guess it's possible I may live here one day, when I'm old and washed up."

Beth laughed. "You planning on retiring from the air force?"

"I will when they push me out. I love what I do. Which reminds me, don't forget my father thinks I have a feet-firmly-in-a-safety-zone desk job."

"What do I do then? I guess you don't want a special forces fiancée, right?"

He did. His parents might not. Shit, what was he thinking?

"I find being an accountant, or a lobbyist, in this town generally stops people asking more questions." He hoped she didn't mind playing a part. He half wished he'd turned his phone off this morning. They would have just gone climbing and avoided this clusterfuck by a hundred miles. But Maisie's call had just about broken him. He hadn't seen her cry since she was about four.

He brought the car to a halt at the back of the house, where workers were struggling to put up the supports for the big marquee. "This is it."

Beth stayed silent for a moment before slowly moving her hand to undo her seatbelt. The eventual click sounded much louder than normal. Almost as if it was a break from the final frontier of safety. She reached for the door handle and he put his hand on her arm. "Beth."

She turned to him.

"I apologize in advance for anything that happens here."

She looked taken aback for a moment, and he hastened to correct her impression.

"I mean with my family. Fuck. I mean, I just wish we were rock climbing right now." He looked out at the activity on the lawn. "Thank you for having my back here. Taking one for the team. And I promise I'll take you climbing one weekend to make up."

"It's okay," she said, resting her hand on his hand. "In for a penny, in for a pound, right?"

He laughed a little at her old-fashioned words. "You're a keeper."

She smiled at him. "Hey, I owe you. And I got some awesome Jimmy Choos. So…"

She was a good sport. Somehow that made him feel even worse.

"Okay. Once more unto the breach…of your telenovela." He opened the door and got out, knowing as he slammed the door shut that the noise would bring at least one of his sisters out of the house. He was not wrong.

"Incoming," Beth said.

He turned in time to brace himself against Maisie, who launched herself at him, legs wrapped around his waist and arms around his neck. Her shriek made one ear ring.

"Get off me, Munch. Let me look at you."

She slid off him and he held her at arm's length. The violet-tipped hair and nose ring were new since he'd seen her last, but the ear-to-ear grin was the same old Maisie. "It's good to see you, Squirt."

She kicked his shin, medium hard. He rolled his eyes.

"You've been gone for too long. I hate your stupid job," she said petulantly.

"Yeah, yeah, yeah. Heard it all before. But I'm here now. *We're* here now." He held his hand out to Beth, who came around the car and took it.

"Whatever. Can you believe all this fuss, just because stupid Sadie is getting married? I'm never getting married."

"I don't blame you." He noogied her head. "This is Beth. Be nice. She just agreed to marry me."

Beth stepped forward, holding her hand out to Maisie.

Maisie took it and gave her hand one hard pump and then turned back to James. "Sadie's super-mad at me for telling you about the e-mails." Her sad face just about broke his heart.

"I'll handle Sadie." He felt something wiggling in his back pocket. Maisie, the fledgling pickpocket. Great. "Put that back or lose your hand. Why you..." He poked her ribs and she squealed and ran around the car with James in hot pursuit.

"James? Can you direct me to the bathroom?" Beth asked.

He pinned Maisie to the car with one hand and said, "Sure. Go through the door here, through the door immediately opposite, and the bathroom is on the opposite side of the hallway to the left. I'll be right behind you, just as soon as I've killed and buried my felon sister here."

* * *

She grinned at the relationship they seemed to have, which wasn't so different from the one she used to have with Tammer when she was that age. Following his directions, she went up the stone steps to the large double door. She went through what she imagined was a reception room, with different sofas and chairs grouped around the room, and found the right door.

The bathroom was luxurious to say the least. Navy blue tiled walls and bright, shiny white fixtures. A chandelier, for God's sake. Really? Who needs a chandelier in the bathroom?

She leaned against the basin and stared at herself in the mirror. She wished she'd thought to change into one of the new outfits she'd bought, but the other dressing-room activities had scattered her thoughts somewhat. She pulled her tank down to smooth the material a little after the car ride and took a deep breath. Well, she guessed this was an adventure. A view into how the other half lives. This house James had grown up in was bigger than the biggest hotel she'd ever stayed in. And that was a strange feeling. They couldn't have more different backgrounds. The military was a great equalizer, but outside work, she couldn't help feeling as much like a fish out of water as she had ever done.

Slowly rebraiding her hair, she decided very firmly to work this. To practice being someone else. To practice blending in to any situation. And hope that the Director of the CIA wouldn't remember her, or recognize her. What were the odds that he was even involved in the recruitment process of protection officers?

They had to be really small. And maybe by being there, she and James could make sure nothing happened to Maisie.

So she tied off her braid and left the bathroom.

"Just what do you think you are doing?" a voice came from above her.

She turned toward the voice. A woman in a light turquoise suit, with platinum hair in a very neat chignon, was coming down the wide staircase. Beth smiled. "Excuse me?" Could this be James's mother?

"You are not permitted inside the residential areas of the house. Your bathroom is downstairs near the kitchens." The tiny woman pointed at a door at the end of the hallway. Completely used to obeying orders without question, Beth took a step toward the small door that she was pointing at. Then she stopped.

"Actually, I think…"

"The only appropriate response from the help is 'Yes, ma'am.' Who is your supervisor?" Her voice was as sharp and unforgiving as steel.

Beth took a breath. Her first instinct was to explain, but she also wanted to take a moment to think about the realization that she was obviously the first Hispanic woman to be in their house who wasn't a servant or maid of some kind. The conflicting thoughts left her speechless.

"There you are," James said, coming through from the reception room. "I thought you'd got lost." He smiled. "I see you've met my mother."

"James, darling. The caterers have their own bathrooms downstairs. You know only family and friends are allowed in the main house." She patted the back of her hair and turned her cheek for a kiss, which James didn't give her.

Awkward.

"Mother. This is Beth. My fiancée." He snaked his arm around Beth's back and pulled her into his side.

Beth played the part. "I'm delighted to meet you, Mrs. Walker. You have a beautiful house." *No sir, no ripples of discomfort here.*

There were at least two or three seconds of silence, which seemed to last forever, before James's mother held out her hand, palm slightly down, as if she didn't really want to shake her hand.

Beth grabbed it and shook it firmly, sending a slightly alarmed look into Mrs. Walker's eyes. Her eyes narrowed slightly as she examined Beth. She gave a half smile and nodded before turning to James.

"Darling. It's been too long. I swear if Sadie hadn't been getting married, we probably wouldn't have seen you until Christmas, would we? Or found out that you were engaged."

"Of course you would have," he said, obviously brushing it off. "So where have you put us? I guess all the upstairs rooms have been taken?"

"Well, in all honesty, we didn't imagine you'd be here this weekend. Sadie told us you were working. And we certainly didn't know you had a fiancée. This is really bad form, James. I'll have to fix all the seating arrangements and..."

"I apologize for the last minute change in plans. But you know very well you won't have to change anything. You'll get the wedding planner to do that."

Mrs. Walker sniffed and paused for a moment, and grabbed a woman in a gray dress and apron who was just coming out of the door she had initially told Beth to disappear behind.

"Gracie. Change of plan. James and...Beth...will be staying in the pool house. Will you make the arrangements? That means that Mr. and Mrs. Walker senior will be in the Blue Bedroom."

"Certainly, ma'am." With those words, she turned a smooth half circle and disappeared back through the door she had come through. Everything seemed like a well-oiled machine, and Beth suddenly felt like the wrench in the works.

"It'll be more private for you, darling." She put her arm through her son's and walked him back out to the reception room.

Beth followed in their wake, all the way outside to the stone steps again. She felt as if she had been thoroughly dismissed. Beth would have been vaguely annoyed. *Fake-fiancée Beth won't be, though. She is much smoother than regular old Beth. Fake-fiancée Beth will just smile and play along.*

"Go and unpack and get settled. I'll send Sadie out when she's finished wrapping the bridesmaids' gifts," Mrs. Walker said as she urged them down the steps to the car.

They both got in and Beth reached for her seatbelt, and watched his mother disappear back in to the house. Beth turned to him and said, "Wow. Just wow."

James winced and tried to apologize, but she brushed his concerns away.

"I'm the fake fiancée. She doesn't worry about these things. She's marrying you, not your parents. She finds this all very amusing." Beth smiled and settled into the car seat. "Fasten your belts; it's going to be a bumpy night."

"Oh shit." He replied, looking as amused as she did. "I can't tell if you being here is going to be awesome or some kind of nightmare that will haunt me for years."

"I'm leaning toward nightmare," she said, grinning as he groaned. Then they turned a corner and all teasing thoughts dropped away. She could actually feel her jaw drop open at the sight of the pool house. When his mom had mentioned it, she'd kind of imagined a tiny outhouse, maybe, that had been made into a room. No so much. The pool house was bigger than her own house in North Carolina.

The pool was designed to look like a Roman spa. There were columns around two sides of the pool, which made it look like a ruined Roman temple. Cushioned sun loungers were spaced out between the columns, and the transom offered shade. *Holy mother of crap.*

At the far end of the pool was the house. It was almost shaped like a Bedouin tent. A drape-shaped roof gave way to ceiling-to-ground windows overlooking the pool.

For a moment the view was obscured by more tall trees as they parked to the side of the building. She jumped out of the car this time and ran around to the pool front. The floor-to-ceiling windows actually housed an invisible set of double doors. She opened one and stepped into the most luxuriously decorated space she had ever been in.

Huge daybeds and sofas faced out toward the pool, with blankets and towels draped at the ends of each piece of furniture. Drapery hung from the ceiling, bringing the outward tent vibe into the living area.

There was a small kitchen with a huge, full wine fridge, and an open archway that led into the bedroom. It was dark and cool, again with the fabric draped low, making the room feel enclosed, safe, but very intimate. She could almost believe she'd walked into a harem.

James called to her from the doorway. "Does this suit you, ma'am?"

"Ha! You may never get me to leave!" she said, still goggling in awe.

"All your bags are here. The closet is to the left of the bedroom."

She looked around. Indeed, the only feature of the bedroom

was the bed and two night stands. There was nothing else there. She looked for the closet and opened louvered doors. A light came on automatically, illuminating a walk-in closet with wooden shelves for shoes and padded hangers by the dozen for her clothes. Phew. It was good they had stopped to get new clothes for her, as she suspected her normal wardrobe would have been automatically thrown from the closet by some kind of built-in ejector-seat mechanism.

"James, this is incredible. I can't believe I know someone who lives like this."

"*Used* to live like this," he said, throwing his own bag on the floor of the closet.

"Well, it's beautiful. I will say that. This debt I'm paying is not such a hardship, you know."

"Well, I feel like I owe you now, after my mother..."

Beth laughed. "No way. That was priceless. I wouldn't have missed that for the world. Although, you might want to talk to her about that later. I mean, if you bring a real fiancée home with you at some stage. If we were really together, I may well have already left."

"No kidding," he replied.

"But then there's this place." She ran her hands along the back of a silk-covered chaise longue. "So maybe a real fiancée would have stayed, if only to experience all this." She winked at him.

"Something tells me that you're not that easily impressed." He smiled back as he opened the collar of his shirt. "Wanna go swimming?"

"Do we have time?" Beth said, eyeing her bags of purchases, wondering where the white swimsuit was.

"I suspect something will be planned tonight, and frankly,

with all the work being done on the grounds, it might be as well to lay low."

"You don't have to ask me twice. I just need to find my swimsuit."

"Okay, let me get changed and I'll meet you out there." He disappeared into what she could see was a marble bathroom, and she looked around for a second, and then threw herself onto the bed. It was like floating on a cloud. Talk about pillow top.

She stared at the dip-dyed material hanging from the ceiling and wondered what kind of person she'd be if she really was marrying James, and really was going to live in this world full of servants and maids. Would she be different?

Ha. No way.

Chapter 7

James came out of the bathroom and did a double take when he saw Beth out of the corner of his eye, lying arms and legs splayed out on the bed. Just the sight of her there made him hesitate, even though she was fully dressed and obviously thinking about something else.

He loosened the waist of his swim shorts, trying to think about baseball and a list of American presidents. In reverse order. But he couldn't take his eyes off her. He wanted her so fucking badly. Now that he knew how her lips tasted, how her skin quivered under his touch, it was agony waiting to touch her again.

He dragged his gaze back to the main room and decided that if he couldn't seduce her here, he'd never be able to seduce her.

He left the door to the pool house open and dived into the clear water. He figured a loud splash would tell her the bathroom was clear. He took long strokes down the length of the pool, counting every stroke and every breath. Emptying his mind of everything except the strain of his muscles and the feel of cutting through the water. It worked for a while, but gradually, strands of Sadie's and Maisie's e-mails wove their way through his consciousness, until they were all he could think about. Why would anyone send them quasi-threatening e-mails? How would someone even get their e-mail addresses? The family was so security conscious, it was impossible to imagine anyone could even find them.

He finished a length underwater and his head popped up at her end of the pool, just as she left the house.

Jesus. Shit. Fuck. Obama, Bush, Clinton, Bush, Reagan . . .

The white swimsuit wrapped around her every curve. She looked like a 1950s movie star, hair wound up high on her head and huge sunglasses hiding her beautiful eyes.

"I had no idea you could hold your breath that long, airman," she virtually purred. In reality, she probably sounded exactly the same as usual, but he couldn't help but imbue his own fantasy on her.

Bush, Reagan, Carter, Ford, Nixon.

She took off her shades and dropped them on one of the double loungers positioned right outside the room. She stood at the edge of the concrete, wriggling her feet so her toes were hanging over the edge. He pulled his hands off the side of the pool and watched as she did a perfect toe touch before diving into the pool.

By the time she surfaced, all he saw was her bottom bobbing as she powered through the water. Shit. Why was her strength, and ability to do just about anything, such a turn-on for him? Every other woman he'd dated in the past ten years had been slight, tiny, and in need of being looked after. Why was he so into Beth? He was going to be a walking hard-on for three days. It was going to be some kind of sweet hell.

After doing a professional-looking flip-turn at the far end, she lazily backstroked her way back up toward him, stopping just short and floating. So close to him. Her forward momentum was bringing her toward him in a kind of slow-motion crash. He could see it coming, but couldn't move out of the way fast enough in the water, and he wanted to put his hands out to gently fend her off, but at the last minute couldn't decide what part of her body would be appropriate to touch in order to push away.

He had just decided on her shoulder, and stuck out his hand to stop her trajectory, when she gave a small kick, moving just a tiny bit faster than he had anticipated. He knew exactly what was going to happen only a fraction of a second before it did.

Yup, right on her breast.

She didn't flinch or raise her head. She just said, "Forward, much?" and splashed some water at him as she came to a halt.

He snatched his hand back, saying, "I was aiming for your shoulder, but the target moved at the last minute." But even as he said it, he knew his grin was the biggest fucking giveaway ever.

Beth laughed, just loud enough to be heard. "Good thing you had better aim in Afghanistan, or neither of us would be here to touch my boob."

The thought of her touching her own breast was almost enough for him to go from zero to "that never happens, I'm so sorry" in just a few seconds. Fuck the presidents.

"Well, that would be a crime. The thought of neither of us being able to touch them." In for a penny, in for a pound, was that what she'd said? "That night in Afghanistan, you know, before you carelessly got yourself shot, when you reached to check the .50-caliber gun, I saw the smallest part of your bra. I never forgot that. And then when I cut off your pants and realized your panties were the same color, it was a feat of superhuman strength that kept my mind on administering first aid and trying to stop you from dying. I mean, for a moment, it could have gone either way."

"Really? Either way, huh?" She flipped herself upright and treaded water next to him, getting closer and closer. Beth took his hand in hers and drew it down. Down past her waist. And touched it to her hipbone. Then, lower, so his fingers were slowly stroking from her hip downward. When he touched her skin instead of her swimsuit, he swallowed. It took every ounce of strength in his body not to press his fingers against her center, slide them under her swimsuit and feel her heat.

Instead she stroked his fingers lightly over her scar. It felt soft, but slightly ragged. In seconds he had flashed back to when he thought he'd lost her. Frantically pushing back the tide of fear, trying to get the pararescuers to land and take her to safety. Some other emotion overwhelmed him, overtook his pure lust for her, and he slid his hand around her wet neck and pulled her the few inches to him.

Her lips were soft, yielding. For a second. Then she slid her free hand around his hips and brought him against her. Electricity shot through him. There was nothing hotter than a woman who took what she wanted. Nothing.

Her mouth opened under his assault and he slid his tongue against hers. He had an overpowering need to hold her, to bask in her, to protect her. His mouth pressed against hers as if he was keeping her alive somehow. Breathing life into her.

Suddenly they were underwater, sinking into the warmth of each other and the water. He maneuvered her to the side of the pool and slid her up the wall so that they could breathe again. Bracing her against the wall, he held her up while he kissed her, pulling away only to bite at her water-slicked neck.

She shuddered under his touch, as if he *had* just brought her back to life.

"We shouldn't do this," she murmured. He didn't hear her as much as felt the tremor in her neck.

"Hmm?" James said, mouth still on her neck.

"We shouldn't do this," she said, a little more clearly this time.

James pulled away to assess his ability to persuade her, but only heard his father's voice.

"No, you really shouldn't," it said.

Beth jumped about a mile at the close proximity of the new voice. He turned her to the wall so she could hold on, and turned himself to address his dad.

"Father. Good to see you."

"Good God, son. How many times have I found you making out with some girl or another in this pool? It's getting a little old now, isn't it?"

Beth prodded him in his butt cheek. He jumped and made a face.

"It wasn't that many." He turned back to Beth. "I swear it wasn't that many."

"Nevertheless, I'm at least ninety-nine percent sure you should be too old for this now," his father continued.

"Dad, this is…"

"Beth, sir. Nice to meet you," she said, holding out her hand.

His father crouched by the pool and shook her wet hand, and as soon as he released it, he put his hand on James's head and dunked him, just like he'd done every day throughout the summers of his childhood. Every day after work, his father would come get James out of the pool for dinner and would invariably try to dunk him in the process.

He surfaced again to hear her throaty laugher. She had a great laugh, too. Shit, he was a goner.

"Your mother and I have a function to go to tonight, so we won't see you again until breakfast tomorrow. Good to see you, James. We'll meet properly later, Beth." He nodded, and she smiled back at him as he turned to leave.

They watched him until he was out of sight, and Beth pulled herself out of the pool.

"Where are you going?" he asked.

"I think I left my dignity in one of the bags in the closet. I'm going to see if I can find it."

"Wait! Are you okay?" He jumped out after her, still slightly poleaxed by the emotions that were playing with his mind.

She paused to look at him. He could see that her nipples had hardened under her swimsuit. Her perfect nipples on her perfect breasts. A shaft of heat stabbed through him as he longed to take them between his teeth. Fuck. He needed an anti-Viagra.

She gave a smile. "Don't worry, I'm just going to take a shower. We'll forget about this. Again." She gestured at the space between them.

"You'll love the shower." He couldn't wait until they were faking it around other people, so he could touch her with impunity. He had turned into a Machiavellian bastard.

* * *

Beth changed into a robe so that she wouldn't get her new clothes wet while she was hanging them up. She was so turned on that she was practically vibrating.

She wanted him. But she was also scared at what she saw in his eyes. The warmth there spoke of intimacy. Emotional intimacy.

She had to nip that in the bud. Sex. Sex she could deal with, enjoy, understand, feel guilty about later. The rest was messy, annoying, and ultimately devastating. But she had a sneaky suspicion that sex wouldn't just be sex with James.

She needed to focus on the mission: pretend to be engaged and look after Maisie. Nothing else. Ignore the heat between James and her, and...she groaned to herself. Why was everything so complicated? She needed...a freaking cold shower.

James was right; the shower was incredible. The bathroom was tiled in a coffee-colored marble. It had two basins, a claw-footed bath, and a toilet inside, and through some glass doors, the shower was outside, surrounded by a wooden slatted fence. No one could see in, or out.

She released her wet hair from the knot on the top of her head and let the water cascade over her. The slight breeze and the rustle of the leaves in the trees were not doing a good job of making her feel less aroused. The wind blew across her aching nipples, and the rest of her skin, like a caress. She ran her soapy hands over herself like a lover. Briefly. Half of her wanted a release that would stop her from feeling like a schoolgirl around James. Half of her knew it would only increase her appetite.

She turned the water temperature down as she washed her hair.

Enough.

She stepped back inside to wrap her hair in a towel and shrug into the big fluffy robe once more. She caught sight of herself in the mirror and laughed. There was absolutely nothing sexy about the way she looked now.

James was still lying in the sun, so she nudged him with her foot.

"All clean now?" he asked without opening his eyes.

"I wasn't *that* dirty before," she countered.

He laughed and sat up. "I am not touching that comment with a ten-foot pole."

"Very wise." She sat at a table, putting her feet up on the neighboring chair. "I was going to get dressed, but I didn't know what we would be doing later."

"Sadie will show up soon. My bet is a bar in the city." He looked at his watch. "We probably have an hour or so before we have to get dressed. Are you okay here? I'll take a shower if so."

"Sure, why wouldn't I be?" she asked, puzzled.

"No reason. I'll be back in a few." He jumped up and went into the house.

Beth unwound her hair towel and ran her fingers through the long waves. She turned the chair so that the sun could dry her hair and settled back.

From the other side of the pool house, she heard the shower splash on, and tried really hard not to think about James and his body under the shower. Really hard. She shifted in the chair and wondered if *he* was really hard. *Damn it.* She clenched her fists in the pockets of the robe to stop them from wandering anywhere they shouldn't. With the cadence of the water she could visualize him turning under the shower head, tipping his face up to the water…

"Excuse me?" A voice came from across the pool.

Beth sat up and saw the source of the voice. Older than Maisie and James. She was either a maid, another Henrietta-type, or Sadie.

"I'm Sadie." She was tall like the rest of her family. She had short dark hair and was very elegantly dressed, with flared white pants and a black boat-neck top.

Beth jumped up. "Of course you are. I'm so happy to meet you. I'm Beth."

Sadie laughed. "I can't believe you're not a mirage. I just heard that he turned up with a fiancée and felt sure I was hallucinating. But here you are. I've been so eager to actually meet you since I heard. I'm happy you were both able to come. When I sent James his "plus one" invitation, it was really just for Mom's benefit. I knew he would never come. But here you both are!"

Sadie looked at the chair next to Beth and then in toward the kitchen in the pool house. "Do you mind if I..." Her voice trailed off as Beth followed her gaze toward the huge wine fridge.

"Oh no, not at all. Help yourself." Beth grinned.

"Will you join me? Red or white?" Sadie asked as she opened the door.

"White please."

Sadie returned with glasses, a bottle, and a wine cooler. Talk about every convenience. She sank onto the chair next to Beth, facing the pool. She cast a look in the direction of the house and winced a little. "As you can probably see, it's gotten a little out of hand. That's Mom and Dad for you. This whole thing started as fifty people in a small church in Bethesda. Now it's kind of a circus."

"I'm sure it will be a beautiful wedding," Beth said.

"I so wish it was already Sunday. I'd be on my honeymoon and all this craziness would be over with."

That would have been an ideal opening to ask Sadie about the weird e-mails, but Beth didn't feel comfortable asking her about them. She wished James were out here already.

Beth took a long, welcome sip of cold wine. "Where are you going on your honeymoon?"

"Oh my God. Turks and Caicos. A private island. I can. Not.

Wait. Seriously. Just Simon and me, on a private beach, doing unspeakable things." She giggled and took her own long drink of wine. "I guess my parents would be super-pissed if we just eloped at this stage." She looked back toward the main house, which was hidden behind a thicket of trees.

Beth settled back into her chair and took another sip. "I won't tell if you want to do a skip. You can take the Audi."

"No, she cannot. That's my baby." James came out with cut-off BDU pants on, and nothing else. Beth saw two tattoos on his torso that she hadn't noticed before. One small one on his far left-hand side above his hip bone, and the other higher, slightly farther in on the right. She wanted to jump up and take a closer look, but that would seem strange, especially since she was supposed to be intimately familiar with his body.

Sadie jumped up and hugged him for a good few seconds. "I'm so glad you're here," she said.

"And yet it seemed as if you and Beth were planning an escape without me. You can't have missed me that much."

"I did...It's just been so...I don't know, full-on with Mom and Dad. You know how they get. Especially with no one to deflect the attention. Even Maisie hasn't done anything horrific in a while."

James smoothed a tendril of hair back from his sister's face. "It's going to be fine. We're going to have a great night, and the wedding is going to go off without a hitch and you'll love every second of it. I promise."

Sadie took another slug of wine and got up. "I'm holding you to that. Anyway. Tonight, it's just drinks at the JibJab downtown. Eight-ish?"

"We'll be there. Now are you going to tell me about the e-mails?"

Sadie seemed to collapse in on herself as her shoulders slumped and she sat back down. "No?"

"Not an option. Maisie was openly sobbing on the phone, her e-mails upset her so much."

A flicker of concern etched across her face. "I didn't know. She didn't let on that she was scared." She placed her hand on James's arm. "It's dealt with. I told Dad's office and they're handling it."

"When did you tell them?" James withdrew his arm from under her touch, leaned back and crossed his arms.

"A few months ago."

"And did they stop?" he asked.

"No. That's when Maisie started getting them." She sat back in her chair and suddenly seemed resigned to the inevitable. She took a deep breath. "Okay. They started very benign. I didn't know the e-mail address, but because I didn't know half the people Mom and Dad had invited, I e-mailed back to be polite. Just basic things like what the dress code was for the rehearsal dinner. Then they got a little more personal. Asking me if I was sure I wanted to get married. Asking me if I really knew my fiancé. Telling me that people were saying he'd tricked me into marrying him." She shrugged. "I mean it was just crazy stuff. I asked around about the e-mail address but no one recognized it. I sent it to Dad's office and they told me they were investigating, but you know how they are. It's just not as high a priority as other things they have to deal with. So far, the IP addresses were from hotspots in coffee shops and places like that. Short of staking them all out, there wasn't much they could do. Especially since there wasn't an actual threat in any of them. They just told me not to tell anyone about them." She took a sip of wine.

"But they kept coming. Then they started going to Maisie, too. She doesn't know that Dad's office is looking into it, so I made her promise not to tell anyone about it. Obviously she doesn't follow orders as well as I do." A small smile appeared on her face, just for a second, and Beth wondered if she was talking about orders from her father's office, or orders from her fiancé. That smile certainly wasn't about the e-mails.

"Maisie got an e-mail this morning that suggested that someone was following you when you went shopping for her bridesmaid dress. Did you know about that?" James leaned forward.

"Oh God. No, I didn't. Following us?" Sadie rubbed her hands up and down her bare arms as if she'd felt a chill.

"We just need to keep it close this weekend. Neither you nor Maisie leaves the property alone. Let's just get through the wedding, and if the e-mails still come after that, you have to get Dad to take it seriously. Deal?"

"Deal." She got up from her chair and finished her wine.

Beth and James got up too, and Sadie gave James a hug. "So glad you're here, Squirt. I'll see you both later. So lovely to meet you, Beth."

"Likewise. And thanks for the wine. See you later," she replied, raising her glass.

As soon as Sadie had rounded the corner, Beth said, "Squirt? I like that name."

James donned some sunglasses, settled back into the chair that Sadie had vacated, and poured more wine into her glass. "You can call me whatever you like, baby."

"What do you think about the e-mails?" Beth asked after taking a sip.

"It's hard to say without actually seeing them. Sadie broke a lot of hearts when she was younger. Could be an ex, or it could be about Simon, or Dad. Difficult to say. I'll ask Simon about it tonight."

Beth nodded, and then changed the subject. "Okay, let me see your tattoos. I didn't notice them before."

He stretched back in the seat so she could get a look. They were black and gray bullet holes. Like the decals some people put on their computers. She reached out and touched one. It felt the same as her thigh. She traced the other one, on the other side of his body, and moved back. She couldn't read his expression with his shades on.

"You've been shot, too?" Her heart dropped at the risk he'd taken when he saved her.

He inclined his head.

"Twice?"

He nodded again. "Two different tours."

"Wow. You are some bad luck bunny." Thank God he hadn't been shot again when they'd been together. Thank God.

"Until you came along. For a second back there in Afghanistan, I thought the third time would be the charm. But you shot the bastard before you passed out. The PJ had to wrestle that sidearm from your hand when he loaded you into the chopper. You were virtually dead but you held onto that gun like it was a baby. I guess we saved each other."

"Oh, so you admit that now? So really you owe me, too?"

"Ha, ha. No. Nice try, though."

"I can't believe you've been shot twice. And your parents still think you're a desk jockey?"

"Only Sadie knows what I do. You know, just in case someone has to make that call. She's listed as my next of kin. I can't go shirtless in front of my parents, but that rarely happens. You know, unless I get caught making out with a girl in the pool." He took a sip of wine.

"It sounds like that happens more than one would think," Beth said, tipping her glass toward him for a refill.

"When I was a kid. I mean, who wouldn't use this place as a teenager?"

"Truth," she said, clinking her glass against his. She took a drink and imagined James as a teenager, enticing young women into his pool. She smiled to herself. "What's the JibJab?"

"It's a bar in downtown D.C. Sadie must be on a nostalgia kick. We used to go there as soon as we were able to fake reasonable IDs." He smiled as if remembering their exploits. "It's actually pretty nice. A rooftop bar overlooking the mall. It was closed for about ten years for security reasons, but it reopened a few years ago. It'll be fun to check out the old stomping ground again."

"Dress code?"

"A little more upscale than your average pub."

"It'll just be Sadie and Simon, and us two?" She really didn't want to spend any more time than necessary with Director Walker or anyone who would report to him. She didn't want him remembering her, or trying to get to know her. If possible she wanted to fade into the background of this whole weekend.

"Probably. Unless they invited any other friends. But I doubt it. They don't live around here anymore, and most of the family guests will arrive tomorrow for the rehearsal dinner, and then everyone else will just be here for the reception after the ceremony on Saturday." He swirled the wine around in his glass as he spoke, concentrating on it as if he was conducting a scientific experiment.

Beth mentally went through her new wardrobe and picked

out some floaty black pants that had slits down each side from just above the knee, and a wraparound white cotton blouse. She wished she'd brought some nail scissors so that she could just trim the ends of her hair. Maybe she'd look for some in the pool house. It seemed pretty well-equipped.

Maybe she'd ask James to help. She closed her eyes and imagined him touching her hair.

Yup. She jumped up. "I'm going to look for some scissors and get ready."

"Kitchen drawer," he replied.

* * *

The sun had dropped behind the trees when James left the pool and headed into the house. The light was on in the bedroom, so he went to his bag in the closet and unpacked his tuxedo and the other clothes he'd bought at Nordstrom. He hung them up on the opposite side of the closet from Beth's new clothes. She'd left her bag open on the floor, and her sultry perfume rode on the air in the small room.

He touched her new clothes—silk, cashmere, cotton, linen— and imagined how they would look and feel on Beth. Where they would touch her skin. Where they may gape a little and show a glimpse of underwear.

He stepped away. He had no idea why he was torturing himself so much. This was so unlike him. He worked twelve-hour days in a mainly male career field. He hadn't dated in a year or so, but also hadn't even seen any woman in that time that he was interested in. It was crazy that he was acting like a hormone-crazed teenager just in the presence of her clothes.

Shaking himself out of it, he grabbed a handful of dress socks and opened a drawer to shove them in. A flash of jewel colors stopped him in his tracks. Of all the drawers in the whole closet, he had to open the one with her underwear in it. He hesitated, looking at them, oh so tempted to be the creepiest person on earth and touch them. Instead he slammed the drawer shut as if it had been filled with rattlesnakes. He threw his socks in the drawer below and heard Beth in the kitchen.

"Did you find the scissors?" he asked, striding out into the main room. He stopped in his tracks at the sight before him.

She was side-on to him, looking in a drawer. She wore black pants that made her legs look miles long. They were tight around the hips and thighs, and flared toward the floor. She shifted onto her other hip as she rummaged in the drawer and he caught a flash of leg up to her thigh. Jesus hell. Who would make pants with slits in them? Surely they were designed to torture him.

"Not yet. Am I looking in the right place?" She turned to him with a helpless look on her face. He slow blinked, grateful for the dimness of the room now the sun had disappeared. Her top was a white shirt that tied at the side, as if it had wrapped itself around her and was hugging her body. Like he should be.

He was never going to survive the night.

"Should be in there somewhere. It's been a while since I've stayed here. Maybe there's a pair in the knife block next to the stove?" He padded toward her in his bare feet, feeling strange because she was dressed and he was still half naked. Strange? Maybe something else.

She spun around to locate the knife block and her pants billowed slightly, showing the length of her other leg. He suddenly felt as if he was in some kind of alternate reality. As if he was living in proximity to a movie star, someone he lusted for but couldn't have. But he could have her. He was just waiting for the perfect time to make his move. If there was such a thing.

He needed a drink.

"Ah-ha. Found them," she said, brandishing them.

He smiled and reached for a beer from the regular fridge. He remembered the time he'd unknowingly stored beer in the wine fridge, only to find that the ideal temperature for wine did absolutely no favors for beer.

He popped the top and leaned against the counter. "You look fantastic, by the way," he said.

"Oh, this old thing?" She laughed and twirled. And then she stopped. "I've left the tags on. You know, so we can take them back."

"We're not taking anything back, Beth. These clothes are yours for being here when we should be climbing, and yeah, the casual racism of my mother."

She frowned. "We'll talk about returning the stuff later. Let's see how clean I can keep everything. Can you help me?" She held up the scissors.

He put his beer down and said, "Sure. What do you need?"

"Just a tiny trim." She turned her back to him and pulled a couple of pins from her hair. Her dark brown mane tumbled down past her shoulders, her waist, and stopped in the middle of the small of her back.

"Shit, girl. I've never seen hair like this before. It's crazy long." He couldn't help himself but to run his hand down its length, feeling the heat from the sun, or the hair dryer or however it had stopped being wet.

She passed a brush and the scissors over her shoulder and said, "Can you just take off a few stray ends? It didn't occur to me to do it before I went rock climbing. I figured I'd wear it up the whole time. But these clothes make me feel as if it needs a little tidying. Do you mind?"

"Not at all. But I have to say I can't see anything untidy about it." He slid the brush down her hair, and had to bend to reach the ends. "Okay, this isn't going to work. I know. Turn around."

She turned to face him and he effortlessly lifted her onto the counter. For a second he paused, hyper aware of being between her legs. Devastatingly aware of how easily he could lean in and feel her. He glanced up, and watched her mouth fall open, so slightly. It was almost an acceptance of a kiss to come. Almost.

He stepped back and swallowed. "If you scoot back, I can reach you from the other side, and I'll be at a level with the ends of your hair. Is that okay?" He went around the island as she shuffled toward the other side of the counter. He put his hands gently on her shoulders and pulled her back a little more. She leaned back, bracing her hands on the edge of the granite.

"How's that?" she asked.

"Much better. Although, I'm thinking that I'd never cut it as a hairdresser."

"Well, to be honest, you don't strike me as a hairdresser type. Too many bullet holes," she replied huskily. Huskily? Was his imagination playing tricks on him again?

He smoothed the hair down from her scalp, allowing his fingers to dip into the heaviness of it. Did she just shiver? He trailed them down, down and then grasped the ends. He tried to remember how he had seen the on-base barber trim hair.

Realizing he wasn't going to get a good straight line, he used the brush to straighten the hair down her back, and snipped slowly at the few ends that fell longer than the rest. He repeated the action over and over until he was reasonably sure he'd done an okay job. And then he did the creepy thing. God he couldn't help himself. He continued to stroke her silky hair, just a few times more, until he wanted to kick himself. Damn it. He was a heartbeat away from tattooing her name on his ass.

Pull yourself together.

"I think you're done. It's as good as I can get it," he finally said, proud for a second that he'd managed to stop touching her.

"Thank you. That was above and beyond. Appreciate it." She pulled herself upright and stretched like a cat.

He returned to the other side of the counter and grabbed her waist to help her back down.

"It's all right. I can manage," she said.

"In those shoes?" He eyed the three-inch spike heels. "I really don't want to have to carry you around this weekend with a support boot on. Not sure it'd go with your new dresses."

"Fair enough." She grinned and put her hands on his shoulders. He effortlessly picked her up and placed her carefully back on the floor. He prayed that he hadn't hesitated before moving away. He hadn't, had he? He couldn't get a good grip on time and space with her so close. *Shit.* He needed to do something about this.

"I'm going to change and I'll be right out," he said as he hurried to the closet.

"Okay, I'm timing you. If you take longer than I did getting ready, I'll be ending this engagement immediately."

He looked over his shoulder to take in her own shit-eating grin.

Chapter 8

She hoped it would take him ages to get ready. She needed to recalibrate from the eroticism of having his hands in her hair. Her heart rate was unsteady, and her breath shallow and unsatisfying. She made short work of opening another bottle of wine. Not that they had finished the one from earlier; she could still see it outside in the wine bucket filled with what was now water.

She poured herself a cold glass, and took a gulp. Better. Much better. Being a little thriftier than the Walkers, she retrieved the half-drunk bottle from outside and put it back in the fridge for later.

After another sip of wine and a few deep breaths, she leaned her shoulder against the glass front of the house, looking out to the pool. What was she doing here, really?

What had seemed like the right thing to do in the car had suddenly plunged her out of her depth, a feeling so alien to her it was beginning to worm its way into her stomach. She wasn't used to this kind of society, this kind of luxury, or these kinds of clothes. And definitely not the glittering, beautiful diamond ring. The fading light refracted off the facets, casting patterns on her skin and blouse. Hypnotic.

It was important to get a grip on her emotions, her thoughts. She wasn't used to not being in control; it felt like all she could do was hold it together and help James keep an eye on Maisie. Until Sunday, at least.

Sunday, she could be regular Beth again. Sunday she could be back home with her beloved dog, her sister, a beer, and some afternoon football. In pajamas. Ratty old pjs. She took a deep breath and focused on Sunday, and her real life.

"Ready to go?" James said, turning the light off behind him and plunging the house into dusk.

"Sure. Just let me…" She placed the wine glass carefully in the kitchen sink, and brushed her hand lightly over her pants. "Ready."

He loomed out of the darkness, dressed in charcoal gray jeans, and a black, tight polo shirt. Fully dressed he seemed even taller and larger than she remembered.

The journey to the bar took less than thirty minutes. The city seemed almost deserted in the summer heat. Their route took them along the Potomac, over Key Bridge and past the Kennedy Center and the Watergate Hotel, places she'd only ever seen before in movies or TV shows. Beneath the quaint streetlights of Georgetown, she could almost believe she was living some kind of Cinderella fairytale. One with a hot Prince Charming.

James pulled into the valet parking area and jumped out to open her door for her. Her heart thumped. How stupid was it to be semi-seduced by mere politeness?

"Now remember, we're engaged. In love. Just for a few hours. Can you handle that?"

"Of course, sweetheart." She looked up adoringly into his eyes and kissed his cheek. "I know what I'm here for."

He swallowed hard, something she took great pleasure in. She wasn't alone in feeling this. But nothing could ever come of it. It wasn't worth the heartache. It wasn't worth becoming crazed with jealousy and uncertainty while she was deployed.

That settled in her mind, she took his arm and smiled at the doorman who opened the black double door for them to enter.

A tiny lobby had two holes in the wall, as if elevators used to be there, but the doors were gone, leaving black holes where the shafts had once been. There were no buttons to press. A sign read ENTER AT YOUR OWN RISK.

"That sign encapsulates my whole life," she said, looking into the elevator shaft.

"This is the fun way to get up. There are regular elevators and stairs at the alley entrance. You know, for the scaredy-cats." He raised his eyebrows at her as if in question.

"Please don't tell me we have to rope up. I'm not sure my pants will survive it."

"Nothing quite as extreme as that. The elevator doesn't stop. You have to step into it as it's moving. But it doesn't move very fast, so it's not too dangerous."

" 'Too' dangerous? Dangerous enough to take my shoes off?"

"No. Don't worry." He looked up as a rumbling noise got louder. "Just step in when I do." He wrapped his arm around her back and tucked her close to him. The base of the elevator came into view, and instinctively she slipped her arm around him, too. "One, two, three…step."

They stepped on at the same time, and instantly descended into darkness. "What the…?"

He held her even closer, as if the darkness made him bolder.

"It's the turnaround point at the bottom. We're sliding sideways into the next shaft."

She gripped his hand for a second. She wasn't scared; it just felt so unusual.

In about ten seconds they were back in the lobby and ascending up through the floors. Some had closed office doors, some looked as if they were being renovated, covered in plastic and wooden work benches. In between floors the elevator was pitch black.

Somewhere around the eighth floor he dropped his arm and wove his fingers between hers. In the dark, she felt him raise her hand as if he was going to kiss it, but he didn't. By the time they reached the tenth floor, he said, "Ready to step out?"

She squeezed his hand in reply and they stepped out into another lobby. This one was all metal and glass and looked like it was part of a different building from the one she'd seen as they passed through the floors.

Glass doors led out to a large rooftop, decorated with millions of fairy lights against the darkening sky. Sofas and armchairs were grouped around the edges of the roof, and at the far end was a busy bar and a dance floor.

A sharp whistle sounded and James raised his hand. Beth just caught Sadie pulling her fingers out of her mouth and beckoning them over.

Maybe she did fit in here after all.

* * *

Still holding Beth's hand, he led her to where Sadie had commandeered a tall table right next to the bar. Score. Close enough to signal the barman, far enough away to have some space. She hadn't changed at all.

James kissed his sister, who then lunged for Beth, saying, "There you are! My getaway driver!"

"Your what? What now?" Simon said, grabbing his fiancée's hand and pulling her back into her seat while simultaneously holding his hand out to shake James's.

"This is my fiancée, Beth."

Beth smiled warmly and held out her hand, which Simon shook.

"Beer or wine?" he asked them both.

James looked at Beth for her answer, but she shrugged. "Either is fine for me. I guess it depends how long we'll be here."

Sadie looked at her watch. "A couple of hours, maybe?"

"Then I'd like wine, please." She turned to explain to James. "If we were going to be here longer, I'd say beer was a safer bet not to have to carry me back home."

"White wine then, please, for both of us." James told Simon.

Simon raised his hand toward the barman, but Sadie had already whistled for him. "Bottle of Chard, four glasses!" His sister had obviously regressed the second she stepped into this bar again. She sat back down and grinned around the table. "Beth, it's so nice to meet you properly. I hope we get to spend a bit of time together while you're here. We'll be family soon. Oh my God, let me see your ring."

She showed her left hand and Sadie clasped her own hands over her heart. "James must really adore you. What a beautiful ring."

Beth reached for James's hand and said, "I know. I'm so lucky. Really." Then she brought his hand up to her luscious mouth and kissed it, just as he had been tempted to do in the dark of the elevator. Her lips were slightly open and the heat from her mouth warmed the center of his body. And other parts. Jesus.

"It's me who's lucky," he replied.

"So have you set the date yet?" Sadie gushed. "I mean, I know this engagement must have only just happened, given that we didn't know anything about it at all until today." Under the table, she kicked him good and hard.

"Ouch. Stop it, Sadie." He rubbed his shin.

Beth stepped in smoothly. "We haven't really got a concrete date yet. A lot depends on my workload, and James's, and also my sister, who's my only family. I need to make sure she's in the country, too."

"Sweetheart," Sadie said, not without a bit of drama, "you have us now. We're your family."

"Thank you. That's kind of you to say."

Thankfully the waiter arrived with the wine. Everyone took a glass and waited as it was poured. Beth caught James's eye and gave him the shortest glare. He let her take a couple of sips, and then said, "May I have this dance?"

Beth was off the seat before he'd even completed his sentence, so he smiled at the others and in a mock-stern voice told them not to drink all the wine.

"Is that how Sadie usually is? She seems a little...I don't know. Manic?"

"This is definitely not normal Sadie. But with the over-the-top wedding and the e-mails, she's probably just on edge. Or maybe she's not buying our sudden engagement? I don't know."

"We can fix that, at least," Beth purred. "Dance with me here, where she can see." She'd found a spot between other couples dancing to the languid lounge music.

With pleasure, he almost groaned. Instead he put his arms around her and dragged her abruptly against him, holding her hips firmly to his. "Like this?"

"Like this," she whispered in his ear. Jesus, he was sure he felt her nip his earlobe. Familial tension evaporated, and a whole other type of tension filled his body. As they moved to the music, damned if her blouse didn't move so that he could see her light purple bra. Just the strap, tempting him as if he could see her naked.

This time he did groan.

"Sorry, did I step on your foot?" Beth asked, rubbing herself, very slightly, against his erection.

"No. You're stepping on my self-control. What are you doing?" Pure desire rumbled through his body.

"We have to be convincing, right?" she replied, her lips a mere inch below his.

"Right." He stopped dead still. His hand buried itself into the back of her amazing hair, stroking her neck, massaging her scalp. Until he gathered as much of it in his hand as he could and pulled it, first gently, and then with a bit more force. As her head tipped back, her lips opened as she swept her tongue slowly over them. She was so tempting.

Her hands found his shoulders, and she slowly slid her fingertips over his chest, making his whole body pulse in time with his heart. Her eyes never left his, and he felt as if he was the only man in the bar.

She reached up and pressed her mouth against his. She kissed him gently, once. Twice. And then laid her forehead against his. Jesus. Everything in him slowed down to revel in the feel of her, soft and inviting in his arms.

"Can you just stay here, right here, for the whole weekend?" he murmured.

She seemed to tense in his arms. "You don't have to say that when no one's listening, you know." She looked around. "At least we seem to have convinced Sadie and Simon. Oh, here they come."

"Darlings! We've come to break up the lovebirds. I thought the bouncer was going to use the fire extinguisher on you."

A familiar face in the crowd distracted him for a minute. Two faces. James pointed over her shoulder. "Is that Jeffrey and…is that William? What the…" He released Beth and took a step toward them. William had been his very best friend in high school. He'd lived on the same road, but they'd lost contact when James had enlisted eight years previously. Considering James rarely went home, that wasn't really surprising. William caught his eye and waved. The bastard hadn't aged at all.

"Oh my God, who would have imagined?" Sadie said, grabbing Simon's hand.

James squeezed Beth's shoulder. "Jeffrey is Sadie's ex from ages ago. He works for my dad now. William was our neighbor, my best friend. We all used to hang out as kids. It's crazy seeing them here."

Simon took Sadie's hand. "Why don't we all go sit over there on the sofas, and catch up?"

James noted the look that they exchanged and figured Simon wasn't too keen on spending the evening with Sadie's ex and an old school friend.

Sadie nodded and let Simon lead her over to the sofas on the side of the bar that looked out over the Washington Mall. James beckoned the newcomers over. Jeffrey acknowledged where they were sitting, and pointed at the bar. James grabbed Beth's hand and followed Sadie, but she pulled her hand free. "I'm going to get our wine."

"Do you need any help?" he asked, looking back toward the table.

"I've got this," she said, and walked back before he had a chance to reply.

* * *

Beth wouldn't have gotten nearly as far as she had in her career if she couldn't get an instant read on a man. And her instincts were telling her there was something odd about Jeffrey. She'd clocked him immediately. The smile, the way he looked Sadie and her up and down. The way he tried to hide his slightly receding hairline, the slightly higher heels than loafers would normally have. They all spoke of an insecure man trying hard to look like the most confident man in the bar.

In Beth's experience, it was the insecure ones who tried to belittle her, tried to make her feel less than she was. And in her eyes, that was a form of abuse.

This was what she would be doing in the CIA, she hoped. Assessing threats. She always seemed to feel danger before it happened. Like during her last tour. Not that it had saved her from being shot.

William made his way over to the others. He was about the same age as James—tall, thinner than James. Floppy hair that reminded her of a young Hugh Grant. Handsome in a more intellectual way. He seemed happy to see Sadie and James, and she leaned on the bar and watched them greet each other.

Their wine had been bussed away—what little there had been left—so she got the bartender's attention and ordered another bottle. While she waited for him to retrieve the bottle from the fridge "out back," Jeffrey acknowledged her silently from the other side of a group of drinkers at the bar. She smiled and that was all it took. He maneuvered around the group and squeezed in next to her.

"Hi. So you're the new family member everyone's talking about?" He laughed. "I'm Jeffrey, a friend of the Walkers, from, like forever."

How in the hell had their fake news traveled so fast? "You're here for the wedding?" she asked, turning toward him.

His expression didn't waiver, but she thought she saw something flicker in his eyes. Or maybe it was just the fairy lights. "I sure am, honey. Can't wait for the festivities to start." He grabbed her hand. "You *are* engaged. When I heard, I was sure it was just idle gossip. Another Walker bites the dust." He threw his head back and whooped in a way that would only work if he'd been wearing cowboy boots.

"I guess?" she said, pulling her hand back, torn between not wanting to give an inch, and wanting to talk to him, just to get a feel for whether he could be behind the e-mails. Well, and giving him a right hook for calling her "honey."

"I guess we'll be spending time together this weekend. I can fill you in on the Walker clan." He looked at her intently. "Don't worry, I've been cleared. I work for her father, if you know what I mean."

"Okay, sure." Ah, the barman at last. She took the bottle, and a cardboard carry pack of wineglasses, and put it on Sadie's tab. She felt bad about that, but she didn't want to give Jeffrey a look at the name on her credit card.

"I'm going to check you out tomorrow at work." He grabbed her hand as if to shake it, but instead he just held it. "And if you're cleared, I'll tell you all about my experience with the Walkers. Why I called off my engagement. How to survive them. Trust me. You'll need the information I have."

Beth smiled, tucked the chardonnay under her arm, and said, "I'm not sure you'll have much luck looking me up without my last name." She wanted to laugh as his face dropped. "But it was lovely meeting you." She decided to play nice, since she didn't want him talking trash about her to James's father. She left without a backward glance.

A little creepy, but probably not dangerous. Really unprofessional and indiscreet about his job and access to background checks, though. That was the problem with guys like that. Always had something to prove. The real men were the ones who didn't shout about what they did. Anyway, she, along with probably every woman at the bar, had been chatted up by worse men. She just couldn't imagine why an ex would be invited to a wedding. But to each their own.

As she approached the sofas, she raised the glasses and bottle and smiled at James's victory celebration. He must have really wanted more wine, and maybe he was regressing too.

"I spoke to Jeffrey. He told me he was spending the weekend at the wedding. You invited your ex to your wedding?"

Simon answered. "We didn't. Sadie's father invited him. In fact, Sadie's parents invited nearly all the people who will be there."

"That explains why I didn't get an invite!" William said with a big grin.

"I had no idea you were in town. Last I heard you were rocking Silicon Valley. What's going on there?" Sadie asked.

William took a swig of beer. "I have this new start-up now. It's looking good. Plenty of investors. It's all about the freedom of the Internet."

"I can't believe you're living in California, dude," James said. "We should come visit you sometime." He slipped his arm around Beth's shoulders, pulling her in tight.

"I love California," she said.

"That would be awesome. You all should. I have this amazing bayside house in Sausalito. In fact you guys can use it whenever you like. Just call my secretary and she'll put it in the diary." He stretched his arms out, draping them over the back of the armchair in the most assertive way Beth had ever seen. She couldn't help but grin at his attitude.

"You have to come to the wedding, Will." Sadie said. We'll send an invitation around to your parents' house tomorrow morning."

"That would be awesome. I'd love to spend some time hanging with you guys."

Sadie shrugged. "At least we'll now have more than just a handful of guests who actually know us. Seriously, this wedding is so far out of our hands that it might as well be someone else's." But she and Simon twined their fingers together as she continued. "Just two more days until the honeymoon. You sure we can't just skip the whole weekend and get on a plane?" Everyone laughed at her plaintive voice.

James poured Beth some more wine and started giving William shit for having a secretary, and a beach house, which segued into recounting the story of how he'd hacked their school's computer system to flunk the biggest bully in the school. Sounded like William had been lucky to escape reform school. She laughed as James described how apoplectic both their parents had been when they'd heard what happened. As they sat back, and she listened to them chat, James put his arm around her shoulders again, snuggling her closer to him.

Thigh to thigh, hip to hip. She expected her mind to wander toward sex again, but instead she felt comfortable, protected. She wondered if she felt that way because he had already saved her life once. Maybe that had taken away a barrier between them. And maybe she had saved his, although that was less clear to her. She had shot a Taliban who was shooting at them, but in all honesty, he might not have hit either of them. On the other hand, James had definitely saved her.

She sipped her wine and listened to the banter and stories that Sadie, William, Jeffrey, and James were sharing. Simon made a head motion to James and held up his empty glass. They both headed out to the bar to get refills. She'd better start counting her consumption, she realized, or she was likely to make a spectacle of herself. She turned to ask James for a soft drink, but he had already disappeared into the throng.

Chapter 9

"How are you holding up?" James asked Simon as they waited at the bar. Hell, he should have brought Beth with him; it seemed like all the women were getting served first.

"You mean the wedding? Oh, pain in the ass, but it's cake, you know? Two days and we'll be alone in the Bahamas. So I really can't complain." He drummed his fingers on the bar as they waited. "It's just...knowing all eyes will be on us. I'm used to being anonymous; we're both used to being in the background. There's just been a lack of sensitivity around that that's a bit mind-boggling. No offense."

James laughed. "None taken. No one could accuse my parents of being sensitive to anything that doesn't involve keeping up appearances."

Simon shrugged and turned back to the bar to try to get some service.

"Something else is bothering you, though," James said. It was true that he'd only met Simon a couple of times in the year or so he and Sadie had known each other, but James could tell that the tension practically oozing out of the man had to be caused by way more than a wedding. This was the perfect opportunity to ask him about the e-mails.

"Just work stuff. A lot of work shit hit the fan on my last day before coming here. I feel bad not being there to take care of it, you know? Leaving it to the team. Oh, thank God." A barman made it over to them, and Simon gave a double order to take back to the table. Sensible man.

"Next time we send Sadie and Beth to the bar," James said, taking the beer and wine bottles.

"Too right. They seem much better at this than I am. I really don't know when I lost my drink-buying mojo."

James laughed. He was looking forward to getting to know Simon better. He couldn't imagine anyone being better for Sadie. He was about to say something new-family-ish to him, maybe something a bit corny, but as he turned from the bar, Simon's eyes narrowed. James followed his look.

In less than a second, between the crowds dancing and milling around, he saw Beth's face. She was standing, and holding her hand out as if to calm down a situation. Instinctively he headed toward her, never taking his eyes off her. Simon moved in tandem.

Then he saw Beth yanked backward. He dropped the drinks and took off, barging through and pushing people aside. As the crowd cleared, he saw Sadie being dragged to the exit by a man in a hoodie. Beth shouted for him, not knowing he was right behind her. She struggled against another man in a hoodie, holding her. James's heart flamed in fury. *Get your hands off her.*

"Simon, get Sadie." James pointed to the exit as he reached for the man holding Beth. Simon vaulted over the sofas and caught her abductor, spinning him around and decking him in one punch.

James tore the man's hands off Beth's arms and held him the

same way that he'd been holding Beth. Anger flared in her eyes as she kicked her would-be abductor in the balls. James couldn't help but wince. He let the guy go so he could collapse to the floor, which he did.

"That bastard." She kicked him again in the stomach, but he didn't make a sound.

"Are you all right? What the hell happened?" James kept his eye on the other guy, still lying prostrate by the sofas.

"They tried to take Sadie. William ran, Jeffrey froze, and I tried to stop them. But he wrapped me up in a bear hold before I could get any leverage. The guy's definitely a pro."

Before she could finish, the man reared up on his shoulders and used his momentum to spring to his feet, a move James had only seen in movies. He reached for him, but the man had already jumped over the sofa and was making his way toward Simon and Sadie.

James ran after him, but Beth's assailant grabbed his almost unconscious partner and threw him in the elevator, diving in after him as the stupid thing dipped out of sight.

"Fuck," Simon said. "What just happened?"

The whole incident had taken less than a minute. Maybe a minute and a half. Sadie was visibly shaken. "Do you think they were the ones who sent the e-mails?"

Simon's eyes narrowed again. "What e-mails, Sadie?" She groaned and rested her forehead on his chest.

"You told me he knew about the e-mails," James said accusingly. "How could you not tell him?" Beth touched his arm, and when he turned to her, she shook her head at him. He looked back at Sadie, who was in Simon's arms, her eyes glistening with tears.

"Come on," Simon said. "Let's get out of here." He nodded at James. "I'll take her home. We'll talk about this in the morning."

James nodded. There was nowhere safer for Sadie than plastered to Simon's side.

"Shouldn't we call the police?" Beth asked. He knew it was probably the responsible thing to do, but all James wanted to do was get her home and away from whatever was going down here.

"I'm not sure there's much point now," William appeared out of nowhere, looking at his cell phone. "My Twitter feed says that the metro police are responding to an altercation at JibJab. We might actually need to go. No sense in answering questions all night, right?"

He was right, although to be truthful, William always had tried to avoid the police when they were growing up, mainly due to his hacking habit. But in this case James didn't think that the added publicity would please anyone, including Sadie and Simon.

He took a minute to say good-bye to William and get his phone number. Jeffrey was nowhere to be seen, which wasn't a huge surprise. He was probably already reporting back to Director Walker. Breakfast was going to be fun.

He took Beth's hand and steered her toward the elevator. Once inside he wrapped his arms around her in the way he'd wanted to do every time they'd been on patrol together. "I'm so sorry. I never imagined coming to the wedding would put you in danger." He pulled her into him so her head rested just under his chin. "I'm sorry."

* * *

Was he kidding? She pulled away from him. "No, *I'm* sorry. I should have been able to protect your sister. I can't believe I let him get the upper hand. I didn't even get a good look at him."

It was true. All her training was in eliminating the enemy, not memorizing their features. She had zero idea what either of the attackers had looked like, except that they were both light-skinned and wore tightly pull-stringed hoodies.

"Hell, Garcia. Don't beat yourself up. They got away from Simon and me, too," he said in a low voice. "That should tell you something."

She tried to suppress a smile. "That you're both lightweights?"

"Unbelievable. Hell, I'll take it, but feel free to tell Simon that tomorrow morning. Forgive me if I stand waaay back when you do!" She was spunky, he'd give her that.

"Who do you think it was?" Beth asked, the smile evaporating from her face.

"I don't know. They seemed like pros, but also really young. One thing is for sure, we need to nail down this wedding. I don't even like the idea of it being at the Washington Cathedral. It would make better sense if we did it all at the house. It's big enough, and at least it's secure. I guess we'll be talking about this in the morning." He pulled her to him again. "Let's just forget about it for now, okay?"

His breath traced her face, sending shivers goose-bumping their way down her body. She wanted his lips on her. Every-where. *Goddamn it. Get a grip, Beth.* It must be the adrenaline. She turned her face so she was looking at him dead in the eye. *Kiss me, damn it.*

His eyes flickered down to her mouth, but just as she parted her lips in anticipation her stomach rumbled. It sounded like an explosion on the military base range. It echoed around the dim elevator. Yeah, that moment was gone.

"Crap, when did you eat last?" He winced when he remembered. "We haven't eaten since breakfast, have we?"

"Nope, but the wine totally counts as a fruit," she said.

"I know the perfect place for a fast meal," he said firmly. When they reached the bottom, they stepped out of the building and paused. James stood slightly in front of her as he surveilled the road. She took a step back and checked the other spaces not directly on the road: the empty entranceways, the alley opposite, and the first floor windows. Nothing.

He turned back to her and held out his hand for hers. "Shall we?"

She grinned and took his hand. He led her to a small square, with grass in the center and a buzz of activity around the edges. Food truck nirvana.

"Bless you," she breathed. "This looks like heaven." She couldn't wait to eat, and honed in immediately on a Taco Taqueria truck. "Tacos?"

"Excellent choice, m'lady. As long as you order."

"Chicken!" she said, laughing.

"Maybe steak?"

"Very funny," she said over her shoulder as she reached the window of the truck.

She ordered two steak soft tacos with everything. The smell from the truck reminded her of her mother's kitchen, and the food she'd never taught Beth to make.

She handed one to James and took a bite of hers. Flavor exploded in her mouth, a little fire, a little fragrance... *Oh my God it's perfect.*

"*Oh por dios, esto es delicioso! Creo que te amo. Definitivamente estoy enamorada,*" she said to the old man serving.

He shrugged and replied in accented English. "Oh, sure you do. They all say that. Get along with you!"

"What did you say?" James asked, unwrapping his taco.

"I told him I loved him," she said with her mouth half full.

"Unbelievable," he replied, and finally took a mouthful.

"Yeah, he didn't believe it either. It's awesome, right?"

"Jesus. I think *I* love him." He wiped some chili sauce from the side of his mouth.

"You should go tell him. I don't think I was his type."

"You're everyone's type, are you kidding me? *Caliente!*"

"Really? You're really *caliente*-ing me? You idiot." She took another bite. And then pointed at a bench. They sat down and scarfed down their food. When every last bit had disappeared, she said, "You look like you didn't realize how hungry you were."

His eyes darkened. "I know exactly how hungry I am all the time, Beth."

She had a feeling he wasn't talking about the food anymore. "We should go back, right?"

"To the house? Sure." He stood and offered her his hand.

Beth rolled up her wrapper and drop-shot it into the trash, then took his hand and jumped up. "I've never been to D.C. before," she said. "So aside from being set upon by some thug in a hoodie, this is pretty awesome."

"You've never been here before? Holy shit. We are definitely not going back home right now, then." He pointed south. "You know what's four blocks in that direction?"

She laughed. "I have less than no idea."

"Everything is. Come on, let's go." He set off at a fairly good clip, and she had to hold him up and take off her shoes.

"Look," he said, drawing her to him, and crossing what during the day was probably a busy intersection to a large expanse of grass.

The Washington Monument loomed in front of them, surrounded by a circle of flags. "White House or Lincoln Memorial?" he asked her.

"Lincoln Memorial." She imagined it as she'd seen it in movies, lit up in the night, quiet, still, majestic.

They walked along the reflecting pool, which in all honesty wasn't doing much reflecting, and climbed the steps to the monument. A few people milled around, taking photos or talking quietly on the steps.

She wondered what he was thinking. About the guys in the bar? About her? In the pool, in the store dressing room, those kisses had been electric. Holy hell did she want him so freaking bad. Maybe just this once. Maybe it was the wine or adrenaline talking. She hadn't had sex for so long, she wondered if she even remembered how.

James let go of her hand and pulled himself on to one of the balustrades and leaned back, looking at the clear sky. "It's beautiful here. Hard to imagine we're in the middle of a capital city, isn't it?"

Beth leaned between his legs, back to the stone, and looked up. "You see more stars in North Carolina. More if you have NVGs."

His hands landed on her shoulders. "Well, everything's clearer with night vision goggles."

"Not everything," she said, rolling her neck under his massage. "Anyway, some things are clearer in the dark."

He didn't reply. His thumbs ran lazy, firm circles along her shoulder blades, turning her insides to warm liquid. She had no idea what she was talking about, no idea why she'd said that. Except it felt true. Complications that felt insurmountable in the cold light of day seemed less complex, and less important, in the dark. He was making her feel too much. No, not too much, just feelings she hadn't explored in years. She turned. "What do you think is happening between us here?" She looked into his eyes, searching for a sense of honesty.

He took a hand and cupped her cheek. It took every ounce of

strength she had not to turn her face into the warmth. "What do you want to happen?"

She couldn't answer, didn't want to answer, give anything away, or just give anything. She was lost in this unfamiliar territory. A place she didn't feel entirely able to control. "I want you, but I don't know if I can do this." She shook her head, either in dismay at what she had said, or as an excuse to feel his hand over more of her face; she couldn't tell the difference anymore.

She did want him. She just didn't want the crushing broken heart that she knew would be around the corner. She could already feel it creeping toward her, as if it was inevitable.

"I want you too," he said. "I can't say where this is going. But I'd never deliberately hurt you." He slid down from where he was sitting and traced her cheek with his other hand. "The first move is yours, Beth."

She took a breath. Was she really going to do this? Embrace a one-night stand and hope she didn't feel anything for him on Monday? His face, so handsome in the moonlight, studied her intently, waiting. To hell with the future and worrying and bad dates from the past. To hell with everything except this warm excitement his very presence gave her. Life was too short.

She stepped toward him and put her hand flat on his chest, taking pleasure in the heartbeat that pumped hard and fast beneath. "I do want you..."

He waited for a second as if to see if the "but" part of the sentence was coming. After a second of silence, he claimed her mouth. In one swoop she was off her feet and pushed against the wall. Equal parts excitement and fear of the repercussions drove her hormones into overdrive. She kissed him in a frenzy of need, winding her fingers around his collar and gently scratching the back of his neck.

Groaning, he tore himself away from her. "Not here. I want you in my bed. In the shower. In the pool. Not in public."

Before she could say anything, he picked her up again, and this time he slung her over his shoulder like he had in Afghanistan. "This feels familiar," she gasped out between the strides he was taking toward the car. She couldn't help but giggle, and that turned into a laugh so difficult to push out that she struggled to catch her breath.

"You all right, ma'am?" asked a man dressed in army PT clothes, coming to a stop as he passed them.

"Yes, thank you, soldier. I'm fine." She laughed again as the soldier shook his head, smiled, and continued his run.

At the traffic light, James put her down and made a big deal of leaning against the lamppost and panting. "Sweet hell, that taco packed on the pounds. You are much heavier than I remember."

Beth half shrieked and half laughed. "You bastard! You better run fast…"

He turned and ran. Ran for his life. At least he should have. Beth found it unreasonably easy to keep up with him, even though she was really not dressed for athleticism.

James reached for his valet ticket while still running. And Beth couldn't really figure out why they were running. He got his beloved Audi and opened the door for her, holding her hand as she got in. Instead of going to his side, he crouched down next to her as she reached for her seatbelt. He kissed her gently on the lips, and then on the cheek. "We'll be back in twenty-five minutes. Please don't change your mind."

She grinned and reached out to touch his inner thigh, stroking her nails down to his knee. "You better hurry." He wasn't going to know what hit him.

* * *

His dick strained against the seam of his pants as he ran around to get in the car. He was on fire for her. The excitement in the club had segued into the very physical reaction coursing through him. The car purred to life as he shifted into first gear and took off toward the GW Parkway. "You are the devil. I'm so hard right now," he said, accelerating through the gears.

"Really? *Dios*, it's hot in here."

Out of the corner of his eye he saw her untie her wraparound blouse. Was she serious? "What are you doing? I mean, what are you doing right now?"

"Nothing," she whispered.

"That"—he swallowed—"doesn't look like nothing." He was beyond caring that his dick was tenting his pants in a way that not even the dark could hide. "You're killing me." He tried to keep his eyes on the road, but she was making it impossible.

She slowly unwrapped her top, first pulling it from one side, then the other, shifting slightly on her seat.

"Look!" she said.

He looked as she flashed her bra. Holy shit. Was he even going to make it back home?

"Eyes on the road," she said in a singsong voice.

"I want you to know I am going to tease you so bad when we get back, you'll be screaming my name, begging me to let you come."

Silence.

He looked over. She was stroking one of her breasts over her bra. Shit. His eyes were off the road a little too long and a horn blared. He swerved back into his lane and took the exit to the GW. He shifted into fifth gear and set the cruise control. With a deep breath, he reached for her. Touched her knee, softly, slowly, belying his utter need to devour her.

He stroked up her thigh to the split in her pants. His eyes remained resolutely on the road, but he was feeling his way by her suddenly labored breathing.

"What do you want?" Beth whispered, her fingers lightly caressing the back of his hand as it played with the gap in the fabric.

"I want to feel how wet you are right now. How much you want me. To feel your slickness. Coat my fingers with it and slide it around your clit. Slip a finger deep inside you and feel you grind against my hand. I want to feel you tight around my fingers. I want to hear you beg for more, for the release I can give you. I'll never get used to you saying my name. I want to hear you say it when I'm so deep inside you I'll need directions to get out." He slipped his hand directly into the gap of her pants, and slowly allowed it to climb.

He reveled in the feel of her skin under his hand. After all this awkward fumbling today, he just wanted to throw her flat on the huge bed in the pool house and spend the night making her insane with desire. Then maybe tomorrow night, and the next night too. There was no way he'd ever get enough of her. His hand slipped up and the tip of his finger came in contact with the heat of her panties. She gasped out loud and tried to push against his hand, but he pulled it back to caress her inner thigh.

"You're making me crazy," she said.

"We're nearly home. We have all night," he said, cringing at the hoarseness in his voice.

"Really, you can wait that long? I'm not sure I can." She put her hands up to her collarbone and stroked down between her breasts. Up and down, making him into a swivel-head again.

Slowly, she undid the front of her bra and sank back into the seat.

No way. No way.

He was seriously about to come. There was no way he could watch her touch herself like that. His hand left her thigh, and he shifted forward in his own seat so he could touch her. Sweeping her bra open, he exposed her to the car's air conditioning that he'd innocently switched on when she'd first said she was hot. He couldn't not look. He couldn't not pull over. He did both. Put on the parking brake and dived for her, taking one sweet dark nipple in his mouth and biting gently on it.

Beth moaned, a sweet, sweet sound that filled his ears and made his body pulse with need. And then her hand made contact with his dick. She stroked him through his pants, pushing hard against it, forcing the blood to pump around it like lava.

His hand slipped up her pants again, and this time he pressed lightly against her hot, damp panties. The mere touch sent shudders through them both. He had to take charge here. He gave her nipples one last lick...and then a little more biting, until she ground herself against his hand.

"Make me come. I'm so close, James."

He pulled away and took a breath. "I'm taking you home, sweetheart, and I will make you come as often as you want." He wrapped her blouse over her and pulled back on to the road. He blasted through the speed limit to get them back in the minimum amount of time. He didn't want her to change her mind, totally absorbed with getting some privacy so he could bury himself in her. Jesus. He'd been thinking about her since he'd met her. She was all he'd thought about. He was a goner.

The nighttime security guard waved them through, and he pulled up to the side of the pool house with a slight skid. He was out of the car in seconds, racing to open her door to help her out. She got out and they stared at each other for a moment before she reached for his head and kissed him, gently this time, slipping her tongue into his mouth and sliding it against his, bringing a friction when she lightly sucked on his tongue.

His hand gently brushed open her top again. He caressed her breast so lightly he could barely feel it himself, but Beth's breath became ragged and she groaned into his mouth.

"Come," he said, taking her hand and drawing her along the path to the pool.

"That's what I'm counting on," she said, walking fast behind him.

Shit. He stopped dead and turned to her. "I'm so sorry." He wrapped her blouse around her and tied it at her side in an approximation of where it had been before their car ride. One kiss, a revoltingly chaste kiss. Her brow furrowed at him—a little hurt, maybe? *Damn it.*

He led her toward the pool. On the double lounger lay Maisie, asleep with her blanket and her childhood bunny, which had seen better days.

"I have to take her back to the house. If they miss her, the cavalry will be called." He sat next to the girl and gently shook her. "Maisie. What are you doing here?" She mumbled in her sleep.

"It's okay. Take her back; make sure she's okay."

"I'm so sorry," he said again.

"No need to be." Beth shook her head and ruffled Maisie's hair as she went into the house.

He sighed and watched her slip inside the darkness of the house. He wanted to kick something.

He lifted Maisie into his arms and made his way to the main

house. Halfway there, she woke up and snuggled into his neck. "Jimmy."

"What were you doing at the pool house?" he asked, taking large strides.

"I thought you'd be coming back earlier. Jeffrey told me that you'd be back at about nine when I told him where you'd gone. I wanted to play cards or something. But you didn't come back."

Jeffrey? Maybe he'd been here with James's father discussing work. That kind of made sense. Maybe that's how he'd found them at the bar.

There was no one around at all in the residence when he deposited Maisie back in bed and closed her door behind him. He went downstairs to see Gracie, who was in the hallway. "I just put Maisie back in her bed. She was sleeping by the pool," he told her.

"That's no problem. I'll go and check on her in a bit. I did worry that she'd be lonely when your parents left this evening. I think she's feeling a little left out. Hopefully when the wedding is over, everything will get back to normal," she said.

He was so eager to get back to Beth, he only half listened. "Thank you, Gracie. I'm going back to the pool house. If she wakes up again, call me. I guess she can sleep in the pool house for the night if she wants."

"Of course. I'll sit with her for a while. Good evening, sir."

He walked back toward the door. Shit, what was he thinking? He left the main house and ran back to the pool house. The lights were still off. He half hoped to get back and find Beth waiting for him with more wine. But, no.

He let himself in and stopped for a second to listen for a clue as to where Beth was. No lights were on. He started taking off his clothes and made his way to the bedroom. "Beth?" he whispered.

No answer. He turned on a lamp. Beth was in her underwear, face down, asleep in the bed. *Fuck.*

He stared at her for a moment, then smiled and turned the light off again, and crawled to the far side of the huge bed.

Un-fucking-believable. Cockblocked by his sister.

Chapter 10

Beth stood in the shower, unable to believe she'd passed out so quickly the night before. She'd woken up as the sun hit the pool, and decided to creep out without waking James. The outside air was slightly chilly, but the water was deliciously warm. She tried to keep her tied-up hair dry so that she wouldn't have to go looking for a hairdryer.

Damn it. She'd been so ready to have sex last night, so hot for him. What was wrong with her? She liked him and had decided to throw caution to the wind last night, but now she was convinced that it had just been adrenaline taking control of her hormones. Maybe he also had regrets. Would things be awkward now? *Urgh*, she hated this shit.

"Morning, sunshine," he said from the door to the outside shower, making her jump.

Her back was toward him, and she couldn't bring herself to turn around. She couldn't bear to see pity or awkwardness in his eyes. Except, if he was feeling awkward, would he have come outside when he knew she was in the shower?

"Can I join you?"

Maybe not so awkward.

Still silent, she closed her eyes. Which way to jump? She turned around slowly and slightly cocked her head at him. An unmistakable invitation. *I guess that's my answer.*

He took a second to kick off his boxers and step in, and in that second, all her insecurities rushed back. She tamped down the instinct to cover herself. But then James was reaching for her, and all room for thought disappeared.

He put his hands on either side of her face to kiss her lightly. He pulled away, just in time for her to see his smile fade.

"Wait. What's that?" he asked, pulling away from her. He looked at her arms.

She suddenly felt very self-conscious. What was wrong with her?

"What's what?" she asked.

"Turn around," he said softly.

She did, worrying what he'd seen on her to break the mood.

"My God, Beth. You are black and blue. Your arms have purple hand marks on them, and your back..." His cleared his throat. "You're bruised. All over."

She turned back around and looked at her arms. "It's nothing. I told you he was a professional. He put his knee in the small of my back while he held my arms back. I couldn't move. If I'd seen him coming..." She paused and rubbed her hands over her bruises. "But I didn't, and that's just the way it goes."

"I'm so sorry," he whispered.

She grinned to try to snap him out of his quiet. "How sorry?"

A spark entered his eyes as he considered. "Very, very sorry?"

"I'm just saying...It says something about a man who doesn't keep his promises," she said, raising her eyebrows disapprovingly. "You promised me something last night and I've been waiting all night for your follow through." She placed her hands on her hips. "Now, *soldiers*—they keep their promises…but maybe airmen…"

He slipped his hands around her waist and pulled her in tight, nuzzling the side of her neck and making her squirm. His body was hard against her. Every part of him that she could feel was tight and firm. The water flowing between them left her rubbing her slick body against his, just to feel his muscles move under her touch.

"I remember exactly what I said last night. And I intend to keep my promise, again, and again…" He moved his lips from her neck to her mouth, but before she had time to kiss him back, he set her away from him.

She looked at him questioningly, knowing full well she was flushed with blood pounding around her body.

"I just want to look at you for a second," he murmured, running his eyes over her body. "You are even more gorgeous than I ever imagined. And let me tell you, I imagined you a lot."

"A lot?" She giggled as he darted toward her, ducked back under the shower and held her, careful not to touch her bruises.

"A whole lot." He grabbed her again, and pinned her with his eyes as he slowly lowered his face to hers. He tasted her lips gently at first, but as soon as she snaked her hand around the back of his head and opened her mouth under his, he groaned and thrust his tongue against hers. After a knee-trembling minute, he gently pulled away from her, breathing heavily. A second later he'd grabbed the soap from a holder attached to the wood surrounding the outside part of the bathroom, and lathered up his hands. He kissed her again as he sudsed up her neck and shoulders, giving them one hell of a massage while his kisses turned her insides to molten lava. He reached again for the soap. "How dirty are you?" A glint flashed in his eyes.

"A whole lot," she whispered back, mimicking him and making him laugh.

He dragged his soapy hands down her arms and took her hands in his huge ones, massaging her palms. She was in heaven, anticipating what he would do next and reveling in the feel of his strong hands on her.

"So, so dirty." She grinned with her eyes closed, head tipped back, no longer caring about how wet her hair got. In fact, when he took the pins out of it and watched it fall down her back and over her shoulders, he groaned.

"I love your hair," he said, reaching for the shampoo. He gently swept the hair that had fallen over her breasts over her shoulders, but her nipples pebbled as her heavy wet strands touched her.

His eyes closed and she watched with pleasure as he swallowed hard, having touched her breasts. He poured the shampoo into his hands and massaged her scalp. Pulling her into him so her forehead rested against his chin, he slid his hands down all her strands and her back until she purred.

Hot liquid flowed through her and settled between her legs. She was incredibly wet for him. She tipped her head back and kissed his chin, rising on tiptoes, nibbling at his bottom lip, sucking it gently and slowly into the heat of her mouth. Then she flickered her tongue over his lip and felt rather than heard a groan vibrate through him.

His hands left her hair at the ends and cupped her bottom, grinding himself against her. His dick lay flat against her stomach and she rotated her pelvis a little to allow him to feel her flesh all around his dick. "Tell me what you want," he moaned against her lips.

"I want you," she said. "I want your hands on me, I want you to feel how wet you make me. How wet I am. I want to feel you inside me."

"Magic words," he whispered, running his hands around from her ass to her waist. His foot nudged her legs farther apart. A frisson of excitement dashed through her as she acquiesced to his demand and opened her legs for him.

He slid a cupped hand between her legs, soapy and slick, from the front to her ass and back again. A tease of immense proportions. She stilled, waiting for his touch, the one that burned in her imagination. He paused, and with one hand tugged at her hair so she was looking up at him. "Open your eyes, sweetheart," he whispered.

Her eyes found his as he stroked firmly along her slit, finding her clit and pressing gently on it. Her eyes fluttered closed and he pulled his hand away. "Open. I want to see you."

She opened her eyes again, feeling his intimate stare right down to her toes. He stroked her again. "You're so wet," he murmured. He pushed a finger inside her and stroked the front of her channel, directly behind her clit. With his thumb, he stroked her bud until she was digging her fingers into his shoulders. She'd never felt such a brewing explosion. Her legs weakened as she felt her orgasm build like a tidal wave. She hovered on the brink of the precipice for a second. "James. *James*," she gasped as it erupted in her.

His eyes bore into hers as she came, shuddering around his fingers. He leaned down to kiss her wet lips, but she pulled away. "I need you inside me. Now." She reached down with her own soapy hands and took his dick in her hand. It was so hard, smooth, and…big. Heat continued to pulse around her, and she drew his dick down and pressed it on herself, using the tip to stroke her clit. "You're killing me, Beth," he groaned. "Are you… do I need to find a condom?"

She couldn't wait. She was on the pill, and all active duty military were tested for other things fairly regularly. "No, we're good," she said.

He didn't hesitate. He lifted one of her legs over his elbow, wrapped his arm around her waist to help her balance, and teased her with the tip of his dick, just pressing so slightly against her opening.

"Please, James," she asked.

With one thrust he was buried inside her. She gasped out loud and felt her heated body expand to accommodate him. She felt complete with him inside her, a part of her.

He lifted her so her legs could wrap around his waist. She dug her heels into his ass to get as much of him inside her as she could. With her arms around his neck, she kissed his mouth, licking and sucking his tongue and lips, needing to give him what he'd given her. He groaned.

She flexed her pelvis, using her legs as her pivot point, but she wanted more. "Put me down," she said softly.

He immediately withdrew slowly from her. "Are you all right?" he asked, a look of concern flashing across his face.

She kissed him. "Perfectly fine. I just want to feel more of you."

He frowned until she flipped all her hair over one shoulder and turned away from him, still looking at him over her shoulder. She braced her hands on the wooden fence and slowly smiled, bending at the waist and opening her legs.

"Fuck," he breathed, putting his hands on her waist.

"That's the idea, Senior." She watched as he took his dick in his hand and guided it into her in one non-stop slow thrust. She wriggled against him to get the perfect angle, and turned to face the wall. She closed her eyes and just felt. Felt him deep inside her, felt him moving inside her. With every stroke, her body, every cell came alive. Something strange was happening deep inside her brain, as well as deep inside her body.

His hands stroked her back from her waist to her ass. From her ass to where their two bodies met. She reached between their legs and stroked his balls. Immediately James started panting, and his cadence picked up. She squeezed gently, and his hands on her hips propelled her onto him faster and faster, until with a groan and a shudder, she felt him come. She waited a second, and then flexed her pelvic muscles, which made him grind out a "Beth."

She slowly stood up and stretched her back, hands above her head. He reached around her and cupped her breasts in his hands, pressing his whole body against her back. He nuzzled her neck and kissed her jawline. She felt wanton. And she really, really liked it.

* * *

He was weak for her. His whole world had just shifted on its axis. He'd just got something he'd been craving for over a year and he didn't feel sated. Not even a little. He wanted her again. Wanted more. Wanted to lose himself in her. He swore if she moved just a little, he would get hard again. It was like fucking an enigma. The most desirable enigma in the world. In the moment she came, he felt as if she was his. But now, minutes later, he felt as if he'd have to win her all over again.

She turned in his arms. "That was spectacular. Thank you." She reached up and gave him a kind of chaste kiss on the lips.

"Thank you? You don't have to thank me. I plan on giving you 'spectacular' any time you ask for it." He grabbed for the soap again and lathered her breasts, reveling in how her erect nipples felt under his fingers. He soaped up again and washed her stomach and then between her legs. No lingering but, oh my God, she felt so hot and welcoming down there. As she had before, she opened her legs for him. This time she grinned at him. He slid his hand all the way around her pussy, up to her ass, pressing a finger against her, which made her expression turn from smug to surprised.

He laughed and she punched his arm. "You're getting me excited again."

"Really?" he said, painfully aware that his cock was transmitting signals of interest. Suddenly he heard the phone ring. "Shit, that's the internal ring tone. If I don't answer it, someone will come down here."

He grabbed a towel and wrapped it around himself, then ran back into the house to grab the phone. It was his father, calling to detail the hour-by-hour plans of where he needed to be and who he would be meeting. He tried to bring up the events of the previous night, but his father cut him off, only saying that it had been handled. That wasn't good enough. James planned on discussing it at breakfast.

As he spoke to his father and made notes about the show times for various events, Beth wandered in from the bathroom wrapped in a big towel. She settled opposite him on one of the daybeds. He smiled at her and mouthed "father," pointing at the phone.

A few minutes later his father was still talking about who would be at that afternoon's gathering and who he wanted James to talk to. Beth lay back and flipped open her towel, showing off her incredible body by stretching one arm behind her. Fucking amazing view. He smiled and slowly let his eyes travel the length of her, taking in the flush of stubble burn around her neck, where he had kissed her.

"Hm-mm?" he said to his father.

"James, are you listening to me?" his father barked. "It's very important to me that the right people are looked after at this damned wedding. I have people from the office, and from important areas of government. It wouldn't hurt you to do a bit of networking. You've done your time in the air force. Serving your country will look great on your résumé, and will get your foot in the door of the next chapter of your life."

James watched Beth hold his gaze as she stroked one hand down her body. His body immediately started to react to the beautiful sight. "I'm not sure I need a new chapter. I like the one I'm in."

"Don't be facetious," his father said.

She touched her nipple, circled it with her finger, and still with her eyes on his, she licked her finger and continued to play with it. His dick hardened under his towel.

He knew his father was still talking, but he felt like he'd heard the speech a couple of dozen times before, so his concentration was on Beth, as her hand slipped lower.

"Hmm-mm," he said into the phone.

Her fingers stroked down, and down, until she deliberately opened her legs, showing herself to him. Glistening and hot. Now all he could hear was the blood rushing in his body.

As she touched herself, his eyes closed for a moment. Then popped open. She moved her hips up and around as she stroked, dipping her fingers into her liquid and slithering them around her clit. Her breath began to speed up.

His cock pulsed with every stroke she made. Slowly he undid his towel and showed her what she was doing to him. Her eyes seemed to gleam at the sight. Lightly he ran his own hand over his dick, feeling it strain against his hand for more friction, more satisfaction.

She widened her legs and slid a finger inside herself. His balls tightened. Watched as she drew it out and spread the moisture over her clit. He'd never ever experienced anything as hot as this in his life. Never felt like this. He needed her in his life. Needed her body, her mind, her utter fearlessness.

"Gotta go, Dad. See you at breakfast." He knew he'd cut his father off mid-lecture, but James couldn't bring himself to care. He disconnected.

"Sweetheart. You started without me," he said, sliding to his knees at the end of the daybed.

"I'm nearly finishing without you, too," she gasped with a low half laugh.

"No fucking way." He gripped her ankles and pulled her toward the end of the chaise. Then he kissed her bullet wound, flicking his tongue over it, and nudged her thighs even farther apart. "I want to see you." He parted her folds with his fingers and lightly blew on her, making her buck under the sensation.

"Touch me, James…" she whispered, and the words, the use of his name, nearly blew the lid off his tightly controlled need for her.

He used the tip of his tongue to dart around her pussy, knowing full well that he was driving her as crazy as she was driving him. She strained against him, against the daybed, seemingly desperate to have his mouth on her.

He flattened his tongue and licked her hard, allowing the tip to flick at her clit at the end of the stroke. Again and again, holding her ass cheeks in his hand, he raised her hips and licked her from her asshole to her throbbing clit. It seemed to grow in his mouth as he sucked on it. He slowly slid two fingers into her.

Her breath was becoming labored and loud, until her hands dug into his shoulders as she embraced her release. She pulsed around his fingers as she came, gasping into the quiet air of the room.

Boo-yah.

* * *

Beth's muscles melted like butter and she sank into the cushions. "*Madre de Dios*, James."

"I take it that's a good thing?" he asked, grinning.

"More than good." She stretched and looked out at the pool. Something flashed in her peripheral vision and she shot upright. James followed her line of sight.

"What is it? What did you see?" He moved quietly to the window and peered out into the undergrowth.

An uneasy feeling prickled at the base of her spine, an instinct that had served her well in the past. "There was something, or someone there. Watching." A chill ran through her. Give her something she could fight, something she could neutralize, and she was in her element. People she didn't know sneaking around? Made it difficult to figure out who the enemy was.

"Whoever it was has gone now. It was probably a worker who stumbled across this place. Don't worry. I've got your back. I won't let anyone hurt you."

There was a huge difference between being in combat, and having some unknown person watching her while she was naked. But his words infused a sense of security in her. He did have her back. He'd proved it before, and she trusted him now. Damn him. He could talk her down from borderline paranoia to ease with a couple of sentences. He was good.

He held out his hand to her. She grabbed it and he swung her into a fireman's carry once again. This time he spanked her bare ass. She squealed at the sharp crack but wiggled against his shoulder. He carried her into the bedroom, where he tore off the covers and threw her down so hard she bounced. He was incredible. This was incredible. The most erotic morning she'd ever experienced, the most erotic she'd ever felt. What was it about this man that brought out this strange brazen hussy in her?

He towered over her, looking down at her, strangely intense. He closed his eyes slowly, as if he was capturing an image, and then bent over her, kissing up her leg, hip, stomach and breasts. Then he kissed her mouth, sending spangles of heat zigzagging through her body. With one hand he held his dick, teasing her still-sensitive clit with the tip, using her moisture to slide up and down. He took her left hand and kissed its palm, then as he slowly penetrated her, he sucked two fingers in his hot mouth. The duel sensation sent tingles all over her body. It was like every inch of her skin was on fire.

She used the fingers in his mouth to draw him down toward her mouth. He slid in and out of her with what could only be described as amazing control. He filled her up. Completely.

The muscles in his arms took all his weight as he rocked against her, pelvis against clit. She pulsed her hips in concert, eliciting a moan from him.

"James. I'm going to come again." Her voice cracked on the last word as his gaze bored into hers.

"Good. But it won't be the last time. Not nearly. The day is long and…"

"So are you," she interrupted, gasping as his length pressed all the way to the top. She ground herself on his pelvic bone, unable to stop herself from giving into the blissful friction. She exploded, crying his name. He roughly thrust into her, watching her the whole time, groaning, suddenly out of control. He came inside her as her vision went grainy with the force of her own orgasm.

He released his arms and lay on her, their breaths in concert as they panted. After a minute he rolled to her side and held her against him. She wrapped her arm around him and stroked his back. He stared at her, and this time she just stared back, trying to take in this man who had saved her life, and then had burst like a tsunami through her defenses and made her want him enough to display herself to him, in the most vulnerable way she had ever been. It was physical. It was a physical vulnerability, but it was also deeply mental, and maybe even emotional. This wasn't supposed to be. And she needed to quash that emotional aspect. Immediately.

She did not need to fool herself into thinking that she'd fallen in love in the space of a day. That would be too ridiculous. This was physical, maybe mental, and that was all.

"You're something else," he told her, tracing her side with the tips of his fingers, giving her skin light goose bumps.

"Something else other than what?" she asked, propping her head up on a hand.

"Unique." His hand moved up to stroke her still-damp hair. "Like nothing I've ever experienced before."

"I'm an *experience*? That makes me feel like a visit to a museum." Beth shifted uncomfortably under his scrutiny. "What are you saying?" She smiled to take the edge off her question.

"I've never been with a soldier before. I'm experiencing the army in a whole new way." He grinned and ducked as if he thought she'd hit him. Which she might have done if she'd had the energy.

She laughed and snuggled into the pillow-top a little further. "Do you want to go ahead to breakfast and have the conversation about last night with everyone? I don't have to be there if you think it would be better…"

"No way. You were affected, too." He looked pointedly at her bruises. "And as far as anyone's concerned, I've chosen you to be my wife, and you're family now."

"I guess the engagement should buy you some time, right? Until you get your heart broken and call it all off." She grinned and stuck her tongue out at him, although her heart clenched as she actually said the words. What was up with her? She knew this was an act. But because they were pretending to be engaged, a tiny bit of her was embracing belonging to him. Nope. No, it wasn't. "I mean, as long as I don't meet someone here…there must be someone here my type, right? Even if he's a caterer." She winked at him. "Don't worry, I'll be discreet."

He gently bit her arm. "I guess I'm just going to have to keep my eye on you, keep you close. Make sure you don't run off with the food guy, like you nearly did with the taco guy last night."

She sat up and slid off the bed, throwing a cynical look back at him. "Are you kidding me? I think *you* would have run off with him if I hadn't been there…You should have seen the look on your face when you took your first bite." She shrieked as a pillow flew at her head, and ran out to the closet to pick clothes.

He yelled behind her. "Breakfast at the main house in twenty."

"Okay," she called back, but inside her a cold hand of dread had already begun to sweep away the passion that had been there just a few minutes ago. Now she was going to have to stand up to the scrutiny of his family, and try not to be memorable at all to the director. She looked at her bruised arms.

Urgh.

Chapter 11

They walked slowly across the lawn to the main house, hand in hand. Slowly because he knew the spell of the most perfect beginning to a day was about to be broken by his family. He loved them, but had nothing really in common with any of them except Sadie. It was too early to tell about Maisie. She always seemed to have something up her sleeve, much like his father, and he kind of hoped she would grow out of that trait.

Beth glowed this morning. She wore loose black linen pants and a long-sleeved top that showed off her toned arms but covered her bruises. His stomach clenched when he thought about how close she'd been to being seriously hurt. He couldn't believe he'd brought her here and she'd been attacked. *Jesus.* She was also strangely silent.

"Are you okay? You're very quiet," he said.

She looked at their intertwined fingers. "I can't help thinking that this is going to explode in a bad way. I mean, we're faking this, right? Your family is going to see right through us. Added to which there's bound to be the pressure of added security after last night, won't there?"

"Are we? Are we faking this?" His breath came a little more quickly just thinking she considered what was happening between them to be fake. Was this a one-weekend stand for her? If so, how was he going to change her mind?

"Our engagement is fake. Look, the ring is already rejecting me." She held up her hand and showed him the ring. It seemed to be moving around on her finger more than it should, as if it was trying to get off. Over his dead…

"We can get it resized for you," he said, before realizing that of course there would be no resizing. "You'll just have to try not to lose it before Sunday."

"I'm trying really hard to keep it on. After breakfast I'm going to try to find a band aid to fatten my finger a bit. See if that helps. Don't worry," she said, looking at him, "I won't scratch it or anything."

That really wasn't what he was worried about. His brain had flashed forward to having to take the ring back to Tiffany's, and that didn't sit well with him. Who wanted to be the guy that needs to return a ring? Who wanted to be the guy who returned the ring that was supposed to adorn Beth's hand? He really hoped his dysfunctional family didn't fuck up any chance he had with her. He needed a smooth weekend, where his family showed their very best side.

He led her up the stone steps, and as soon as he'd opened the door for her he headed toward the shouting. He guessed they weren't going to show their best.

Beth stepped inside the doorway and pulled a face. "You think we should wait for backup? Let the fighting die down? You know I don't like walking into a war zone."

"Except I know you love walking into a war zone, you big chicken. You can face down the Taliban, but you're scared of a little family disagreement?" As the words left his mouth, there was a huge crash, and a scream.

"I hate all of you. I'm leaving." This was Maisie.

Beth kept her eye on the door. "Attack or retreat?" she asked.

"How about a little 'hearts and minds' diplomacy?" he said, drawing her toward the dining room.

"I missed the 'hearts and minds' class at the academy," she said. "Also the 'how to win friends and influence people' one."

He dragged her through to the dining room in time to see Maisie at the end of the table, holding three plates in her hands. As they both entered the room, she threw them all to the ground.

His parents were at the table but ignoring her, which he knew only made her behavior worse. Some therapist had told them to ignore her tantrums at some point, and so her bad behavior had continued, largely unchecked.

"What the hell is the matter with you, Maisie? Pick that up. It is not Gracie's job to clean up after you've deliberately made a mess," he said to her. It pissed him off that his parents didn't stop to consider the other people who would actually have to clean up after they'd let her run amok.

"They won't let me wear my boots," she wailed. "I want to wear my boots."

"Jesus, Maisie. You're acting like a five-year-old. You should know by now that this doesn't accomplish anything."

She reached for another plate, but Beth stepped up to her and took the plate from her hands. Maisie looked totally astounded.

"What kind of boots are they?" Beth asked.

"Knee-high biker boots. They're Doc Martens," Maisie said with a brow too deeply furrowed for a thirteen-year-old.

"The ones with the laces up the shins?" Beth asked.

"Yes." More disbelief at her words.

"Why don't you pick up the plates and take me to see them? I always wanted a pair, but I was worried I wouldn't have anything to wear with them. Come on." Beth bent over and picked up a couple of pieces of broken plate. "What size are you?"

Maisie started picking up the rest of the shards. "Seven."

"Ha! Guess what size I am?" Beth laughed triumphantly.

"Seven?"

"Got it in one. You going to let me try them on?" she said, holding her arm out to her.

As if they'd known each other for years, Maisie slid under her arm, allowing Beth to steer her toward the door.

"We'll be right back," Beth said as they walked past and out of the dining room.

All very well, and he was completely impressed, but now he was stuck with his parents and he knew they would probably ask questions that good manners dictated they couldn't ask in front of Beth.

His mother patted her lips with a napkin and set it on the table. "Is she pregnant, dear?"

Okay, so not "probably."

"Don't." He knew he had to head this off at the pass before he blew his top and left. He had to hold this together for his sisters.

"It's a reasonable question, all things considered. We hear nothing about her, and then you show up engaged." She relaxed back into her chair and crossed her arms.

Okay, so she had a point.

"No, she's not pregnant," he said, taking a seat at the table.

"Do we know her family?" she asked.

He tucked a serviette onto his lap. "I doubt it." *Come on Walker, move it along.*

He thanked Gracie for a coffee that she poured and added milk and sugar to the brew. "So can we talk about what happened last night?"

His father pulled down his *New York Times* and peered over the top of his glasses. "Yes. Simon briefed me last night."

James fought hard to resist rolling his eyes. "And?"

"And it's being handled." His father picked up the paper again and started reading.

"Dad. My fiancée was attacked last night, and my sister was nearly abducted. Can you please give me a slightly more detailed answer. What exactly is being done about it?"

"The correct people have been informed, and we're moving the high-profile part of the wedding back here."

"So the ceremony will be here?"

His father sighed. "Yes." He eyed his wife. "Your mother is taking care of the wedding arrangements. My people are taking care of everything else."

"Okay. I want to be updated if there are any more threats. This is now affecting all the women I care about."

His father looked at him impassively and gave a short nod. He guessed that would have to do.

"So remind me of the schedule." James refused to be drawn into feeling like a kid again, and he definitely wanted to keep the conversation away from Beth and certainly on an even keel.

"We'll have a small cocktail hour for friends and family around lunchtime, and then we will be getting ready to leave for the rehearsal dinner. That's all we need you for today. Tomorrow will also be slow for you, until the wedding at midday." His mother intoned the words as if she was reading from an itinerary.

"When you say 'small cocktail hour,' do you mean regular small or Walker small?"

His mother looked blankly at him, as if she'd never seen him before. He'd been on the receiving end of that look pretty much every time he'd seen her in the last ten years. She couldn't understand why he'd chosen the military over Harvard and D.C. politics. James couldn't understand why his choice was such a surprise to her, and had stopped explaining it a few years ago.

"Head count?" he explained.

"Oh, no more than fifty for cocktails and appetizers. We're shifting the rehearsal to here, and then we're going to Jamison's," she said, naming a famous Washington restaurant. "Your father's made sure to have extra security there, so everyone will be able to relax. Right, dear?"

"Right," his father agreed from behind the paper.

There was silence for a few seconds, during which he really hoped Beth would come back. But no.

"So." His mom's attention drifted as she paused. "Are you really marrying that girl?"

"That girl, mother? Do you mean my fiancée?" He could hear his own voice hardening.

"Now, don't be like that. You know Sadie has Henrietta at the wedding for you, don't you? In the hopes you'd get back together with her."

He laughed at her. "Mother, I think you're projecting. Harry is Sadie's best friend; that's why she's at the wedding. And I can tell you that she has zero thoughts about getting back together with me. That is all in your head."

"No it isn't, darling. Is it so wrong that we want you to make the perfect match? Besides, we never imagined for a second you'd show up with a fiancée. Why would we? We'd never heard a word about her before you dropped that bombshell on us."

"Mom. Please don't interfere. I love her, and I'm going to marry her." As the words came out of his mouth, for a second, one true sweet second, he wanted them to be true.

"Well, you'll have to explain that to Harry. I'm afraid she's under the impression that you're still up for grabs." His mother carefully stirred her tea, not touching the sides of the cup with her spoon at all. With a practiced swipe, she replaced the spoon on the saucer, knitted her hands together and considered him levelly.

"I introduced Harry to Beth yesterday. She does not think I'm up for grabs. Nothing could be further from her mind." Of anything in the world, he was at least sure of that.

"And I'm perfectly sure she doesn't. Well, at least she's never known exactly what she wants, and without parents of her own, it's the least we can do to look after her." She sniffed. "Harry told me that you were buying a lot of clothes at the mall. That makes me somewhat suspicious. But whatever you say, dear. Remember. You're getting old. Soon there will only be divorcées for you to choose from. No one wants that."

James pinched the bridge of his nose and took a breath. "Mom. I just want a nice weekend with my family. I want you to like Beth as much as I do, and maybe, if you behave, and don't make her feel in any way awkward, I will invite you to our small wedding in North Carolina. And you will show up, be very nice, and welcome her to the family. Are we clear?"

"Whatever you say, James." Except the way she said it was definitely in a placating tone, rather than a sincere one. His father hadn't even acknowledged the conversation, so deep inside his newspaper was he.

James wished Beth would come back. He was hungry but didn't want to eat without her. And of course, her very presence would stop this line of conversation for good. He hoped. Sweet Jesus, he was twenty-seven years old, and still, with a look, his mother could make him feel like a six-year-old who'd turned up for dinner with dirty hands.

And this? This was why he'd never had any intention of coming to Sadie's wedding.

* * *

Maisie took Beth up the same staircase that Mrs. Walker had descended when she'd accused Beth of being the "help." The memory made her smile.

The second floor of the house was split two ways from the staircase, with a few doors on each side of the opposing hallways.

Maisie took her left, past the first door. "That's Sadie's room when she's home." She pointed at a door on the opposite side, a bit farther down. "That's James's room. Have you seen it yet?"

"Not yet, no," Beth said. "But I'm a lot more anxious to see your boots."

It was the right thing to say. Maisie giggled. "Cool. This is my room." She opened the door and barged ahead of Beth, who smiled in her wake.

Her bedroom was huge, with three double windows along the length of it that overlooked the front gardens, down toward the security booth. The walls were a gunmetal gray and covered with posters of rock bands.

At the end of the room, farthest away from the door, were two doorways—one a closet and one a bathroom. Beth knew this because the bathroom door was open, with two wet towels strewn on the floor on the threshold; the closet door was also open, with shoes and books decorating the floor, making it impossible to close that door either. Maisie reminded her so much of Tammer when she was younger. Her heart squeezed.

"They're here," Maisie said, reaching into her bed sheets.

"You slept with them?" Beth laughed at her.

"I didn't want them to get all scratched up before the wedding. Although I don't think I'll be allowed to wear them now." She sounded so sad, Beth couldn't help but sympathize. Tammer had been the same way—full of tantrums and fights which could mostly be calmed with some interest in whatever had annoyed her. Looking at James's parents, she wasn't sure if sometimes no parents were better than parents who were too busy to pay attention to their kids.

"You know what I would do?" Beth said with a conspiratorial air.

"No?" Maisie sniffed and watched Beth stroke the boots.

"Okay, is your bridesmaid dress a long one?"

"Uh-huh," Maisie began to unlace the boots carefully.

"Agree to wear whatever shoes they want you to wear, then just before the wedding change into the boots. No one will notice anyway, and if they do, it will be too late to do anything about it." She knew full well that she wasn't giving her entirely sterling advice, but she saw so much Tammer in her that she just wanted to hug her and make everything better.

"Oh my God, that's an excellent idea. I probably would have done that anyway." She sniffed again and shot a glance at Beth.

"I bet you would. And this way, there will be no arguments, and you can tell them that I said it was okay, and they won't say anything to me because I'm a guest." She certainly hoped that was true. One of the adults in the family was certainly going to kill her for this.

"Are you going to marry James?" she asked after a pause.

Oh crap. She didn't want to lie to her. Lousy, lousy... "Would that be okay with you?" she hedged.

"I guess." A long silence, then, "Do you want to try them on?"

"Hell, yes!" Beth said, grabbing the left one and easing her foot into it. It fit perfectly. She really did want a pair of these boots. They felt so badass; no wonder Maisie loved them.

When she'd laced the other one up, she rolled up the legs of her pants and walked up and down in front of Maisie. "Do they look good?" she asked.

"They look awesome."

"Go on, now you put them on and show me," she said as she took them off. And now she knew she was stalling to go back downstairs. Maisie's stomach rumbled. "Or would you prefer to go get some breakfast with me? I'm starving, too." When she nodded, Beth asked, "So what's breakfast like here?"

"Gracie's ham and cheese omelet is awesome. Crispy around the edges, and soft and squishy in the middle."

"Sounds perfect. Want to go back downstairs?"

* * *

When Beth and Maisie got back to the breakfast room, they were greeted with an icy silence. But they both smiled brightly at James, who was relieved they were back. "Hungry?" he said, standing up to pull out both Beth's and Maisie's chairs for them.

"Starved," they said in unison, then laughed. Beth continued, "I have it on good authority that Gracie's omelets are incredible."

He sat down, suddenly feeling calmer and happier.

With Beth and Maisie back in the room, there were no more awkward conversations, just harmless chatter about the wedding and who his mother had invited from her group of old school friends. He wondered just exactly how many of the guests Sadie and Simon would actually know, and figured that it must be a pain for poor Sadie to have to meet a bunch of new people on her actual wedding day.

When they'd consumed the last of the omelets and coffee, they all got up to leave the room so it could be cleared by the staff. Maisie insisted on taking them out to see the portable bathrooms. He wasn't so keen to see them, since he spent a lot of time downrange in portable bathrooms and couldn't quite imagine how the wedding guests would feel about them.

As they were leaving his father stepped up and took Beth by her arm. "May I have a word with your fiancée?" he asked James.

"Dad, she doesn't belong to me. If you want to speak to her, ask her, not me." He realized immediately he should have just said no, but he'd been so incensed that his father had treated Beth like she was a piece of property, he missed the opportunity to answer for her. He frowned at the thought of Beth being alone with his father and hoped she'd say no.

"Of course you can," Beth replied. "I'll see you guys outside in a minute."

James left the house with Maisie, but paused on the steps and looked toward the window of his father's study. No. He wasn't going to interfere. He trusted Beth to say or do the right thing. "Okay, Minxie, show me these amazing bathrooms."

She took his hand and dragged him beyond the grand wedding tent until they found red carpet. Only his mother would have red carpet going to the johns.

Instead of Portajohns, which were what he had been expecting, there were actual rooms, tiny room-sized trailers—ten of them in a semi-circle like an old-fashioned motel. "Wow. Are these really the bathrooms?" he asked his sister.

"Come look!"

He opened one of the doors to find a marble bathroom with brass fittings. His own bathroom in his temporary lodging paled in comparison. "Shit, this is nicer than my whole home. You think I can drag one back behind the Audi?"

Maisie giggled and turned on the faucets and flushed the toilet like she'd never seen running water before. There was even a velvet love seat in one corner. Well, at least now there was somewhere for him to escape to if the wedding became too much. Him and Beth. On the love seat. He shook his head. More importantly, what the hell was his father talking to her about, and was she able to hold up the charade in front of him?

"Come on, Minx. Let's get back. We don't want to desert Beth."

"We do not," she said as she reluctantly turned off the taps and then shut off the light. "Let's go find her."

When they got back to the front of the house, James looked in the study windows again. This time his father was standing at his desk, holding something out to Beth. He squinted. What was it? Beth took the piece of paper and looked at it.

Blood rushed from his head, and he shivered. No way. Not again. The bastard was buying her off. He'd done the same thing to Sadie's ex, the one before Jeffrey. His breath hitched as he watched. She was smiling at his father. Was she really going to take the money? He was suddenly really confused. And angry. She could take the money, because they weren't really engaged, but what did that say about her? Nothing good, right?

Fuck. Fuck.

* * *

Beth literally couldn't believe her eyes. She blinked again and again at the check. Five hundred thousand dollars to leave James. *What the hell?*

"Before I write your name on that check, I want to be sure that you are not pregnant. If you are carrying my grandchild, things will get a lot more complicated for you. Now James assures us that you're not, but I would like to hear it from you."

James assured them…? What the…? A rush of emotion flooded through her like boiling hot water. Anger at James, sadness for him, sadness for his family, who thought they knew who the right woman for him was. God, she felt sorry for James's real fiancée whenever he found one. Anger flared in her belly but she kept her expression blank. Fought to keep it there as she considered her options. She was pretty sure it would break James's heart if she told him about this. Absolutely sure it would create a nightmare wedding for Sadie, who was obviously stressed enough already. She'd tell James when they were on their way home.

Maybe.

She kept her mouth shut for as long as she could, but she was so pissed she could visualize smoke coming out of her ears. Gone was her determination to stay unmemorable to Mr. Walker, to fade into the background.

"I can't accept this," she said evenly, holding it back toward him.

"You need more?" he asked. "Let me tell you, if you marry James, he won't be a part of this family's inheritance. You won't get more money just because you married a cash cow."

"James is not a cash cow. What's the matter with you? You

don't see what a great person he is? He's a hero. He's funny, and kind...Surely you can see that?"

Director Walker rolled his eyes. "A hero? Really? He flies a desk at Fort Bragg. I can't even persuade him to move up to the Pentagon where the real decisions are made. He's frankly an embarrassment, but at least he's not delivering pizza."

Delivering pizza? She wanted to explode on his ass. He thought serving the country was the same as delivering pizza? He really didn't know anything about James. He didn't even know the difference between Fort Bragg and Pope Army Air Field. Sweet hell. Now she was stuck between a rock and a hard...Her mind flicked for the briefest of all seconds to him on top of her in the bed. She fought to regain control of this terrible situation.

"This is your only chance. If you say no now, if you run out of here and tattletale to James, I will ruin you. Not in a conventional way, but five, maybe ten years from now, you may find it difficult to renew your driver's license, maybe find it hard to get on a plane. I want you to understand that I will do anything it takes to protect my family from freeloaders and bad influences."

Beth fantasized for a second about leaping over the desk and kicking him in the nuts. But she had a fake identity to uphold. This wasn't her fight. Wasn't her family. Ideally she could get out of this weekend with minimal impact on this family. Her only job was to make it through the wedding. And then regale Tammer with stories from the Walker Telenovela.

"I will make you a promise. I won't say anything to James, I'll take the check, and if I really am as bad for him as you seem to think, you should have no worries that I will cash it and leave him, all right?" She had no idea if this was going to work or not; it just seemed like an ideal way to keep the peace for two more days.

He frowned at her as if he was trying to figure her angle. But he fingered his pen as if he was buying it.

"But you, in turn, have to promise to leave me alone. Do we have a deal, Mr. Walker?" She suddenly wondered if he was likely to run her fingerprints, but hoped that because this was a family affair, maybe he would do the right thing. She had to believe it, actually. She was going to work for him one day, and if he used his incredible power on a personal matter, it would speak volumes about his abuse of that power. An abuse of power in an organization she would then want nothing to do with. She hoped this was all an empty threat designed to scare a woman with no idea what she had gotten into.

"Who should I make the check out to?" He said, twisting the top off his fountain pen.

A beat passed.

"Beth Cojones," she said, pronouncing it as if it was spelled "co-jones." "That's C-O-J-O-N-E-S."

Director Walker scribbled her name on the check, staring at her over the top of his glasses. "I have to admit, I thought you would be a harder sell," he said. "What do you do?"

"I just want an easy life," she said, taking the offered check.

"You're a beautiful woman, Ms. Co-Jones. I can see why you turned James's head. But you had to know a marriage into this family would never have worked."

Kick. Kick. In the cojones. "Pleasure, sir." She folded the check into a tiny square, and tucked it in her pants pocket, then stuck out her hand. As he shook it, she didn't let go. "I just wish you knew your son better. Appreciated him the way others do. He's here for this whole weekend. Talk to him. Talk to him about what he wants in life, where he wants to work, who he wants to be. You might be surprised."

"I don't like being surprised, Ms. Co-Jones. A fact you would do well to remember yourself."

Shit. She nodded, released his hand, and left the room. She closed the door behind her and released a breath of relief. What a piece of work. Maybe her career in the CIA was a pipe dream anyway.

"What did he want?" She looked up to see James leaning against the doorjamb of the reception room.

A friendly face. "Nothing. He just wanted to welcome me to the family. Sweet, really. And you were all worried! Where did Maisie take you?"

He was silent for a second, and then pushed himself off the wall and held out his hand for hers. "The temporary bathrooms in the gardens. They're in better shape than my current housing, which is a little embarrassing. Maisie is so taken with them I suspect she will commandeer one tomorrow and just stay in it all day."

She laughed. "I can't wait to see them. I expect they'll put mine to shame, too."

"Come on. We're free until the early cocktail thing." He nodded toward the door and studied her as she walked by. He seemed tense, but maybe that was just from being here. Now she kind of understood why he needed her as backup.

"Swimming pool? Can we just laze around all morning?" she asked, suddenly needing to be alone with him again.

"Sounds like a plan," he said and started off across the lawn back to the pool house.

She slipped off her sandals and strode to keep up with him. "Is everything okay?" She laid a hand on his arm.

He patted it almost absently and said, "Sure, why wouldn't it be?"

She let it go. Smooth and detached. Clean entry and clean

getaway. That's what she'd taken from her conversation with his father. James hadn't lied about the Hammer House of Horrors, but he wasn't responsible for the behavior of his parents. Maybe she should tell him about the check. Maybe he would laugh. But knowing him as little as she did, she was sure he would storm back over to the house and rip his father a new one. And then leave.

Damn it. None of this was good for her. None of it was good for James's family life either. She'd never imagined she was better off without a big family...but the Walkers made her count her blessings that it was just her and Tammer.

She knew plenty of people who got stressed when they went home to their families. Sometimes she felt like some of the people she met in the military had actively decided to join up just to get a little space between the claustrophobic feel of home and the freedom of service. She would have joined up sooner if she'd been able to.

James interrupted her thought process. "I'm sorry. I didn't really expect to feel so hemmed in by my family. Sometimes it seems that just being in touch with them, just here for the weekend, leaves me feeling tied up in barbed wire and unable to get myself free without drawing blood. Either from me, or them, or..."

"Me? I promise I can handle whatever they throw at me. Remember, we're just here for the weekend, and then we'll be driving home and all this will be behind us." As she said the words, they didn't feel right either. "Well, *they* will be behind us," she added.

"I wish we hadn't come. I'm sure it would have been more fun climbing." He took his sunglasses from his pocket and put them on, almost as if he was hiding behind them.

Beth looked away and fell silent. In a second she had processed what he'd said and didn't want him to see the gut wrenching his words had given her. He wished all of this away? The...intimacy? She'd made herself so vulnerable to him and that was what he thought? He'd essentially rejected her. How stupid was she? This was exactly why she never allowed anyone to get close.

"I think this might have been less stressful without me here," she replied. "Honestly, if you want me to leave now, I really don't mind. I'm happy to just disappear and you can hang with Harry, keep your folks happy, and then come on back to North Carolina after the wedding. A day and fifty beers later and this will all be a distant memory."

"Really? Ten minutes with my father and you're ready to bolt? Why ever could that be?" He slowed to a stop. "Tell me what he said."

A shot of inexplicable fear rushed through her. He was acting like he knew what his father had done, but he couldn't. "You just said you wished I wasn't here, so I was giving you a painless out. That's all." A coil of terrible emotions tangled in her stomach. Pity at the family life James must have suffered through until he'd left. Desperate concern that she'd fucked over her dream career because of this stupid weekend.

She wished she could walk away. Complication was something she avoided at any cost. She had her work, which she excelled at, and she had her home with her dog Jubilee, and sometimes Tammer. No drama, no anxiety, no stress.

This situation was the polar opposite. And now James was obviously angry, wondering what his father had said to her. As she'd said the words, she'd known that "he was welcoming me to the family" rang all kinds of false. But what could she do? It was a weekend to help out a guy who had not only saved her life, but who'd risked his life to save hers. There was nothing she wouldn't do to give him the weekend he'd hoped for. So allaying his concerns had to be her priority. Giving him what he needed. She would make this work.

"Seriously, Beth. Do I need to go ask him myself?" They rounded the corner to the pool area and the reflected sun made it suddenly feel like Afghanistan in August.

She needed to distract him. "Sure, you can if you like, but I'm sure he'll just tell you to ask me." She took his hand and led him inside. She wasn't stripping for James *and* the phantom peeper.

As soon as the door closed she started to undo her pants. James stopped in his tracks and did a double take.

"What are you doing?" he asked in a rough voice.

"It's so hot. And you need to be not thinking about your father right now." She let her pants fall to the floor and turned slightly so that when she bent over to pick them up, he'd have an eyeful of ass.

Boy, did that ever work.

Before she stood up, he had cupped her ass cheek and undone the zip at the back of her top. She reached up so he could slide it off her. His breath caught as he realized she wasn't wearing a bra. From behind he moved his hands to her breasts, stroking them into points. She shivered against him.

With one last squeeze of her nipples, he spun her around. In seconds he was on his knees, pulling her panties down around her ankles. He lifted up each foot to remove them, and without pausing or removing her high heels, his tongue was on her, forcefully pushing against her clit, laving the whole area with the flat of his tongue. He was still angry, she could tell.

Heat spiked through her and her skin fritzed as if she was

bathing in champagne. Liquid heat pooled between her legs. She held his shoulders to steady herself.

He stood abruptly and held her to him. "Taste yourself," he said, and kissed her, sliding his tongue into her mouth. Her knees became fluid at the forcefulness of his words. She sucked the essence that he'd created within her from his tongue, slowly pulling it into her mouth.

Then his fingers were back, on her clit, almost punishing her. She moaned at the pressure. On the edge, she clung to him as his fingers slid into her, hard and fast while still rubbing her clit with his thumb.

"Come for me, Beth. Right now." He bit the side of her neck and the pleasure and pain of it had her teetering on the edge. It was rough and fast, and the sensations danced along the pleasure-pain line.

She would have cried out when she came, but his mouth swallowed the sound. She throbbed all over. His fingers didn't give up, but took the liquid that had flooded her and gently smoothed it all over her. So gently...but still making her flinch when he touched her clit.

Beth wanted to feel him, wanted him naked. She pulled up his shirt and dragged it over his head. Then she paused and slowly undid the fly of his pants.

* * *

James was as still as a statue. Frankly he was worried that if he moved, he wouldn't be able to control himself. He was so angry with his father, with her. He saw her taking off her damn pants for what it was: a distraction.

He didn't blame her, not really. But he was worried whether

he could even have a future with her after this disaster. He didn't want to think about what her accepting a payoff from his father meant. If that's what it had been. He didn't want to ask her. He didn't want to know for certain the depths to which his father had gone to control him. But he also *did* want to know. He wanted to know what was in Beth's head. She was so strong, so able, and now he was worried that she was too capable of compartmentalizing what they were doing, that she'd be able to close the door on this when they returned to North Carolina.

But right now, she was pulling his pants down. He kicked off his shoes and shucked off the pants when they hit the floor. His erection strained against his boxers. Would he ever get enough of this woman?

She stepped back from him. Her glorious body was bathed in refracted white light, shimmering across her shoulders and breasts. Her legs were accentuated by the impossibly slender heels she was wearing. Magnificent. And fucking hot.

And then he remembered the person or thing that Beth had thought she'd seen earlier. He didn't doubt for a second that she'd seen something; her instincts were usually spot-on. A coldness settled over him when he thought of anyone else seeing her the way she'd shown herself to him.

With the flick of a switch, cream-colored roman blinds cascaded from the ceiling and covered the picture window completely.

"You couldn't have done that this morning?" She stood, brazenly naked with her hands on her hips.

"My mind was on other things." He reclined on the daybed where they'd been before. It was now his lucky lounger. He grinned.

She crouched slightly and kissed the bullet wound on his right side. She touched her tongue to it, and it might as well have been a soldering iron by the amount of heat it generated. He wanted to touch her, feel her hair at least, but he didn't trust the amount of control he'd be able to muster.

She kissed him just south of the old wound. Then played with his waistband with her teeth. Teasing him, rendering him unable to think.

Her kisses fell on his stomach. He felt her tongue in his navel, then tasting the tattoo on the other side. Then without any warning, her open mouth puffed hot air onto his dick through the thin material of his shorts. He nearly exploded right there.

She worked his shorts down his legs and pulled them off. Naked. They were both naked in the reflected light from the swimming pool. Ripples from the breeze across the water outside cast patterns through the blinds onto her skin. He'd never wanted anyone so bad in his whole life.

For a second she stood before him, legs slightly open, lips slightly open. As if she was considering the best way to devour him. He didn't care, as long as she did.

She hitched one leg up onto the lounger and dipped her hand between her own legs. In seconds he saw her juice glistening on her hand. She hesitated for a second, and then slowly climbed on to the bed with him.

Abruptly she opened his legs and knelt between them. Using her own lubrication, she stroked his dick from the base all the way to the tip, swiveled her hand around it and stroked back down. The feel of the friction, abated a little by her own liquid, sent red hot blood pulsing through his body, making its way between his legs. He felt enormous, like every molecule of blood was in her hands.

He closed his eyes and groaned at the sensation. And then her hand was replaced by her hot wet mouth. Her tongue swirled around the tip, probing its hole, and then the length of him. She licked him like an ice cream. Base to tip, base to tip. And then, as she reached the top, she drew the whole of him into her mouth. The light scrape of her teeth, the hot wetness of her mouth made him forget the rest of his body existed. But not the rest of hers.

The sight of her crouching between his legs, naked, with his dick in her mouth, gave him a slam of desire. Her breasts bobbed as she slid up and down his length. He reached for one, and relished the feel of her pebbled nipple in his fingers. He wanted to come so badly, but more, he wanted to see her, wanted to be buried so deep inside her that her eyes glazed over. He needed to hear her say his name. His name on her lips was suddenly more important to him than having his dick on her lips. He wanted to watch her as she came.

In a second she was in his arms. He knew exactly where he wanted to have her. After kicking open the door to the bathroom, he deposited her on the vanity between the two sinks. It was the perfect height, and there were mirrors behind her, behind him on the wall, and to one side. He'd get a spectacular view of her as he fucked her. He pulled her so her ass was just on the edge of the counter.

There wasn't time to play nice. He took his dick in his hand and placed it right at her entrance.

Beth grabbed his chin. "Inside me, James. I want you inside me."

Her words slayed him. "Yes ma'am." He dug his fingers into her ass cheeks and pulled her onto his dick. At the same time he thrust hard, no practice pushes, no waiting for her natural lubricant. Hard, into her. Her warmth squeezed him as she moaned for him.

"Again," she whispered into his ear, her breath fanning heat over him.

He turned her head so she could see their reflection in the mirror to the side. Her eyes grew dark as she saw. She drew one leg up, bending it at the knee, so she could see him sliding in and out of her. It seemed to drive her crazy. He watched as she looked at them, first in the side mirror, then in the one behind him.

Her tight pussy pulsed around him as he thrust into her. Hard, unrelenting, making her gasp and moan. Her eyes opened wide as she watched his dick drive into her. He slipped his hand between their frantic bodies and slid it over her clit, circling it, not touching it, and then pressing directly on the bud, rubbing it with the same cadence as he was fucking her.

"James." Her voice cracked on the most beautiful sound she could make, and she came, gasping every breath as if she was dying. His own balls contracted slightly at the sound as the trail of fire hit the small of his back, signaling a release so strong he wondered if he would be able to stay upright.

Buried fast inside her, she rocked her pelvis in small thrusts, milking his orgasm out of him. If he didn't have the vanity to lean against, he wasn't sure if he'd still be standing.

* * *

Beth's head dropped onto his shoulder. How was it possible to stay coherent when it felt like her whole body was filled with warm honey? Contentment flooded through her as he wrapped his arms around her. She peeked into the mirror opposite and saw his face reflected in the mirror behind them. He looked at peace—blue eyes closed, lips pressed into her shoulder, completely still.

"Nap time?" she murmured. To hell with the fact that it was still before lunchtime.

He didn't answer her, just picked her up and took her into the bedroom. This time he placed her on the bed and tucked the sheets around her. He left the room and came back with some bottles of water, and climbed into bed with her. She turned over to face him.

"When do you deploy next?" she asked him, wanting to know more about his life, or at least his life away from his family. She also thought it might make him happier to think about the military rather than his dysfunctional family.

"I guess some time next year. It depends on the state of the war, I suppose. Are we leaving Afghanistan? Staying? Will we be in a different war next year? All things being equal, next year sometime. You?" He rolled so they were bent knee to knee, and face to face on the pillows.

"I filed my 'fit for deployment' paperwork when you saw me at the gym. So anytime," she said.

"Do you like what you do?" he asked, stroking her arm and making goose bumps pop.

"Love it. Well, for now. I'm not sure what my future holds, but I'm not getting any younger and I suspect my days with special forces are numbered. If I have to sit behind a desk all the time, I'll leave. Go do something exciting." *If your father doesn't ban me from working at the CIA.*

"Did you do the Army's SERE training?" he asked, referring to the Survive, Evade, Resist, and Escape training that everyone had nightmares about, but was a rite of passage in some parts of the military.

"Yeah, I wasn't supposed to in the beginning. I got into the Cultural Support Teams. That was my first role in special forces.

But after my third deployment, that role kind of segued into just another regular S.F. one. So I did the SERE training a bit late. Did you?"

"Yeah, I only deploy with special forces, so I did all their training as well as all mine."

"Funny thing is, my last deployment, I was in a Humvee with the training guy who slapped me around in my SERE. He didn't know where to put himself." She shifted in the bed. "I enjoyed that." She laughed softly. "He was terrified of me. He'd left a training role to deploy, and, well, I guess it's like a cop being sent to prison. You never know who you're going to meet again. But I never forgot him."

"Did you get your own back?" he asked.

"Are you kidding? I owed him. Totally. What use am I if I don't know how to take a punch? No one else in all my training laid a hand on me. He hurt me, but you know, afterward I knew that no matter how hard someone hit me, I'd be okay, and I'd survive it. So now I'm not scared of getting handy in combat."

"I knew before I joined up that I could take a punch," he said, rolling so he stared at the ceiling.

She propped herself up on one elbow. "How so? Were you a troublemaker?"

"Sadie packs one hell of a punch. Trust me. She's five years older than me and used every inch she had on me to her advantage. Yeah, it's a miracle we're still friends."

"What are you going to do now that you're a Senior Master Sergeant? They're not going to let you kick in doors anymore when you're downrange, are they?"

"Probably not. Maybe I won't have to lie to my father anymore about what I do."

"Except you'll still be deployed."

"Good point."

An elite combat airman wouldn't take being out of action very well, she was sure. "So what's next for you?" she asked.

"I have a friend who's a private military contractor. He's always looking for guys with my training. So that's always in the back of my mind. But part of me wonders if I'd be able to do that. I chose to serve my country, but doing the same job for a private contractor, well, it feels…"

"Weird," she finished. "Yeah, I know. I often wondered if I'd be able to take orders from someone whose main concern was making a profit, rather than doing something for the good of the country." She mentally struggled against the comfort she felt with him. They even thought the same way about serving in the military. She half wished he'd do something gross, just so he didn't seem so damned perfect for her.

Her eyes fluttered, heavy. "We're practically the same," were the last words she remembered saying before she fell asleep.

Chapter 12

When Beth woke, she was alone. She wrapped a sheet around her, looked out at the kitchen clock, and saw that it was nearly one in the afternoon. Shit. She'd slept nearly three hours. What was up with that?

James was sitting at a table near the pool. She went out into the main room and was about to make her way outside when she realized he was talking to someone. A woman. She hated herself, but she couldn't not listen. She recognized the voice. It was Harry. What was she doing here?

"Please don't go," James said to her. "You're killing me."

Beth inched closer. Was he talking about their fake engagement?

"You think too much. You should be more like me," Harry replied in a soft voice.

"If I were more like you, I probably would be dead by now. So don't wish that on me." He sounded annoyed.

"Oh, sweetheart, don't look at me like that. You know I'm fine."

"I love you. Remember that, whatever you do, okay?" James said.

Her answer was muffled, as if they were hugging...or something.

Beth's breath stuck. The top of her head felt as though it was melting through her skull, dripping napalm through the rest of her body. He still loved Harry? She blinked back moisture in her eyes. No way. No way was she going to cry over a one-weekend stand. No man was worth that. Not ever.

Her eyes didn't listen. She backed away from the window and shut herself in the bathroom. She needed time to think. Why did she need time to think? She knew this wasn't real, knew she was going to walk away from him on Sunday. Why was she so upset?

She threw off the sheet and paced up and down the length of the room, giving herself a good talking to. Shutting down those pathetic thoughts of a happy ever after that had obviously penetrated her subconscious. This was a toxic family, and this was merely a three-day relationship. They would go their separate ways after the wedding. Simple.

The CIA's recruitment process usually lasted nearly two years. By that time, James's father would have forgotten about her. And—added bonus—he didn't know her real name.

Ha! She really hoped Director Walker did a background search on Beth Cojones. Or even better, asked someone else to do it.

But James...How could she have been so stupid? She'd been so wrapped up in his spectacular body and the spectacular sex, she'd forgotten everything else. Her rules. She was *not* involved here. James was a diversion. An itch-scratcher.

Damn it.

She was madder than hell at herself.

She turned on the shower and concentrated on home. On Tammer, on Jubilee. The view from her bedroom, the smell of the pines in her yard. Making popcorn before a TV marathon with her sister. Her Mini Cooper. Taking Jubilee for a walk on the trails around her house.

This weekend was make-believe. She was here as a favor, repaying a debt. Wearing Jimmy Choos? When would she ever wear them in her real life? She almost laughed to herself at her stupidity. *Embrace this for what it is.* No more sex, though. If James was in love with Harry, he shouldn't be doing anything with anyone else. She didn't know him that well, now that she came to think about it; could she have been that wrong about him? That he could love one woman, and make love to another?

Inexplicably her heart clenched, and a soft pain radiated through her. For one idiotic moment, deep in her subconscious, she'd picked up the idea this had all meant something. But now she knew.

Now she was here just for the open bar, just as she'd joked in the car on the way here. And that felt like months ago, already. That was yesterday. Her spine straightened, and her resolve came flooding back. She was not going to lose her mind, or heart, over a guy she'd only really known for a couple of days. Even putting aside the months they'd spent together in Afghanistan. She was better than this. Stronger.

Just because he'd saved her life didn't make him the right man in her life.

She turned off the shower and wrapped her hair and her body in warm fluffy towels and left the bathroom. James was inside the house.

"I was going to join you, but you locked the door," he said. "Is everything all right?"

"Sure," she smiled. "Must have just been automatic to lock it. What time do we need to head off for cocktails?"

"Soon. I asked Maisie for her hairdryer when I heard the shower turn on." He brandished it like a trophy.

More like he got rid of Harry when the shower came on. "Thank you. That's sweet of you to think about my unruly hair." She took it into the bedroom with her, plugged it in and switched it on, basically putting a stop to their conversation.

* * *

Beth was acting strangely and James wasn't sure why. Maybe she was trying to freeze him out so she could pocket however much his father had offered her to leave him. Was she really like that?

He quickly rinsed off and got dressed for cocktails. Man, he needed a drink. Beth was blowing hot and cold, and whereas he'd thought he'd had a firm handle on her character, she seemed to continually change. First after sex, then after taking the check from his father, and then again after her shower. Was it her, or were all women like this? It had been so long since he'd been with someone, he'd all but forgotten. Or maybe he just hadn't been interested enough to notice.

He wished that she'd let him in again. Being closed out, watching her smile very definitely not make it to her eyes, filled him with dread. It felt as if she was a bad actress playing a role, except that's exactly what he'd asked of her: a telenovela role. Shit. Basically this clusterfuck was all his fault. Everything. They should be climbing, not here. Damn. He needed a drink, and it was still early.

Who the hell cared?

He poured some wine and sat on the daybed where Beth had seduced him that very morning. What had changed? He wanted the giving, open Beth back. He closed his eyes and listened to her move around the house. The hair dryer stopped, she padded into the closet, then into the bathroom, and eventually came back down to the kitchen.

"Are you ready?" he asked, still with his eyes closed. His image of her was much nicer than he feared her real face would be.

"As I'll ever be. You said open bar, right?" she said.

He opened his eyes. She was wearing a light blue slim skirt suit, with the material just hitting her knees, and spiked heels. Her hair was up in an elegant do, decorated with small pearl clips along the seam of the twist.

He almost hated her.

She was perfect in every way. Literally every way. Perfect for him, at least. He wished she would come to him. Wished she would be honest about what was going on in her head. Wished he could be honest, too. This whole thing was such a mess, he wished they could just go home and spend the rest of the weekend at her house, making love and watching cheesy movies.

"Come on sweetheart, let's go get drunk."

* * *

By the time they reached the house, the majority of guests were already milling around, champagne in hand. James impatiently shook a few hands and introduced Beth to people, and kept moving, propelling her to the source of the alcohol.

It took fifteen minutes before they got their cocktails and took their first gulps. This was what they had in common right now. Demons needing to be quashed by booze. There seemed to be so much between them now that they could no longer talk about anything. Alcohol seemed like a plausible short-term solution.

"Listen. About when we get home…" James started.

"Yeah, yeah, it's okay. I totally agree. We'll pretend this didn't happen. It's definitely for the best, right? What happens in D.C. stays in D.C." She laughed and took another gulp, finishing her mimosa and grabbing another from a passing waiter.

Is that what she wanted? Shit, maybe he'd read all this wrong. It wasn't like he could blame her. This was probably so far out of her scope of "usual" it was no wonder she wanted to forget it all.

Fuck. Just fuck all around. He'd totally ballsed this up. He'd had the brief idea in the car that he could triple prong this: see Sadie get married, make sure everyone stayed safe, and spend some quality time with Beth when they weren't getting shot at. That was all, really. The complete and utter animal attraction between them had been a bonus. Hoped for but not expected.

But now she just wanted to forget it all. Well, he wasn't about to beg.

"Sure, if that's what you want. I promise we'll forget this and the drive back to North Carolina will be like we're on a patrol." He smiled as best he could. "Jokes and farting. Nothing more."

She took a sip this time. "Great. Although please no with the farting. I had enough of that with Bastidas...remember that? Never ever would I have imagined that a diet of ramen would have produced that toxic smell. I swear if I could have patrolled with a hazmat suit on, I would have. Sweet Jesus, that was bad."

James laughed out loud. "How could I forget? But you never said anything to him. Never ragged on him, never ordered him out of the vehicle. I thought you were immune to it. We all did, actually." He shook his head at the memory. In truth he'd wondered if they'd been a couple, as unlikely as it had seemed, and not to mention illegal. That was why he hadn't really bought that. She had never once put a step out of line, said or done anything even marginal in the few months he'd been riding with her patrol.

He watched her looking around the room, sipping her drink, and his heart just crushed in on itself. His memories of her in Afghanistan. His crazy daydreams about her, and other dreams. And now she was in front of him, blowing him off like he was a guy at a bar.

"It wasn't his fault. It's not like anyone would choose to smell that bad. Though, I won't lie, I wasn't crying when he sprained his ankle and had to ride a desk for a while." She pulled an adorable "what can you do" face and...Fuck, he had to get away from her. And punch something.

"I see...someone. I'll be back in a minute." He strode off purposefully toward someone he didn't know and opened up with the traditional wedding gambit of, "Who do you know, the bride or the groom?" The man looked surprised, but seemed happy to talk to him.

As the man answered, James's eyes were drawn to Beth again. She stood looking as if she owned the world. Christ, he wanted to penetrate that inscrutable exterior of hers. But he was prepared to let her go to save his sanity, because being around her and not being with her was going to be a level of torture they definitely hadn't prepared him for at SERE school.

* * *

Beth looked around the room at all the happy people bubbling with excitement for the wedding. Yesterday she'd been right there with them, but today—after the talk with Director Walker, then with James being cold and his declaration to Harry—everything had changed again. And this—exactly this—was why she didn't do this shit. No involvement, no dating.

For a second—okay, a few hours—she'd felt something. Felt everything, actually. Damn him all to hell. Who was he that he could make her feel that way and then tell his ex that he loved her? She did well to jump in before she had to hear the "it's not you, it's me," speech.

Thank God she had gotten there first.

The people around her all looked happy, excited, maybe thrilled to be on the inside of the director's house. She spent a little time examining faces for unease, guilt. Maybe the phantom e-mailer/abductor was here, making nice along with the other guests. She watched their behavior, trying to note anything that would give her a clue—and anything that would take her mind off James, frankly. She looked at her glass and wondered if she could have another one without making a fool of herself. She voted yes. Except she knew it was the mimosa voting yes.

Don't care.

Suddenly the double doors opened and Mrs. Walker made a grand entrance. Several people applauded. Sweet hell, were these people for real? Beth didn't clap. James's mom air-kissed the people nearest to her, and then waved her arms as if to encourage everyone to carry on.

Beth eased herself slowly through the throng and into the relative peace of the hallway. She eyed the bathroom longingly, wondering if she could hide there, and if so, for how long. She stopped a waiter exiting the kitchen with a tray of ice water, and grabbed one to sip on after she'd finished her ill-advised cocktail.

She just had to wait this one out. She'd be home on Sunday, no harm, no foul.

James came out of the reception room just as she was chugging the last of her cocktail. She put the empty glass on a side table and he immediately picked it up. "Sorry. Chippendale. My mom will have a heart attack."

"Of course she will. I'll take it to the kitchen," she said, happy for an escape. But damned if a waiter didn't come out at that exact moment.

James slipped the glass on the tray and cocked an eyebrow. "You can't get away from me that easily." He smiled.

"Want to bet? I can get away from you so fast you won't even know I've gone," she said, only half joking.

James looked worried. "Don't do that. Don't leave me here with the crazies. And I know I'm talking about my own family, but still."

"I'm here until Sunday, don't worry," she replied, trying to figure out why she wasn't just running for the hills, or at least Fort Bragg. Every cell in her body was vibrating at his proximity. Damn it. Where were the mimosas again?

Just when she was about to make another break for it, Harry left the main salon and waved.

"I'll leave you two alone," Beth said, dodging under the arm that he'd just slipped around her.

"Why?" he asked. But she didn't stay to answer.

* * *

"Goddamn it," James said as Harry approached.

"Something I said?" she asked, slipping her hand through his arm. "You want to walk me out to the marquee?"

"I really, really don't. But I will." He sighed and navigated the reception room, which was slow going as everyone was being ushered outside.

"Something rotten in the state of Denmark?" she asked.

"Stop quoting Shakespeare, for Christ's sake. And yes," he ground out, knowing she wouldn't take offense.

"What happened? Did you let your grumpiness show too much? Because you can overdo that, you know. What gives?" she asked, concern showing on her face.

"I have no idea. I saw her take a check from my father…"

"Oh." Harry said. "I heard about that routine. Cara told me that he wired her a hundred grand to leave you."

Cara was another ex. "Fuck. But it does explain my pathetic love life. Jesus, I thought he only did that with Sadie's boyfriends. God, if he weren't my father, I'd kick the shit out of him."

"I suspect if you look up all the girlfriends who've finished with you since you were eighteen you'll find them in nice houses, with expensive educations and lovely cars. Maybe nicer than yours."

"No one has a better car than mine. And hell." He couldn't believe what he was hearing. And from Harry, of all people. His father, controlling his love life. A red fury filled his head. "She took the check," he ground out before collecting himself. He gave Harry a glance before scanning the crowd again for Beth.

"And yet she's still here," she said lightly. "Although you might want to hurry—it looks like William has set his sights on her." She nodded over to the tables under the white tent.

William was pulling out a chair for her. James had to admit he looked pretty smart. The last time he'd seen William in a suit was when they'd both graduated from the private high school they'd attended. This suit looked even more expensive than that one had.

"Sadie told me he has a beach house in California," she giggled. "He's suddenly much more attractive, don't you think?" Harry elbowed him in the gut.

"Right. Right. I'd better get going, then." No way was he going to let him sweep Beth off her feet. William had done that more than once to him—sweet-talked a girl he was interested in. He was not going to stand by and let that happen again. Not with Beth. He strode over, Harry following in his wake.

"You better back off my girl, Wills," he said, putting a possessive arm around Beth's shoulders.

William grinned and held up his hands in submission. "You know I wouldn't dare. Not after Anna-Lyn."

James couldn't help but laugh. He pulled out a seat and sat next to Beth, who was looking expectantly at him.

"Anna-Lyn was the neighborhood dreamgirl. I'd got her to go out with me one time..." he began.

"All I did was ask if she'd seen the new X-Men comic, honestly," William said, leaning back in his chair and crossing his arms.

"And before I knew it, they were snuggled up reading it together." James took a mouthful of champagne.

William continued, to Beth and Harry's rapt attention. "He totally called me out, and before I knew it, he'd wrestled me to the ground and was pummeling me."

"I taught him how to do that," Sadie announced as Simon pulled out a chair for her.

James lifted his glass and clinked it with Sadie's. She really had taught him how to beat someone up. Suddenly he relaxed as he looked at the faces around the table. Sadie and Simon, William,

Harry, and Beth. His Beth. He had to figure out a way to make that happen. The only person missing was... He looked around the grounds and smiled as he saw Maisie and another girl chasing a boy about the same age around the garden bathrooms.

He felt a hand on his leg. "So you've all known one another for years?" Beth said to the table.

Sadie answered. "Some of us. The rest, it just feels like we've known each other that long!"

A couple of people groaned, but she clarified. "Harry and I met at college, Simon and I met... recently"—she flashed an intimate smile at him—"William, James, and I have been friends since kindergarten. Harry and James used to date, of course."

Beth smirked. "Yeah, I got that already."

Everyone laughed.

"A long time ago," Harry said firmly. "Much more importantly: Sadie. You're looking really stressed. Is it about last night?"

Sadie and Simon looked at each other, with Simon looking particularly inscrutable. "Is everything okay?" James asked.

"We've just been thinking about blowing this joint," Sadie said with the strain suddenly apparent in her voice. His stomach dropped.

"What do you mean?" he asked gently.

"I mean leaving today, going on our honeymoon a day early, and getting married somewhere else, quietly, just the two of us," she said, reaching for Simon's hand. "After last night, this just all seems too much."

Tension flared in Simon's jaw. "We just feel like being here has made us a target somehow. This... circus..."—he took a gulp of his beer—"seems to be the cause of last night's attack. I'm just not comfortable putting her at risk again. And frankly, I feel we're all sitting ducks in a shooting range. Not a feeling I'm easy with."

It was probably the most James had ever heard him say at one time. He couldn't argue with the man. Everything had been hinky since they'd arrived. Nothing had felt right until they'd all sat at this table. But if Sadie needed to escape, he'd do anything to help. "What do you want us to do?" he asked.

"We haven't really thought about anything other than getting away from here. Canceling the wedding. From a distance."

"Really?" William asked, leaning forward. "After all this?" He gestured around the grounds at the guests and the champagne fountain in the marquee, and the waiters bringing out hors d'oeuvres. "Your mom will kill you." He looked around, grinning. "Probably literally."

He wasn't wrong, but James wanted to kick him nonetheless. William had never been great at picking up on social cues, but he'd always said that his obliviousness made him better in his virtual world of code.

"Look, you can't go off on your own. We didn't exactly cover ourselves in glory at the JibJab. You need to be safe. That's the most important thing," James said.

"She's safe with me," Simon said in what was probably a huge understatement.

"Yes. She is. But she can't be in your sight 24/7. And we still don't know what this is. What the threat is," James said.

"It was professional," Beth said, rubbing her arms where her bruises were. "And they knew where we were going to be."

"It also wasn't random," Simon said. "I just don't understand how they got away. Why they gave up so easily if they *were* after Sadie. I've got some people looking at traffic cams around the time it happened. They'll call when they find something."

"Wow. Who are you? A cop or something?" William said.

"Nah. Just have friends," Simon said.

James jumped in to avoid any other stupid questions from William. "So do you want to sneak out? We can easily get Maisie to create a diversion." He smiled.

"A diversion for what?" His mother appeared, stealthily, like a vampire.

"Nothing. It was a joke, Mother," he said.

She narrowed her eyes at him like she'd done a thousand times when he was a kid. He jumped up and pulled out a seat for her.

"They were thinking about eloping tonight," William said baldly. "We were trying to talk her out of it."

A silence descended. *Fucking idiot.* Simon tensed in his chair, and Sadie's eyes misted over.

"We were joking, though," Beth said. There was a pause as his mother regarded her.

"No we weren't. Not really, anyway," Sadie admitted.

He half expected his mother to explode, but instead she slumped back in her seat and looked at the partygoers on the lawn and in the marquee. "It's fine. If you want to go, you can go. I know this wasn't to your taste. But with the new political appointments being made, we thought it would be a good idea to bring the key players here and we could, you know, take care of your father for once."

Well played, Mom.

Chapter 13

As soon as James had sat down with his friends he'd seemed at ease. Now every single person seemed to be on edge in sympathy with Sadie. What a nightmare for her. Beth half wanted to help spirit both of them away.

Sadie's face fell as soon as her mother laid the guilt trip on her. "Of course, Mama," she said almost pleadingly. "But maybe we can have the ceremony here, just with family. No other stress. And maybe early in the morning so we can get a head start on the honeymoon?"

Mrs. Walker rallied from her slump and perched on her seat, reminding Beth of a jackal. "That doesn't sound too unreasonable. Rehearsal dinner as planned at Jamison's in Georgetown, and then we'll send word that due to security, the wedding is closed to family only. Then your father and I can still have the guests for dinner." She cocked her head as if considering how it would play out. "Yes. That sounds like an acceptable compromise. Are we agreed?" Beth marveled at the manipulative woman.

The whole table turned to Sadie and Simon.

Simon looked incredibly uncomfortable under the scrutiny.

Beth thought he must love Sadie with the power of a thousand suns to have agreed to the whole wedding circus to begin with. She wondered what James was thinking. Was he imagining his own wedding being like this? He'd been so inscrutable recently that she couldn't begin to fathom his thoughts.

"I'm sure we can do that," Simon replied to his mother-in-law-to-be.

A now-familiar tension twanged her stomach. She was at war with herself inside, and usually, the only people she liked being at war with were very definitely outside. It didn't help that everyone was tense. Really tense. Even William seemed anxious, and he'd just dropped Sadie in it without even realizing what he'd done. She was beginning to see why James stayed away as much as he did.

She reached for her slightly warm champagne and was about to take a sip when sharp cracks sounded from the other side of the house. Simon and James stood up immediately. No one else seemed to pay much attention. Beth's heart rate kicked up and her fight instinct kicked in—the army had beaten ninety percent of her flight instinct out of her.

"Wanna take a walk?" James said, holding his hand out to her.

She gave him a nearly imperceptible nod and said, "I could use the bathroom."

His warm, dry hand encased hers as he helped her up. She tried to steady her breathing, although she couldn't tell whether her erratic heart rate was because of James or due to the sinister-sounding bangs.

Simon kissed Sadie on the cheek and told her he'd be right back. Then he hesitated. His eyes met James's.

"Stay with Sadie. We've got this," James said.

Simon gave Beth a strange look, as if he was wondering what

on earth *she* could do that would help. They walked away from the table then sped up, going toward where the sounds had seemed to originate and looking for telltale smoke or ejected shells. "What do you think it could be?" she asked as they walked faster. "It sounded more like a sidearm than anything else."

She looked at all the people they passed and wondered if they would be victims of something awful, or if someone had excessively loud party crackers. It wasn't close to being dark enough for fireworks, and she couldn't help but think that the Walkers would have made a bigger deal of a display like that.

"Incoming!" a man shouted.

James ran toward the voice. Beth kicked off her shoes to keep up and sprinted after him. White heat pumped around her body and her legs took over. Running *toward* trouble was what made people who'd undergone military training different from most others.

James cleared the back of the property, where all the guests were, and ducked behind a large oak tree. She slid in behind him, watching to see if anyone was approaching from their rear.

No one.

Beth's hand instinctively went to her side where her sidearm usually nestled, and she berated herself for not remembering she wasn't actually in uniform.

The front of the house was all but deserted. A few cars belonging to the family's closest friends were parked to one side. Where the driveway peeled off toward the road was similarly dead-looking.

Another crack sounded—this time coming from the part of the yard closest to the huge walls that acted as a security barrier. He turned to her, nodded in the direction of the noise.

Beth took another look around. Where the hell was Security?

And who had shouted "incoming" like a mortar or a grenade was coming over the wall?

James stayed very still, and then his shoulders sagged a little as if all the tension had left his body. He turned and smiled.

She opened her mouth to question him, but he headed her off at the pass with a kiss. A hot, relieved kiss. A familiar heat washed over her slowly as his tongue stroked hers, almost languidly. Suddenly she felt like a teenager with her first boyfriend. All rampant need and hormones. She dragged her mouth from his.

"What was the noise?" She swallowed hard, trying to regain her equilibrium. She tried to peer around the tree to get a look.

"It's the worst terrorist known to mankind, of course." He took her hand and led her along a path beside the boundary wall. About thirty feet down the path was Maisie with two friends, throwing very large fire crackers at the wall.

The boy shouted "incoming!" again.

Beth shook her head and grinned. She wanted to join them so badly.

"Munch. What are you doing?"

"William gave me these. He said he found them in Pennsylvania. They're called Pegasus Pipe Bombs." She showed them one. It was indeed some kind of firecracker on steroids.

Beth laughed and looked behind her. "Can I try one? Do you have enough?"

Maisie held it out to her. "William bought us a hundred of them."

James smiled. "I'm going to kill him. Or maybe I'll just throw one in his bedroom when he's sleeping."

"I wouldn't, not unless you want to change his sheets," Beth said. She took a step back and launched one at the wall. It made a glorious noise, like a huge lightning strike. "I love the smell of gunpowder at lunchtime."

James laughed and dragged her away from the kids.

As they drew closer to the house, Beth's stomach rumbled in a very unladylike manner. "Urgh. I feel like I'm always hungry around you."

"And I feel like I keep forgetting to feed you," he replied.

"I'm going to duck into the bathroom and then maybe hit Gracie up for some sly food in the kitchen. I'll catch up with you later."

* * *

He should have gone with her, he thought. Ten minutes later she still hadn't found her way back to him.

Instead, Harry found him. "Why did you bolt off like that?" she asked.

"Just checking on Maisie. She and her friends are playing with firecrackers on the front wall." He slipped on his sunglasses so he could see her better. "Have they served any food yet?"

"They're just about to, I think. About time, really. I swear half of your parents' guests are a bit drunk already."

"Maybe that was the idea. Mom did seem to want to grease the wheels of the politicians. What was decided about the wedding?"

Harry started walking slowly back toward the table, and James fell in beside her. "What you heard. Sadie agreed to the wedding being open only to family and her close friends, giving your mother the opportunity to host the dinner afterward. But without them. Simon was pretty firm that they'd be leaving at around midday tomorrow."

"Can't say I blame him. At all," he said. "What about you,

Harry? Found anyone to put up with your war-zone, globe-trotting, death-wish ways?"

He'd been convinced throughout their whole relationship that she'd had some messed-up desire to be with Danny, her dead husband, again. James hadn't been able to live with her exploits, never knowing whether she would come back alive from them. Solo canoeing down the Amazon? Hiking the Australian outback? Walking across Africa? She'd done all that and more. She was afraid of absolutely nothing. Certainly not death.

"Let's not do this here. You're stressed out being here, and you're taking it out on me. That's not fair," she said evenly.

He stopped and looked down at her. "You're right. I'm sorry." He wrapped his arms around her tiny frame and squeezed her tight, all the time wondering about Beth. Wondering if they had a future—wondering why she could definitely have his back in some situations and then take a check from his freaking father. He felt an uncontrollable urge to beat his head against a brick wall.

"Look. Go find Beth, and try to forget your crazy family for a while. You're all safe here at the house, and you know, just have a bit of fun. You were a real catch. Still are. She'd be stupid if she didn't see that. And she doesn't seem stupid," Harry said.

He wanted to confess his whole scheme to Harry, to ask her advice. Figure out why Beth didn't trust herself, or anyone else, to stay in a relationship when she was away on deployment. But he couldn't. He didn't want to admit to Harry that he was still useless at relationships. Or even at starting one. This attempt already seemed to have imploded in a spectacular way.

He let Harry go and wandered the grounds, looking fruitlessly for Beth and chatting distractedly with his parents' guests, all of whom seemed to have met her.

After an hour or so, he finally caught up with her. Guest after guest had come up to him to tell him how lucky he was to have found Beth, and ask when their wedding would be. He had no idea how to respond. He just wanted to find her, take her back to the pool house, and forget everything else. Weddings, checks, Sunday—everything.

He eventually found her in the kitchen, chatting in Spanish to the caterers. He watched her for a moment before making his presence known. She glowed, and the aproned people around her seemed happy: laughing at her, with her. She seemed at home. He wanted her to look like that when she was with him.

Her gaze eventually found his, and her smile dimmed a fraction. The tiniest amount, but that fraction splintered in his heart. He held out his hand. "We're off the clock. We have a few free hours until we have to get ready for the rehearsal dinner."

She slipped off the counter and took his hand. He couldn't help but kiss it like he'd done in the elevator.

As they left the kitchen, she said, "You don't have to do that, you know. Not when it's just us."

"What do you mean? Do you think when we're in the pool house I'm kissing you for an audience?" He squinted at her, as if he was trying to understand her.

"I heard you tell Harry that you loved her." She stared at the ground. "By the pool."

"Jesus, don't you start. I get Harry shoved down my throat enough by my mother. I love Harry, but just as an old acquaintance. We were never hot and heavy. I actually think I was just an experiment for her, to see if she could be with anyone after Danny. The answer to that was a resounding no."

"Okay," Beth said, but she only sounded about fifty percent convinced.

He said nothing, just held her hand tighter and towed her through the few remaining guests, back down to the pool house. He opened the glass door for her.

"Listen. Don't mistake this"—he gestured toward the daybed and the bedroom—"for what we're pretending to be out there. They are two completely separate things. I know things are complicated, and my family is bound to have done a number on you. But I am not my family. Don't confuse the two." He dragged her against him, kissing her as if he already had her permission. But he wasn't asking.

Chapter 14

His kiss messed with her head, her heart, her whole body. She kissed him back, pushing her tongue against his, and reveling in the heat that flooded her body. Her resolve not to be intimate with him again evaporated into nothing. Once again, the intoxication of his proximity slayed her. How had she survived those weeks in the MRAP without knowing him like this? Everything had changed in the space of a couple of days. His steady gaze pinned her.

James pulled away, took a step back and released her. "This is on you, sweetheart. Your choice. I'm not going to take advantage of the rush we're both on from this evening. Take a moment to decide whether this is what you really want. Whether *I'm* what you really want."

She could follow him, or not. Decide to sleep with him or not. Every part of her mind told her it was a bad idea. Every part of her body tingled with the anticipation of the way she knew James could make her feel. She'd worry later. Right now, she did want him. She followed him into the bedroom.

Wordlessly, he pulled her toward him. Every touch was gentle, deliberate. The intensity in his light eyes took her breath away. Her breath hitched in her throat as he carefully unbuttoned her jacket, unzipped her skirt. In seconds she was in her underwear, her skin prickling under his fingers. He left her panties and bra on while he made short work of his own clothes. Then he was naked, all hard muscle and glinting eyes. He laid her back on the bed and her whole reality faded. Just this moment in time was hers. Was real. She touched his leg with her foot, and he caught it, raising it to his lips. He kissed her arch and she squirmed under the hot tickle of his stubble.

He leaned over her and kissed up the outside of her leg until he was next to her on the bed. She struggled to hold everything together as he stroked her face, kissing where his fingers had been seconds before. He touched the tip of his finger to her nipple through her bra, his eyes pinning hers.

It was…intimate. As if he was seeing her every emotion. Every thought. She gasped as her body responded to his, nipples hardening and liquid pooling between her legs. It was as if her whole inside was on fire, and her outside was cool and vulnerable. Too vulnerable. But she liked being vulnerable with him. It made her feel honest, and real, and open to him. And if she couldn't bring herself to be those things in public, she could be those things here.

She kissed him and swung her leg over his and then sat up, reveling in the feel of his hardness between her legs. She leaned over him, pretending to kiss him, grinding lightly against him. Her face moved over his; her hair fell over his chest. He groaned at the tease, but his eyes stayed open, watching her every move.

His eyes closed as he nibbled on her lip, teased her with his tongue. She slipped off her bra quickly, so when she pulled away from him and sat up, he would see her.

His breath pulled in abruptly when he opened his eyes again. She rubbed herself gently along his dick, knowing he could feel her heat through her panties.

He raised a finger to her lips and slid it into her mouth. She sucked on it and teased it with her tongue. He withdrew it and slipped the wet finger onto her nipple. Glossing it, sliding around it until he squeezed it gently. She couldn't help but moan. The way he touched her... she'd never felt anything like it before in her life. Her head fell back and he gasped as her hair fell again, this time over his thighs.

"Do you want me?" she asked hoarsely, trailing her fingers over his smooth chest, flicking his nipples and basking in his responsiveness.

"In every way," he choked out.

Beth wriggled against his dick and then rose to her knees, feeling it spring up beneath her. As he watched, she pulled her panties to one side and lowered herself onto him.

His eyes darkened. She suddenly wanted to leave him wanting her, unable to think about sex without thinking about her. Irrational. She wanted him thinking about her forever.

She moved her pelvis, adjusting so he could slide inside her. As he did, she squeezed her eyes shut, hiding tears from him and from herself. She rocked herself against him and then raised herself so he came out of her almost entirely, before pushing down on him again and making him shake under her.

His fingers found their way past her panties and gently, so gently she could barely feel it, he stroked her clit. She felt as if all the moisture in her body flooded between her legs. She was scared to let go, scared to come, as if by doing so she would lose control and never regain it.

She slid up and down his dick until he was bucking beneath

her. It got faster and hotter, and his fingers stroked and teased her until the universe spun out of her as she climaxed. As she cried out his name, tears sprung from her eyes. His hands grabbed her hips and he drove into her—once, twice—and then groaned, shuddering under her. She relished making him come; it was like having the ultimate power. Except it was a power he had over her, too.

His thumbs swiped the tears from her face and he gathered her to him, cradling her in his arms, laying her on his chest.

* * *

He couldn't bear that he'd made her cry. All this messing around, pretending to be a couple—why couldn't he have just switched off his phone and gone climbing? Or just fucking manned up to begin with and told his father to go fuck himself, that he'd date and marry someone of his own choosing.

He wanted to ask her what was wrong, what he could do to make it better, but he didn't want to push his way into her head that way. It was like seeing people cry downrange: it happened for all kinds of reasons, and if you saw it, you pretended you didn't to allow that person some privacy and dignity. He worried that if he asked her she'd never forgive him for pointing out her weakness.

Shit, but this wasn't downrange, and she was here as a woman, not as a soldier. He looked down, hoping to see the expression on her face, but her eyes were closed, her breathing even.

Shit. Too late.

* * *

When he woke up, she was gone. The first time ever he'd regretted his ability to sleep like a log.

He scrubbed his eyes with the heels of his hands and jumped out of bed. They really had to talk. Like really. He went out into the living area and looked at the clock in the kitchen.

Crap. They only had about twenty minutes until the transport left for the restaurant.

"Beth?" he called, but there was no sound in reply, not even water dripping. Then he looked outside and there she was—fully dressed for dinner and walking slowly around the pool, talking on the phone. She looked at peace, and he wondered who she was speaking with. He couldn't take his eyes off her. Her eyes danced playfully as she spoke, and her expression appeared open and happy.

She hadn't looked like that at any time while they'd been together—not at war, not during the weekend. She looked comfortable, softer somehow. He'd do anything to be the one who gave her that peace, but this whole weekend had turned into a mistake of epic proportions. She didn't do relationships, he didn't do casual, the sex was the most electric he'd ever experienced, but unfortunately that didn't seem to be enough to bridge the gap between them.

As if in protest, his dick twitched. Damn it. He turned away to get dressed, convinced he was going to have to cut her loose for his own peace of mind. And his dick's.

* * *

"I wouldn't say that exactly," Beth almost laughed at her sister's question.

"What exactly would you say, then? A nine? An eight? For the love of God, tell me he wasn't sub-zero," Tammer said, clearly latched on to the topic of grading James's performance.

"I am not having this conversation with my little sister. It's all kinds of wrong. But definitely a nine point five, maybe point six." She touched the smooth surface of a column as she strolled by.

A shriek from her sister made her pull the phone away from her ear. "Sweet hell, are you trying to deafen me? Look, don't get all excited about this. I'm just here with him for the weekend, then we're back to our normal lives, okay? Don't put more importance on this than there is."

"You've gotten laid for the first time in...what is it...ten years? Of course it's important. He's a cute, sexy hero. What's not to love about that?" Tammer was clearly not going to let this one go.

"It is *not* ten years, and I can't get involved with him. There's another very good reason I can't get involved. Remember I told you there was a job I really wanted after leaving the army? Turns out his dad is the boss of the...company. And he really, really doesn't want me to be with James. If I stay with him, what will I do for a career? Right now, I'm just hoping that I can get into the company without him knowing." Suddenly she started feeling slightly nauseated again. She'd been shot at more times than she could count, but this whole situation was making her so tense and nervous. So out of her comfort zone. Hell, even the Jimmy Choos were out of her comfort zone.

"Beth. That's just your career. Some things, like life, are more important than a job."

"Not to me. My career is my life, you know that," Beth said.

"I do know that. But it doesn't have to be." Her voice was small, and Beth could tell Tammer was giving up the fight.

"How's the pup? Is he missing me?" she asked a little wistfully.

"Nope, Jubilee doesn't even remember you, so go out and have a good time, get laid, then come back here and just live on the memories for another ten years." In the background Beth could hear the dog howling as he did whenever Tammer made a hand signal to him. The sound squeezed her heart a little.

"I miss you both so much," she said. "Wait...it *wasn't* ten years!"

But Tammer had already hung up. She smiled for a second at her phone and stuffed it in her purse.

"Are you ready?" James called from across the pool.

She looked up. She was glad he wasn't close enough to see her slow blink at the sight of him, in a charcoal gray suit, pristine white shirt, with a deep blue tie. *Wow.*

"Ready to go," Beth said, making her way to him. "Are we driving, or is there some other arrangement?" She needed to keep everything neutral. She was Switzerland.

"There is transportation available, but I thought we'd take the Audi so we don't get stuck there."

Beth grinned. "Can I drive?"

His face fell. He looked at his keys, and then again at Beth. "Well, I don't...it's just that I never..."

She burst out laughing. "It's okay. I didn't expect you to give up your baby that easily. You drive." The relief that flooded his face made her laugh harder. "Seriously? It's like I really asked you for your baby."

"You did," he replied weakly.

"Come on, let's go, you sad, sad person," she said, nodding toward the car.

The journey didn't take long, and Beth was careful to talk about things that couldn't be segued into any awkward areas. She had to keep it together for one more day.

When they arrived they were assigned to different tables at the restaurant. It seemed as if the Walkers had taken over the whole floor of the eatery, with ten round tables seating about seven people each. *Some "small, intimate" rehearsal dinner.*

Sadie met them at the door and hooked her arm through James's. "You're so lucky I didn't ask you to be an usher or anything. The rehearsal blew the big one. None of us could remember what we were supposed to be doing and Simon's Blackberry kept going off. He's got some work emergency going on and is only half here." She sighed. "I'm just focusing on the honeymoon now." Then she seemed to snap to attention. "Oh, you guys. Sorry, Beth, we had to split you up. Dad's put James at a table with Maisie and several people from The Hill, so I've put you at the fun table. You'll be sitting with Harry. Keep her company, won't you?"

"Of course I will. Which table?" Beth asked, half relieved and half worried that she wouldn't be sitting with James. *Gah.* He'd probably prefer to switch with her and sit with Harry. With a slightly rueful look at James, she followed Sadie's pointing finger and immediately saw Harry alone at a far table. She was staring at a half-empty cocktail glass. Beth intercepted a waiter and asked for another drink for Harry, and a mojito for her.

"Harry," she said as she approached the table.

"Beth! I'm so glad you're at our table. Where's James?"

"At a table with some bigwigs, I think. I ordered us some more drinks," Beth said, looking over her shoulder for the waiter.

"Then I love you, and I feel doubly bad for what I've done." Harry took another sip from her glass and flipped her long blond hair over her shoulder.

Beth found her place next to Harry and inspected the seat for...she didn't know really, a whoopee cushion? Thumb tacks? Eventually secure in the fact that the chair hadn't been booby trapped by James's ex, she sat. "What did you do?"

"For some unknown reason I ended up sitting next to Jeffrey, Sadie's ex. So I swapped places with you. Even knowing he's at the table is making me drink more than I should."

Beth looked at the card next to hers and yes, it was indeed marked "Jeffrey." Great. "It's okay. I've only met him once, at the JibJab bar. He lived to tell the tale, so I swear I won't try to kill him. Not at the table, anyway."

Harry's eyes widened and she laughed. "I really do love you."

Their drinks arrived and they clinked glasses. "So you know Sadie from college? Or was it mostly because you were dating James?" Beth asked. "She told me to keep you company, you know."

Harry's smile dropped a fraction. "Sadie and I go way back. And no, I knew Sadie first. Then James. But Sadie's just worried for me." At Beth's inquisitive expression, she continued. "This is the first wedding I've been to since my own. I think she thinks this is going to trigger some kind of meltdown."

"Oh, I'm sorry. Bad ending?" As soon as the words were out of her mouth, she remembered what James had told her about Harry being a widow.

"The worst." Harry took a huge gulp of her cocktail. "He was killed in Afghanistan."

Cold washed over Beth. James hadn't mentioned that she was a military wife. "I'm so sorry. That *is* the worst."

"Really it's okay. It happened seven years ago, and I have to say, my wedding was nothing like this one is going to be. I don't think she need worry that something among all this...opulence will be a trigger for memories."

"I don't think any wedding will ever be quite like this one," Beth agreed. "So, not talking about weddings, what do you do?" Multitasking, she held up her fingers to a passing waiter for more drinks.

Harry leaned back in her chair, looking at ease for the first time since Beth had sat down. "I'm a freelance archaeology advocate. I know. You're going to ask me what that is...that you've heard of archaeology and advocacy, but not together, right?" Her eyes lit up and she leaned forward as she talked about her job.

"I advise on the cultural significance of archaeological finds, particularly on private property, or on property that is about to be developed. You know how you sometimes read that a Stone Age village has been found while construction workers are building a road or a supermarket? I'm the expert the courts call in to help them decide whether it's important to preserve the site or not, and how to preserve it if it's necessary."

"That's really interesting. Do you make a lot of enemies? I wouldn't imagine arguing with a huge corporation about whether they can build a mall would be very good for your health."

Harry grinned. "Well, sometimes that's the fun of it. The only downside is that your whole world starts to revolve around lawyers. And that's not fun for anyone."

Beth held up her glass to clink in agreement. As they drank, a shadow loomed over the table and Harry groaned into her glass.

"Ladies," Jeffrey said as he took his seat next to Beth. "Henrietta." He nodded to her. Harry responded with a subdued hello.

"And Beth. How nice to see you again. I'm looking forward to chatting with you tonight. I specially asked Sadie to sit us together so we could get to know each other better."

Gag. He was either lying, or Harry was. She put her money on Jeffrey being the liar. Either way, thanks to Harry, she was stuck with him. She kicked Harry's shoe under the table, making her laugh into her drink.

A very handsome, tall man approached the table and introduced himself as Matt, a friend of the groom. Beth could tell

he was some kind of military—some unspoken mix of deport-
ment, haircut, and degree of confidence. He sat next to Harry,
who gave him an enthusiastic welcome. She wondered if Harry
could pick up on his military vibes, too, and whether she steered
clear of military men now.

Matt held Harry's hand as he sat, only releasing it when the
waiter arrived to take his drink order. "Bourbon for me, and
whatever the ladies are having," he said, slipping the waiter a
hundred-dollar bill. "And keep them coming."

Harry leaned in and stage-whispered, "I think the drinks are
free."

"But now we have our own drinks waiter," he whispered back.

Harry threw both arms in the air. "Score!"

Beth smiled at Harry's new exuberance, which she suspected
was driven not a little bit by her three cocktails. "So what do you
do, Matt?"

He leaned back, shoved both hands behind his head and
smiled at the pair of them. "I can turn my hand to most things."

Cocky, much? Beth took a sip and shook her head.
"Unbelievable."

He tipped his head to the side. "What? You don't believe me?
I swear I'm pretty handy to have around."

Harry took Beth's side. "Oh, honey. I can see you are. You
obviously think you're very capable. But some women don't need
men for anything."

His eyes lit up under her push-back. He sat forward, arms
resting on his legs. "Nothing at all? I find that hard to believe."

Harry pretended to think, finger on her chin as she appeared
to consider the one thing she could possibly need from a man.
"Well, maybe I can think of one thing. One...very delicate task
that I frequently need help with..."

Beth was certain that Matt was set to explode at Harry's teasing, which was amusing in itself, but her mind was still on James. She looked for his table again and saw him deep in conversation with one of the elegant blond women seated next to him. His table wasn't only stacked with people from The Hill. It felt like she was watching a dream slip out of her hands. Her ring sparkled as she moved her hand for her drink, and she couldn't help but pause to look at it. To touch it quickly with her thumb. The problem was, the ring was the only thing that *was* real.

Her attention was brought back to the table by Harry's laughter. As Beth turned back to them, Matt pulled his chair much closer to Harry's, wearing a very confident cat-that-got-the-cream smile. Shit. Good for Harry, but that meant she was left with Jeffrey.

"How are you enjoying the wedding festivities?" Beth asked Jeffrey evenly. All the alcohol in the world might not be enough to endure a whole meal with Jeffrey.

"Oh, they're okay. Such a shame tomorrow was downsized. I'll only be around for the evening reception." His face was flushed and she wondered how much alcohol he'd consumed already. She felt a pang of sadness for him. He was a strange man, no doubt, but Beth wondered how much of that was driven by pain at being rejected by Sadie. She wished she'd asked Harry why she didn't like him.

"At least all the important people will be there, though," Beth said. "Plenty of people for you to threaten with background checks." *Whoops.* She softened her words with a smile.

He took a drink and smiled ruefully. "Sorry about that. It was a stupid move. I just wanted to warn you about the Walkers. They're a hard family." In a gulp he'd finished his short drink. "But I think you've worked that out already. I see you worry your engagement ring as if it's bothering you. There are no prizes for going through with a wedding you're not sure you want. A true friend would provide an escape route."

She guessed his CIA training was apparent even while slightly drunk. She kicked herself for giving him an in to her situation by playing with the unfamiliar ring, but he didn't seem to be that concerned with her; she noticed his eyes flicked to Sadie at the head table. "I don't think she needs a getaway driver. She seems happy, doesn't she?"

"She seems happy, yes. But I know her better than anyone." He shifted in his chair and brought his gaze firmly back to her. "Are you absolutely sure that James loves you?"

She was taken aback. With no quick response, she took a drink. As she was about to defend James's deep and abiding fake love for her, he interrupted.

"I felt the same way with Sadie. The Walkers are strange in that way. They can only ever give sixty percent of themselves. To anything. Anyone. They keep people at arm's length, ready to push us away if we don't suit their goals."

Beth wanted to defend James and his family, but in truth she didn't know if what he said was false or not. "People are different. Situations are different. Who really knows if anyone loves anyone?" Wow, that had slipped out without her meaning it to. She looked at her empty glass. That was probably why.

"Well, James has left you all alone here with me...so maybe... love the one you're with?" He stroked a finger down her arm.

Was he kidding? Beth flicked it away this time. "You think that will make her jealous? I doubt it."

Jeffrey's face fell and in a second she felt a weird compassion for him. She shook that off pretty quickly. Could he be the phantom e-mailer? Could he have been trying to persuade Sadie not to go through with the wedding? Surely not. Would someone who worked at the CIA be clumsy enough to send e-mails? Also, by the mooning look on his face, she didn't think he would want to physically hurt Sadie, like the hoodied man at the bar had.

"So what do you do at work?" She changed the subject, hoping he'd be as indiscreet as before and keep talking about how important he was.

"I'm Director Walker's right-hand man. I do whatever he needs me to. I'm honestly quite surprised he didn't fix this wedding a long time ago, but apparently, on some things, he lets Sadie have her way. It's the first time I've ever been unimpressed with the way he manages the people around him." He took another slug from a fresh glass the waiter brought and gritted his teeth as he inhaled after the whisky.

The appetizers arrived at that moment, as did four other guests, who introduced themselves as Sadie's friends from work. They greeted Jeffrey with slightly overdone gusto, and introduced themselves to Harry, Matt, and Beth with good humor.

Matt jumped up and asked Harry to go to have a smoke with him. Beth recognized a suppressed pain in his eyes. He needed to get away from the crowd. She'd seen it many times before. She kicked Harry under the table, and the tiny blonde leapt up and followed him out onto the restaurant patio.

As they all started to eat, the conversation became restaurant-oriented, with everyone chiming in about their favorite D.C. places to eat.

Beth's thoughts drifted as the others spoke. Harry and Matt had seemed to be in a world of their own, conversing in low voices and with the occasional touch to an arm. For a second, Beth had been jealous of Harry meeting someone in such a totally benign way. Who doesn't dream of meeting a man at a wedding?

The newcomers to the table seemed happy to take up Jeffrey's attention by talking about people at work, being sycophantic in a way only government employees were. She should know. She was one of them.

After a dessert of crepes suzette prepared tableside, James came over to suggest they head out. Beth bid good-bye to everyone at the table, hugged Harry who had made a reappearance, and left with him.

As soon as they cleared the restaurant, she breathed a heavy sigh of relief.

"Was it that bad?" he asked, wrapping his arm around her shoulders.

"I was sitting next to Jeffrey. How was your table?"

He opened the car door and paused as she got in. As he closed his own door he said, "My table was rigged. It was me, two senators looking for chiefs of staff, and one military contractor looking for operations managers. And then there were two single women. I guess they all owe my father a favor." He ground his teeth as he slid the car through the gears until they hit the parkway again.

She felt bad for him. For a second. "I guess it must be hard to have parents so concerned about you and your future. I get how you feel, I do. I told you I kept my mother happy for years before I eventually did what I wanted. But I would give up my whole career in the army for another year with her. To give Tammer another year with her. A month even. So don't take them for granted. Don't not see them because they annoy you." Her voice trailed off as she looked out of her side window. "Or fake a relationship just because it makes your life easier."

There was an extended silence before he spoke. "I'm sorry about all this. You probably think my family and I are a bunch of jerks." He looked around. "Don't get me wrong, we are a bunch of jerks. I especially feel like a jerk for dragging you here. When we talked about it in the car, it sounded like fun, but I guess it's turned out the opposite of that for you. I just liked you and I wanted to spend a little time with you.

"I know our weekend kind of went to shit somewhere along the line, but some parts of it worked out okay, don't you think?"

She remained silent. They both knew the answer to that. How could the sex be so good and the in-between parts be so sketchy? Urgh.

"What do you want?" he asked. "What's your ideal outcome here?"

Yesterday her answer would have been to just enjoy the weekend. This afternoon it would have been to just see what happened when they got back home. But with the job she so desperately wanted in the CIA and the craziness with his father's check, all she really wanted now was to go home. She needed to deploy, he needed to…She had no idea what he needed, except for a quick fling, but there was no way anything could work. "I just want to go home on Sunday and get on with my life."

There was another long silence in the car before he simply said, "Okay."

Chapter 15

They said very little as they prepared for bed, except for the odd "excuse me" when they bumped into each other going between the bathroom, the closet, and the bedroom. James's every instinct was to grab her and tell her how much he liked her, to tell her how much he'd wanted her in his life since they'd first met. This whole weekend he'd found it impossible to keep his hands off her, but tonight he was going to.

He kept his mouth shut, offered her a t-shirt to sleep in, and stretched out on his side of the huge bed. In the king-sized bed with so much acreage between them, there was no way he could accidentally brush up against her.

They had lain in the dark for about twenty minutes when he heard her yawn. Sleeping people don't yawn. He reached out and dragged her toward him, wrapping his arm around her waist and tucking her against him. She protested for a second, wriggling away, but then seemed to sink into it and relaxed against him.

With the scent of her hair in his nose, he fell asleep. The last words to run through his mind were *Complete. Clusterfuck.*

* * *

The morning brought clouds and shadows to the pool house. Rain threatened as thunder rumbled in the distance. It fit his mood perfectly.

As they dressed for breakfast, the same awkward silence permeated the small pool house, to the extent that he was itching to leave for breakfast even though it meant getting up close and personal with his family. There was no way his family was better company than Beth but he really needed time—to think, to put together some kind of a declaration that wouldn't scare her off.

Fucking hysterical. He was a man of action, but now that he was concerned about losing Beth, he was reduced to planning conversations. What was wrong with this picture? Problem was, he'd already done the action thing, and this was where they'd ended up. At least after the wedding, he'd have a good five hours in the car to talk some sense into her.

He wanted her in his life, and he wasn't going to give up until she agreed to even try to squeeze him into hers.

"Are you ready for breakfast?" he asked her as she emerged fully dressed from the bathroom.

She smiled. "Starving."

Just her smile and the way she looked slayed him. He was doomed. Fucking doomed. She was wearing a dark pink skirt suit, the same color as the bra and panties he'd found on her in the dressing room. It felt like that had happened weeks ago, but it had only been two days. He wondered if she was wearing the matching underwear as he held out his arm for her to take.

As they entered the main house, his father was disappearing into his study with a few gray-haired, gray-suited work colleagues.

His mother and Gracie were in the hallway, going over some written notes.

"Are we late for breakfast?" He looked at his watch.

"No, go on in," she replied, gesturing toward the breakfast room. But before they could, a door slammed upstairs.

* * *

Sadie came running down the stairs in her underwear as if her hair was on fire. "My dress is too big! It's sagging around my ass."

James winced and turned away, as if the sight of his sister in her wedding underwear was a little too much for him. To be fair, it seemed to be a little too much for everyone there. "Can't you call the dressmaker?" he asked.

She couldn't stay in the hallway like that with Director Walker's colleagues only a closed door away. Beth put out her arm to usher her back upstairs. "It's okay; I've got this." She nodded reassuringly at Sadie and they both headed upstairs, leaving James behind.

"When you come downstairs, please bring Maisie with you." Mrs. Walker intoned, patting the back of her head. Beth wondered if she ever spoke in public without touching her chignon. Maybe it was a nervous affectation.

"I'll wait for you in the snooker room," James said.

Yeah, where the family's bar was. She guessed breakfast had been abandoned. "I'll see you there in a bit," Beth said.

Sadie took her back into her room, where she was immediately enveloped in a cloud of perfume. Harry was sitting on Sadie's bed. "Sorry. I wish I could help with the dress, but that kind of thing is so very definitely not my area of expertise," she said.

Beth laughed. "I'm just surprised to see you managed to shake Matt off. When I left you last night, you seemed inseparable."

Harry fluttered her eyelashes. "It was a one-evening thing. Simple, fun…" She ducked her head and grinned.

"She's just an old tart. I'm almost jealous," Sadie said.

Beth turned to Sadie. "Well, let's get this on and see where the problem is."

As Sadie and Harry carefully slipped the dress over her head, a flush came from the en suite, and Maisie came out, looking fabulous. Her violet-tipped hair hung down against the violet of the dress. When she saw Beth, she grinned and hitched her long dress up so Beth could see her boots.

"Awesome," Beth said. Then took in the whole picture of the two bridesmaids and Sadie in her sheath dress. "All of you. You all look beautiful. Wow." She grinned at them and Harry handed her a full-to-the-brim champagne flute. She took a sip. "And now you all look even more beautiful."

They all laughed.

"Right. Where do I find a sewing kit?" Beth asked, putting the glass down. It wouldn't do to be dizzy while stitching a dress that in all likelihood cost more than her yearly salary. It looked as if the waist seam needed to be taken in at least half an inch, but that shouldn't take her more than fifteen minutes, if that.

Maisie claimed to have her grandma's sewing box in her room and ran off to get it.

"So, you and James," Sadie said. "Have you named the day yet? Or has this whole shindig put you off marrying into the family?"

Wow. She was not going to let that question go.

Do not ruin Sadie's wedding day. Do not ruin Sadie's wedding day.

"What do you think the odds are that your parents will let us marry somewhere private? On a beach, maybe." Beth couldn't help imagining being barefooted with flowers in her hair, wearing a floaty dress, with daisies in her hand. And James. James wearing sunglasses on the beach. She shook herself. *Never going to happen.*

"Oh, slim to zero," Sadie replied. "You have to understand, my father has every intention of pushing James into politics."

"But he doesn't want that." She paused. "You know your father put him at a table with people who were all looking to recruit him last night? He wasn't interested in any of them."

"Of course he isn't. But I never wanted to be a lawyer, yet here I am, working for the government. It's hard to say no to Father." She spun around, absently watching her train float up around her.

A pop came from downstairs. Harry giggled. "I guess we're not the only ones getting an early start!" She reached for the champagne bottle again and topped off the glasses.

Beth froze. That hadn't been a champagne cork. She knew that sound very well, and her blood ran cold. That was a gunshot.

Another pop. "Holy shit," Harry said. "They really are getting the party started. Maybe we should go down."

Beth held up her hand. "Shhh."

Everyone went silent. Sadie frowned at her. "What is it?"

Beth's worried eyes met hers. "I'm not one hundred percent sure that was a champagne cork. But I'm going to check. Stay here, okay?"

"Beth. This place is a secure compound. No one can hurt us. Stop worrying."

"It's okay. It's probably nothing. I'll be back in a minute." She inched the door open.

Sadie said, "Seriously. Don't try to freak me out on my wedding day, okay?"

Beth cast one last look at her as she slipped out into the hallway. Silently she crept along the upper corridor to the stairs. She got down on her hands and knees, cursing her tight skirt. God help her if she was caught like this and the sounds really had been just popping champagne corks. Embarrassment, much?

She stuck her head out from a corner in a super-fast move. She saw nothing downstairs. But as she moved back and stood, she heard a scuffle. She took another fast look—this time she saw a man with a Glock and a balaclava mask going into the reception room.

Shit.

She took a second to consider her options. James was in the snooker room, Director Walker and his guests were probably in his study. Maisie...

She whipped around just as Maisie came out of her room with the sewing box. Beth kicked off her shoes, picked them up, and ran toward her. She placed a finger to her lips when Maisie noticed her.

Beth pressed her mouth to the girl's ear and whispered, "Something weird is going on downstairs. Don't say a word, don't make a sound. Come with me. Understand?"

Maisie's eyes bugged but she nodded. Beth took her hand and quietly opened Sadie's door. They both slipped back into the room.

The women were still drinking and giggling. Beth took a deep breath.

"There is at least one masked gunman downstairs," she said quietly. "Don't panic, and do not make a sound." *Whoops. Not so subtle, maybe.*

Sadie went white and plonked onto the bed. "Are you sure?"

She held her arm out for Maisie, who ran to the bed and threw her arms around her sister.

"Can you lock this door?" Beth asked. "What about the bathroom door?"

"Yes to both," Sadie said, rocking Maisie.

Beth took a second to think. "Maisie. I need your boots." Without waiting for an answer, she flipped open the lid of the sewing kit and found a pair of large tailoring shears. She quickly slit her pencil skirt nearly to the waistband. Maisie was trying to undo her boots, but her hands were shaking so much she was having trouble.

"Hey, it's okay. Let me help," Beth said quietly. "I won't let anything happen to you." She hoped she could live up to that. She slipped on the boots and tied them up carefully.

"When I leave, lock the door behind me, and take the key with you. I need you to all get into the bathroom. Lock the door. Sit away from the door, and away from the window. Wait until I come back for you. I will shout at you through the door. Do not open the door for anyone who isn't me. Do you understand?"

Sadie put her hand out to stop Beth. "I don't mean to seem rude, but I think you should sit tight with us and not get us into any more trouble. Let the professionals handle this. I mean, what the hell can you do with an armed gunman?"

Beth tied the final double bow on her laces and stood up, sliding the shears into the top of one boot. "I'm an army of one." Then she smiled genuinely for the first time since she'd arrived. She was in her element. This was her comfort zone.

* * *

James had been racking balls for a quick game while he waited for Beth when the first shot sounded. He knew immediately what it was, but wondered if maybe an eager security person had had an accidental discharge. Then he heard the second shot. His adrenaline spiked in a way he had never felt outside of Afghanistan, or out of uniform. He moved silently to the door that led to the dining room and quietly locked it.

He looked around the room for a weapon. Nothing but pool cues and bottles of booze. He tried not to think about his whole family in the house, about who had been shot.

He wondered for a moment if his father had organized any additional security, but he wasn't going to wait for the cavalry. Some of the guests might have been CIA, but neither his father nor any of his cronies ever had this kind of combat training. The best he could hope for was that they'd sit tight in the study. His father's usual security detail would likely still be at the gate. They weren't scheduled to make rounds until the guests arrived. James *was* the cavalry.

He unscrewed the two heaviest cues and discarded the smaller ends so he was left with two easily maneuvered bats.

Where was Beth? He did a mental accounting of the people he thought must be in the house. His parents, about three of his father's colleagues, Sadie, Maisie, Beth, and Gracie and Harry. Everyone else was outside, making finishing touches to the marquee decorations, all beyond the bulletproof and soundproof windows. FUBAR.

He eased the door open and slid into the hallway. Almost immediately he heard someone else open a door. He pressed his back to the door, but kept it open. He held perfectly still, knowing that people always noticed something moving before they noticed something stationery.

A masked man was creeping slowly toward the bathroom, apparently not familiar with the layout of the house. He didn't look like a professional. He wasn't clearing the area properly—ignoring what was over his shoulder and in his blind spot. James was fine with that.

As the intruder passed the shadow of the doorway where James stood, James grabbed his gun and took it right out of his grasp. In the next second, he had the man in a headlock and dragged him into the snooker room.

James held his forearm across the intruder's neck until he passed out and fell to the floor. He ripped off the man's mask but didn't recognize him. What? This takedown had been too easy. James realized his target had hardly struggled at all and also hadn't panicked. It was a contradiction. He ripped a piece of braid from the snooker table and tied the man's hands and feet.

Checking the gun's magazine, he found two rounds missing. He chambered one and slipped out of the room again. The hallway was empty, but he heard a scuffle and clanging in the kitchen. He headed in the opposite direction of the main door to see if his father's security detail was outside, but found the door locked.

Clever. Very clever. The intruders had gotten in, then triggered a lockdown. It would take the best part of half an hour for the protocol to be reversed. He went to investigate the noises in the kitchen. No one else was going to surprise him. He held the gun at eye level and kicked in the door of the kitchen just in time to see Beth remove a large pair of scissors from a masked man's thigh as she slammed a cast-iron frying pan into his face.

Relief, admiration, and anxiety competed for space in his head. He tucked the gun into the waistband of his pants at the small of his back when he saw the man drop. Beth picked up the unconscious man's gun and grimaced. "I'm hoping he wasn't an entertainer at the wedding."

"Doubtful. Where is everyone?"

"The girls are all locked in Sadie's bathroom. At least that's where I left them." She went through the same process James had, checking the gun's mag. She pressed the top down. "Full. I heard two shots, though."

"Yeah, I've got another guy in the snooker room. His gun had two missing rounds. The front door is locked. This one's locked. I think it's safe to say that we are on a reverse lockdown. We're stuck in here with the bad guys."

Beth took a step toward him, and he reached out and dragged her close. He kissed her forehead, again overwhelmed with knowing she was safe, and better than that, that they were now in this together.

"How do you want to play this? I cleared the rooms upstairs that weren't locked before I came down but I've been in here for a few minutes so I don't know if anyone else went up there. I'm worried that there are more men moving around the house. If they wanted Director Walker, he's in the study down here, right? Why would they need to find anyone else?" James wondered why she'd used his father's work title instead of just saying "your dad," but he couldn't argue with her logic.

"Yes, he should be in the study, and I hope he stays here. I wish I knew where my mom was. If she isn't upstairs, I don't know where she'd be." He tried to look out of the kitchen window, but because they were in the basement, all he could see was grass and the bottom of the marquee.

"Could she have gone outside to supervise something?" Beth asked. "What about Gracie? I thought she'd be in here but she's not."

"Fuck. This is a nightmare."

"Split up?" Beth asked, chambering a round.

Nothing about this situation made him want to split up. He wanted her right by his side where he could protect her. Okay, and where she could have his back, too.

She continued. "I know it's best to stay together, but we're more dangerous apart, since no one knows we're, well, us. We can cover more ground and find more people."

James nodded once, knowing she was right. "My mother's salon is at the opposite end of the house to my father's study. The house is symmetrical. I guess it's the only place she could be."

"I'll find your mother and Gracie, and get them upstairs to Sadie's room. Then I'll come look for you," she said.

He looked at the man on the floor wondering if he should tie him up.

"Don't worry," Beth said. "He won't wake up until next Tuesday, I promise you that."

He nodded. "Okay, I'm going to try to clear the ground floor."

"Deal." They bumped gun-holding fists and gave each other identical smiles. Yeah, who would have thought they'd be under fire in the United States? Afghanistan was one thing, but McLean, Virginia was something different. Or should be, at least.

James headed to the door, but turned just before he went through it. "This,"—he said, motioning between them—"I'm sorry about this. About everything."

She shrugged and said, "Good luck out there. Don't get shot."

He grinned. "You either."

Chapter 16

Beth watched him go and gave him a few seconds. As soon as this was done, she was out of here. She was fairly convinced that she was falling in love with him, which was crazy. Literally bone-deep nutso.

Damn him. She assessed her surroundings before heading out into the hallway.

No gunfire, no scuffling. Just on the off-chance it was working, she picked up the kitchen phone. It was dead.

She left the kitchen, looking up the stairs as she went. No movement, still quiet. This time she went past the staircase to an area of the house she'd never been in before. It was a mirror image of the other side of the house, as James had told her, but the hallway was painted a dusky purple.

She had to find James's mother. For him. Then certainly her debt to him would be paid. Going through and clearing each room as she went, she eventually found the counterpart to the masculine study where she'd had her lovely meeting with the director.

Ear to the door, she listened for movement. There were no voices, no sounds of movement within. She quietly turned the handle and pushed the door open. She'd never kicked in doors by herself before; she'd always had someone at her back, so she'd decided upstairs that stealth was the best idea.

The room seemed empty so she stepped inside and closed the door silently behind her. There were two other doors in the room. Maybe they were closets. She held very, very still, and heard someone breathing. She edged around the room, back to the walls. A stiletto peeked out from under a large antique-looking desk.

"Mrs. Walker?" she whispered. "It's me, Beth."

A head poked out from under the desk, and James's mother saw Beth with her gun. "I knew you were no good. I knew it. My son would never want to be with someone like you. Thank God. Now, what do you want? What is all this about? Put that gun down."

For someone sprawled on the floor under a desk, she was still full of poison. Beth took back the kind words she'd said to James about her. She sighed.

"Get up. I'm not going to hurt you. Have you seen Gracie?" She didn't have anywhere else to put the gun, so she let her arm fall to her side.

"If I knew, I wouldn't tell you."

"Sweet hell. Mrs. Walker, I'm not involved with this. James sent me to find you. The other girls are in Sadie's room," Beth tried to explain.

"A likely story. Where is he? What have you done with my son? If you've hurt a hair on his head, I will kill you myself." She spat the words at Beth.

Wow. Just... wow. Now what was the plan? Whenever she'd rescued people before, which in all honesty wasn't really her specialty, she'd been in uniform. She'd never had to convince anyone she was a good guy before.

"I don't know what to tell you. There are masked men in the house, your security is nowhere to be found, and all the external doors are locked. James is looking for your husband and his colleagues, and I said I'd come look for you."

One of the other doors in the room opened and Beth immediately took a shooting stance and aimed her gun at the door. Gracie came out of a closet. Beth lowered her gun, mentally if not physically swiping her brow in relief that she hadn't shot.

"I believe her," Gracie said, shrugging.

Mrs. Walker covered her face with her hands in apparent desperation. "Okay," she said when she lowered her hands. "But I swear to God, if you are lying, I will put my Louboutin through your eye."

Beth didn't doubt it, but didn't want to waste time placating her. "I'm taking you to Sadie's room. Harry, Maisie, and Sadie are in the bathroom. That's where I'm taking you, okay?" She used a military strategy—keep repeating the goal in case anyone was distracted the first time it was stated. "Please stay behind me, and don't say anything when we are outside this room." She looked at the women. Mrs. Walker's nod was somewhat reluctant, but Beth took it as acquiescence.

The hallway was quiet, making Beth think that this could all really be just about the director and his work cronies in the study. She wondered if it was a secure study, like a panic room, or just a regular room. She cleared the hallway, and motioned for the two women to exit the room.

They followed her down the hallway until Beth, by habit, put up her fist. They stopped obediently as if they were her troops. She would have smiled if her heart wasn't beating a tattoo in her chest. She crouched and took the corner, pointing her weapon first up the stairs, and then down the hallway beyond the staircase.

Nothing. She led them up to the second floor. But halfway there, she heard a commotion.

She took the rest of the stairs two by two and peeked around the corner toward Sadie's room. The door was open. Shit.

Beckoning the ladies to her, she whispered for them to wait, backs to the wall on the opposite side of the corridor.

Heart pumping and echoing through her ears, she crept up to the doorway. Inside, Sadie was slung over a guy's shoulder, kicking and hollering. Maisie was trying to hold on to her. *Jeffrey? What the fuck?*

Ah. Jeffrey. The jealousy over the wedding, the e-mails. She sighed to herself.

"No, she has to come with me. I'm saving her. I'm taking her to safety. William told me…"

"Put me down," Sadie was yelling over and over, while Maisie was crying, holding on to her hands.

William? What does William have to do with this?

Whatever he was doing, he could stop right now. Beth wasn't scared. She could take Jeffrey. But then she saw he had a gun in one hand. Fuck it all sideways. Well, that made it all a lot clearer. She raised her weapon but then realized that he could easily start shooting, and there were too many people that could be in the way. Cursing inwardly that she didn't have a waistband to tuck the gun into, she carefully put it out of sight on the floor, just on the other side of the door.

"What's going on?" she asked as if she'd just walked in.

Maisie screamed, "He's trying to take Sadie! You told us to wait here."

"I did. Jeffrey, it's not safe down there; you should stay here with us. Put her down."

Her reasonable tone seemed to penetrate his mania and he put

Sadie down. She tried to step away from him but he grabbed her around her neck. A kind of uber-violent hug. "I'm rescuing her. She needs me to rescue her. William told me that I could take her out."

"Take her out? You're going to kill her?" Beth inched back toward her gun.

"No! That's not what he meant. He meant I could take her outside."

Did he?

"Where is William?" Beth asked, trying to sound calm. This was getting more complicated by the second.

"He's downstairs with his friends. He told me he would create a diversion while I rescued Sadie. I told you I could tell she didn't want to get married."

Sadie's mouth opened but Beth shook her head sharply to stop her from saying anything that would further derail Jeffrey.

"William seems to have friends with guns downstairs. Look." She retrieved her gun and held it by its muzzle so he wouldn't feel threatened. "See? I took this off one of them. I don't think this is a prank diversion, Jeffrey. I think William is doing something real."

He loosened his arm around Sadie's neck and squinted as if trying to figure out what to do next. "No, I'm taking her to safety," he decided. He dragged her toward the door, gun waving wildly.

Beth swallowed. She really just wanted to shoot him. "That's great, Jeffrey. But you can't expect her to want you to rescue her without rescuing all of us, too, can you? How will she be able to look at you again knowing you left us all behind in such a dangerous situation?" She figured fucking with his head was the right approach.

Sadie leveled a stare at her, and Beth hoped that she was getting the hint. "Beth's right. What if my sister gets killed, or my best friend? How will I ever be able to forgive you for leaving them behind?"

He scoffed. "No one is going to get killed." And then his mouth snapped shut as if he'd said too much.

"How do you explain the men downstairs with masks and real guns, real bullets?" Beth asked. He was crazy. Certifiably crazy.

An arm snaked around her shoulders. She jumped and looked round.

James. Prayers answered. Her breath steadied, and the adrenaline pulsing through her abated. She wanted to hold on to him. Forever.

"What's going on, Jeffrey? Isn't it bad luck to see the bride before the wedding?" He smiled at his sisters as if he couldn't see Jeffrey's gun.

"I'm saving your sister," Jeffrey said, tightening his grip on Sadie.

"From what?" James asked, still smiling.

"The men. The masked men who are in the house. They have guns. They will kill everyone unless..." He hesitated as if he didn't know what to say next.

"Unless what?" James dropped his arm from Beth's shoulder after squeezing it, sending a little comfort through her.

"I don't know. All I know is that I'm saving Sadie. Taking her away from this. It's dangerous here. It's dangerous for her to get married here. To Simon. William told me he was dangerous, and I couldn't find anything in our databases about him. He's fake. He doesn't exist. I couldn't get the director to see sense."

Holy shit, he sounded just bat-shit crazy. There was no way

he was leaving the room with Sadie. But at least James was here. Then she was jostled, elbowed out of the way by Mrs. Walker. *Oh good, now everyone's here.*

"James, we should do as Jeffrey says. Let's not cause any problems."

"Yeah, that's not going to happen, is it, Jeffrey? You have a gun, and try as you might, you can't shoot all of us."

Jeffrey paused and looked at his weapon as if he could count the bullets inside, and James took the opportunity to suddenly lunge at him. The gun went off as he jerked Jeffrey's hand upward. Plaster fluttered down from the ceiling as Beth ran forward, shoving Sadie and the other women back into the bathroom.

By the time she had turned around, Jeffrey was on his back with a bloody lip and a half-closed eye. James flipped him over, then took a stocking lying on the bed and tied his hands. Jeffrey tried to speak, but he just dribbled incoherently.

"I think your arms are broken, so try not to move too much," James said conversationally. Beth watched him finish knotting the stocking. God, he was magnificent. She wanted him—not sexually, not right now—but next to her, forever. She slipped that thought into a pocket as Mrs. Walker picked up the gun Jeffrey had dropped. She handed it to Beth in what Beth could only think of as a vote of confidence.

"You don't know what you're doing. Simon doesn't exist. She can't marry him."

"Of course he does. How you stayed my father's secretary so long without him realizing how stupid you are amazes me," James said.

He was right. Jeffrey should have figured out that the reason Simon wasn't in any database was because he was a covert operative.

"I'm his right-hand man," Jeffrey protested weakly.

"James, thank God you're here," Sadie said from the bathroom. "You were awesome."

He smiled back at her for a second, and then glanced at Jeffrey again. His fight was gone and he was looking at the bullet hole in the ceiling.

"They were supposed to be blanks. William told me they were blanks." He closed his eyes, and Beth could have sworn he was trying not to cry. "I can't believe I was so stupid. William convinced me Simon was a terrorist. That I'd be a hero if I saved the family from Sadie marrying him."

"They're supposed to be blanks? Not live rounds?" Beth asked, ignoring the rest.

"Yes!" Jeffrey said.

"Blanks can still kill people, you idiot." James said, kicking Jeffrey's leg.

Jeffrey just closed his eyes and shook his head.

Beth looked at the ceiling. "These *are* live rounds. They're not blanks." She looked at James. "Do you really think this was just a plot to kidnap Sadie?"

"I think William told Jeffrey that he'd make a diversion so Jeffrey could have Sadie, but I'd guess this was a diversion for something else William wanted to do."

"Does that sound possible, Jeffrey?" Beth said.

Jeffrey looked at the ceiling and shrugged again.

* * *

Beth left the room, allowing the family members to hug and reassure each other. She watched them through the doorway from the outside. Just as it should be.

James instructed his mother and Gracie to stay with the girls, fixing to leave Jeffrey trussed up like a chicken out in the hall. Beth had stepped back out of the way when a hand grabbed her around the throat. She went cold and reacted instinctively. Stepping backward she swung her head back to head-butt the assailant in the face, but he was ready for her—he turned to the side so that her head only made contact with his shoulder.

She must have made a sound because James stood and turned with his gun up at eye level. He lowered it a second, as if to check that what he was seeing was really happening.

"No way. Put her down." He aimed his weapon at the guy's head. "I can take you from here."

"I don't think so." William pressed a gun to Beth's temple. Everything went quiet and still. Her vision became blurred, and only then did she realize that he was still choking her.

"If she falls, the second she's down you're dead," James said evenly, advancing on them. William released the pressure on her neck, but dragged her backward and off balance.

"Untie him." The man pointed his gun at Jeffrey.

"No. Not until you release her," James said, still coming.

William dragged her toward the stairwell. Great, one shove and she'd break her neck on all that marble. She tried to think of a way to get out of his grasp, but her brain wasn't working as well as it should be.

"I'm not letting her go," William said.

"Me either," James countered. He lowered his gun for a second, then pinned William in his sight again. "What the fuck, dude? What's this about?"

"Freedom of information. The people I'm working with are going to publish everything in the CIA database. Americans have a right to know about all the government lies and cover-ups, what their government really does with taxpayer money. I'm going to be the next Julian Assange."

"Julian Assange lives in a tiny room in a foreign embassy," James countered. "Is that what you really want?"

Out of the corner of her eye, Beth could see two men, guns up, carefully sweeping the hallway below as she and James had done earlier. She was sure one of them was Simon. When the other caught her eye, she realized it was Matt from the rehearsal dinner. Matt held his finger to his lips and she nodded. And then she remembered her shears.

Carefully she raised her knee so the top of her boot was in reach. She looked meaningfully at James, who could see what she was reaching for. Distraction time.

"Why do you want Jeffrey untied? What could you possibly need him for?"

"He has all the codes, too." William laughed. "If my guys downstairs have no luck with your father, he's my backup plan. I meant what I said: you can stay at my beach house whenever you want. The Russians kindly extended diplomatic immunity to me. I'll be in Moscow before the end of the day."

"Jeffrey doesn't have any codes. I think he may have...overemphasized his importance in the CIA to you. And if you're working for the Russian government, then you really are a traitor. You can't play the WikiLeaks card if you're selling information to a foreign power. Are you? Are you planning to sell this data to them?"

William's grip on Beth loosened just a tiny bit, and she hoped that the conversation was making him lose his focus on her. But as that thought occurred to her, he pressed his arm around her throat, sending a new flash of panic through her. He could kill her easily in that position.

"I never meant to. My intention was…" William said, his voice getting louder and more desperate.

"I don't care about your intentions. What you don't understand is that everyone here is willing to die to stop you from accessing the systems. My question is, are you willing to kill everybody here?" James squinted as if he was trying to find a target on him.

Jeffrey whimpered and Mrs. Walker kicked him.

Beth tried to fall sideways to give someone the shot they needed, but who knew a hacker could be so strong? He held her in place, rock solid.

"Yet you seem attached to this one. Maybe I should give you five minutes to get the codes from your father, or I kill her?"

James swallowed. "I think you underestimate me if you think I'd choose a woman over national security."

He was doing the right thing, diminishing her worth to him, but hell if that didn't sting. She got her fingers in the loops of the scissors and pulled them out. She had one chance to make the move right. She mouthed a countdown to James. He nodded, nearly imperceptibly, along with her. On one, she pushed William's gun hand from her head and twisted, sticking the shears into his side, and then dropped out of the way. Three shots rang out, and William dropped next to her.

Beth slumped on the floor, trying to catch her breath, which abject fear had taken. James kicked William's gun out of his hand and bent over to help her up. She wrapped her arms around him.

Matt stayed on the stairway, smoke still wafting from his gun, while Simon took the stairs two at a time. He blew past Beth looking for Sadie.

"What's the point of having a cavalry if it arrives late?" James bit out.

Simon slapped him on the back as he passed. "Sorry, brother. There were four other men outside who kept your security team busy, while Matt and I had to figure out how to bypass the lockdown. That took us a little while. Anyway, looks like you had it all handled. And we still have to liberate the study. I persuaded one of the guys outside to talk. There are nine of them. Five inside, four outside. They're definitely Russian, but I don't think they work for the government. They told William it was about freedom of information to make him feel important, but I think they just intend to sell the data to the highest bidder. They used him to get in."

Beth pulled herself out of James's arms and looked at him, counting off the men. "There's one in the kitchen."

"One in the snooker room, and William here. That leaves two unaccounted for."

"Everyone back in the bedroom. At least everyone who doesn't have a gun," Simon said.

The women edged back into Sadie's bedroom, and Beth picked up the Glock she'd set down near the doorway earlier.

"Sure you can handle that?" Matt asked.

"She's special forces, dude," James said tightly. "Don't even look at her. I know you too well. I'm serious."

Beth just shook her head at both of them. *Boys.*

* * *

Simon and Matt headed back down the stairs first. As soon as they left the landing, James pressed Beth against the wall and kissed her. Less passionate, more like staking a claim. He hoped she would stay long enough after this clusterfuck for him to be able to explain.

Explain what, he wasn't yet sure.

He led her downstairs and they both made their way along the hallway as if they were back in Afghanistan: guns up to their eye lines, swiveling to cover all angles and blind spots. He should be loving it. Should feel comfortable that they were so in synch in this situation. But it was all a very different proposition when you were looking for your father.

The door to the study was closed. Simon and Matt braced their backs against the wall on either side of the door. Shouts from within carried quite far down the hallway, and they stopped to listen. James was glad Beth had his back, but he was petrified something might happen to her. He would never be able to live with himself. Ever.

They moved into position. Beth crouched down and aimed into the room from in front of the door and James prepared to kick it down. He looked at her and waited for her nod. When he got it, he kicked. Six faces turned toward them; two of the men had guns. One raised his weapon toward the door and James shot him in the forehead. He didn't want to risk that any of them were wearing bulletproof vests. The next seconds slipped into slow motion.

Beth threw her crouched weight at James to knock him aside as either Simon or Matt shot the second man. They got him, but he had already released a shot that would have pierced James's chest had Beth not shoved him. Instead it entered his shoulder with a burn. The pain invaded every part of him as everything went black.

* * *

"Help! Medic!" Beth shouted, hoping they had at least a first-aid kit handy.

No one moved for a good second or two. Then Director Walker's three colleagues sprang into action. Two of them secured the two shooters, and the other one went for help. Beth removed her jacket and pressed it to James's wound, but soon found it wasn't really bleeding too much. She figured the bullet had probably shattered his shoulder bone. She took advantage of his unconsciousness and brought his elbow around so his forearm lay in his lap. She figured it would be less painful for when they picked him up with the helo. *Ambulance*, she meant. She was losing it. They weren't in Afghanistan, they were in D.C. Everything was fucked up.

Liquid dripped on her hands as she bent over James. She looked up to see if anything was leaking from the ceiling, but realized it was coming from her. She was crying. They were in D.C.; James had just been shot. It was okay; she was allowed to cry. She wasn't at war. Choking sobs came from her as she pressed a bloody hand to her face, as if to stem the tide of emotion pouring from her eyes, nose, and mouth.

"Don't...ugly...cry," James whispered, barely able to hold his eyes open.

She jumped at his words and gasped out half a laugh. "It's okay, James. You're going to be okay. Just because you got shot for a third time, I promise I won't start calling you a pussy."

He choked out a laugh. "You're a lightweight. I beat you by two." His voice was so faint she was gripped by a fear that she had never felt before. Never. Not when she'd been shot, not even when her mother had died and she was left alone with her sister.

The director's security team rushed in, their faces equally worried and embarrassed, and in a matter of minutes, Matt was directing two EMTs up the hallway as Simon got the women out of the bedroom upstairs. For a short while, it was pure chaos. Beth took a step back and watched as they worked on James. As they loaded him onto the stretcher, Harry came running.

"James, sweetheart. James. Are you all right?" She all but shoved Beth out of the way and grabbed his hand. "It's all right. I'll come with you." And before Beth could even react, Harry was running alongside the stretcher as they took James out of the house. Matt stood at the end of the hallway and watched them leave, too.

Numbness oozed into her as Matt shrugged at her.

* * *

"You have no idea what you're talking about," Beth said into the fray. No one stopped talking and yelling, though. The police had eventually arrived and taken the masked men away. It seemed as if William had instigated the whole episode, mostly using Jeffrey as a patsy. Kind of served Jeffrey right for indicating he was privy to the crown jewels of the intelligence community instead of just being an administrator. Not that she cared anymore. James was with Harry, who he probably still loved. Which meant she was on her own now. Again. Why wasn't she happy about that?

She'd saved his life, and now they were totally even. She could leave without regrets. And she was *so* out of here. As soon as she straightened out his stupid family.

They seemed to care less about James's well-being than about whether Sadie's wedding could continue, what people would think, and worst of all, what to tell the media.

"Shut up!" she shouted.

A sudden silence descended in the study as they all turned to look at her. "Shouldn't you be with James?" Sadie frowned at her.

"The question is, why aren't any of you?" Beth countered, looking around the room. "I really don't know any of you, but let me introduce myself. My name is Beth Garcia."

The director frowned and opened his drawer. She assumed it was to remind himself of whom he'd written the check to. "I thought your name was…" He looked at his checkbook. "Beth Cojones?"

"Let me see that." Sadie snatched the checkbook out of his hand and read the receipt. She barked a mirthless laugh. "Dad. You really thought her name was Beth Testicles? It's *cojones*." She pronounced it with a pretty good accent. "It means nuts, balls. And really. You're still doing the check routine? You know I managed to set up at least five friends with college funds just by pretending to date them, don't you?"

Director Walker looked at his checkbook, at Beth, and then at Sadie as the information he'd just been given rattled around his head. Then he sunk to his chair.

"No disrespect, sir," Beth felt compelled to say. She didn't really expect him to say "none taken" and indeed he didn't.

"So, Ms. Garcia? Just who are you, and what are you doing here?"

"I'm a special forces soldier, based at Fort Bragg, sir. I met James in Afghanistan when he saved my life," Beth said, desperate to explain to his family what kind of hero he was.

"Now I know you are lying, young lady. My son has never deployed," he said.

"Yes sir, he has. He didn't tell you he had a combat position because he didn't want you to use your influence to shuffle him

into a desk deployment. He's a TACP, he's in the AFSOC—
Air Force Special Operations Command. He has two purple
hearts."

Mrs. Walker gasped at that, clutching her pearls to her chest.

"Actually, he only has one," Sadie interjected. "He refused to
be nominated for his second one. He thought it made him look
careless."

Beth couldn't help but let out a short laugh.

"You knew about this?" James's father asked her.

"I am the only one who did. He didn't want you to interfere, or to worry." Sadie sat heavily in one of the green leather
armchairs.

"I want to tell you what he did," Beth continued. "James
had been part of our team for a couple of months, going out
on patrols with us to protect us with airpower. One night we
were ambushed, and the vehicle behind us came under intense
fire. I left my vehicle, which had been disabled with a rocket-
propelled grenade, to offer the other vehicle some cover fire."
She was aware that she was basically reciting her report word for
word, and you could have heard a hand grenade pin drop in the
room.

"I was shot in my leg, damaged an artery. Despite orders to
stay in the vehicle, James got Strike Eagles to lay down close
air support, to the exact location of the Taliban, and then left
the safety of the M-RAP to get me. He carried me, while being
shot at, to an extraction point, where"—her voice cracked a
little at the thought of Marks—"*most* of our team was safely
evacuated by Combat Rescue Officers." She took a second and
cleared her throat, thinking about the soldier they'd lost that
night.

"So I'm here, pretending to be his fiancée, because I owed him, and he wanted the wedding to go smoothly for Sadie. I guess he didn't really get his wish, all things considered."

"That wasn't anything to do with him. That was Jeffrey and William." Sadie turned to her father. "The one man you should have paid off but didn't. I can't believe you work with him every day, and didn't notice anything off about him."

The director's face paled noticeably. "Oh my God. A month or so ago, he came to me asking what he could do to win you back. I won't lie; I would have been happier to have a company man in the family than another military one. So I told him to make a grand gesture. I didn't think it would involve armed men and a kidnapping." He groaned and placed his head in his hand.

"Okay," Sadie said, brushing off her wedding dress. "I'm going to the hospital. Want to tag along? Or have you seen enough of this crazy family?" she asked Beth.

Beth hesitated. Her every instinct was to get far away, but she owed him a hospital visit. She owed her heart some closure. "Sure." She turned to the family. "It was…nice to meet you." What a big fat lie. Mostly.

Sadie offered to pick her up at the pool house, since Beth's jacket and skirt had James's blood on them. Once there, she examined herself in the mirror. Was this the amount of blood that James had been covered with when he'd tried to stop her bleeding? More, probably.

An eye for an eye. Her debt was paid, in blood, as it happened. But there was a neat parallel to it that made her feel as if it was meant to end here. When the adrenaline left her body, she felt calm. But she knew she was holding down some feeling, something unfamiliar. And that was fine. As long as it stayed submerged.

She took off her suit and felt rueful that she wouldn't be able to take it back to the store. She shoved it into the kitchen trash can. She slipped on the clothes she had arrived in, and placed the bloody engagement ring on the counter. She rinsed her hands, grabbed her bag, and left the Walker family home with Sadie. She would go to the hospital to say good-bye.

Chapter 17

The hospital was a busy suburban one, but Sadie bullied her way past the gatekeepers and up to the floor where James was. As they got out of the elevator, the first person Beth saw was Harry.

"Harry! What are you doing here?" Sadie frowned at her, and Beth realized Sadie hadn't seen Harry leave with James.

"I just wanted to be sure he was okay. You understand," she replied, looking into a room that nurses were flitting in and out of. "They're just dressing the wound. He'll be fine."

Sadie put her arm around Harry and cooed. "Of course I understand."

Suddenly Beth understood, too. She understood everything. Harry wanted to be sure she wasn't going to lose James like she had her husband. Beth understood in that second that she did not belong in this world. Being with James would not help her work, and definitely not her career prospects. Her life would be easier, simpler, without any of this. No, she wasn't going to do this. She needed to be away from James, Sadie, and the rest of the crazy family, and away from the hospital.

Beth held on to the elevator doors, unable to get out. Sadie looked back at her in confusion. "Aren't you coming to see him?"

"No, I've just remembered, I need to…Anyway, tell James to walk it off, from me, will you?" If she hurried, she could get a flight from National back home to North Carolina right away.

Sadie nodded, still frowning, and turned away from her. Beth let go of the doors and pressed the button to get the hell out of there.

As soon as the elevator started moving, she started shaking. It was almost as if leaving him was causing a physical reaction. She was determined to get back home. Leave the crazy here. Leave James here. It felt wrong suddenly, but she knew it was for the best.

The airport was nearly empty, and a heat haze obscured the view of the Washington Monument in the distance. She paid for a one-way ticket to Raleigh and went through security and to the gate.

Tammer picked her up at the airport, and she avoided answering all of the questions her sister peppered her with. She felt a frisson of longing at the thought of being home with her dog again, of having this weekend fade into a distant memory, or maybe feel like a movie she'd once watched.

The problem was she was almost sure she was a little bit in love with James. When she'd seen him go down, she'd been petrified that she would lose him before she could tell him what she felt. But then, as soon as she'd realized that it wasn't a life-threatening wound, those words had dried up in her throat.

She squeezed her eyes shut and willed them to be as dry as her words.

* * *

"Where is she?" James had asked Sadie back in the hospital room, looking past her in the hope that Beth would appear.

"Who? Harry or Beth?" Sadie asked with an arched brow.

"What? I mean Beth." He lay back on the hospital bed, trying to think past the drugs they had given him when they'd removed the bullet from his shoulder.

"I brought her here, but she didn't get off the elevator. She told me to tell you to 'walk it off.'"

He rubbed at his eyes with one hand. "What happened? I don't remember anything after being shot." Then he laughed quietly. "She told me to walk it off? I told her to do that once. Where is she? Can you get her up here?" He looked at the door again as if she'd just walk in.

Sadie dragged a chair forward and sat, reaching for his good hand. "Squirt. Beth has gone. She left. Harry jumped in the ambulance with you. I think she panicked, seeing you bleeding. I'm fairly sure that's more to do with Danny than with you, but maybe Beth thinks it's something else. But don't worry about it. None of your relationship was real, right? She told us it was fake after they carted you off."

"She said that?" James felt his voice fall to a whisper, although it felt like he was talking at a normal volume.

"She said the relationship was fake, and it was over, and we were a bunch of idiots. I'm paraphrasing of course, but she was right, mostly."

It was over? What...? His brain fritzed, but somehow he didn't have the energy to do anything about it. The last thing he saw was his sister's concerned expression as everything went black again.

* * *

It was a week before James left the hospital. A reaction to Vicodin had messed with him quite badly. He hadn't been able to speak, and one of his lungs had stopped working until the drug worked its way out of his system.

When he recovered, he realized that he had no way of getting in contact with Beth. He couldn't call her because he didn't have her number, and he didn't know her unit or who her commanding officer was. He only had her address, but she was still more than six hours away. It wasn't like he could just show up at her door. While he could have asked his father for help, it didn't seem the right thing to do now that he'd heard everything she'd blasted his family with. Getting her information covertly sounded like a very bad idea to him. He sensed Beth would never forgive him.

His shoulder was still killing him, which he enjoyed. It took away the focus from other areas. He couldn't miss her, feel bereft without her if he couldn't move without wanting to throw up. But it turned out he could lie to himself about all those things.

When he'd returned to the pool house and seen the ring on the counter, it felt like a punch to the gut. Which he'd known was some kind of weapons-grade stupidity because it hadn't been a real engagement. Wasn't real.

Was fucking so. Well, maybe not the engagement, but the something between them was. He was sure. Sure as his aim with an M-4 rifle.

And now…now he needed a plan. A foolproof one this time. One that didn't involve his family, climbing, weddings, or anything else.

Chapter 18

Afghanistan, four months later

Beth had come back from a thankfully uneventful patrol and was doing a little paperwork before heading to the chow hall. It was Italian Day, so she was looking forward to carb-loading before her evening workout. That was what this deployment had been for the months she'd been there: sleep, eat, patrol, eat, work-out, sleep. For her it was a comforting routine, but she knew it drove some people crazy.

It made it easy for her to forget the days before. To forget James. Really forget him. She knew that her heart had been dam-aged, but time and distance always fixed that war wound. She tried not to dwell on it…or think about how often she slept in the t-shirt of his she'd swiped on her way out of the pool house that last time.

For the first week it had smelled of him, and she'd taken to sleeping with it under her pillow. She refused to think about him during the day, but at night, as sleep overtook her, her thoughts always skipped away to James. But like it or not, eventually she'd had to wash it, and since then she'd worn it. Like her Purple Heart, it was a kind of battle trophy. A symbol of a near miss, or a lucky escape.

The chow hall was packed as usual. Italian was a popular day, as was Surf and Turf Day. She lined up, grabbed her food and sat at a table with some guys who waved her over. "Hey, Sarge," one of them said with his mouth full. Really full.

"Hey, Monster Mash." She winced at the sight of his food almost spilling from his mouth.

"Dude. Swallow first, then speak," one of his friends said, slapping him on his back, making him nearly cough up. By habit she grabbed her plate and leaned away from what would surely be a food reappearance one way or another. Miraculously, it all stayed in his mouth, and she put her pasta down and started to eat again.

The guys were unusually silent, but she took it in stride. Sometimes meal times were not all fun and games. Sometimes people wanted peace and quiet. She did notice, however, when two of them slid apart on the bench.

Then, in the gap between them, the Airman at the next table turned around. She choked on her tortellini.

Her eyes watered as she was thumped on the back by one of the guys beside her. She held her hand up to get him to stop. Then she swallowed what was left in her mouth.

"James?" she whispered. He was in uniform, but had a black sling on his arm.

"Garcia." He gave her his shit-eating grin and stood. "Never let it be said that I wouldn't travel to the ends of the earth to track you down."

"What the hell are you doing here?" Her heart was racing ahead of her words. Was he deployed? Unlikely, because he was injured. He couldn't be here just to see her; no one was allowed to do that. This had to be something else. Didn't it? Tears welled in her eyes and she used all her willpower to not have them drizzle down her face. *Back in. Back in.*

"This seemed to be the only way to get hold of you, I mean really get hold of you. Not like trying to get in touch with you via e-mail, when no one knows your deployed e-mail address. Except for Tammer, who was being particularly closed-mouthed. It took me this long. Four. Months. But I'm here now."

Tammer hadn't mentioned anything to her about being in touch with James, and she e-mailed Beth every day. She blinked.

"You ran out on me. When I was in the hospital," he said, as if reciting from a list of terrible deeds.

People around them, an obviously rapt audience, began commenting. "No way…"

"That's cold, Sarge," Monster Mash said. "In the hospital? Brrrr." He shivered as if she was a cold chill rushing by.

Beth rolled her eyes. "You were going to live. That's all I needed to know. Besides…" She looked him dead in the eye. "You had company."

Baxter, sitting next to her, gasped theatrically, and said to James, "You didn't. Who else was there? Was it another woman?"

"There wasn't another woman. She was just a friend. Besides which…" He raised his voice a couple of decibels. "I'd. Just. Been. Shot."

Beth sniffed, then shrugged. "You get shot a lot."

People laughed. Shit, this was becoming embarrassing. Everyone in the chow hall was now listening. Probably better than eating in front of a TV at home.

"So here's the deal," James continued. There was absolute silence. Even the cooks had stopped clanging pots. He pulled out the light blue Tiffany's box that he'd thrown at her all those months before.

Beth felt lightheaded. Blood rushed to her face, and she felt herself shake. No way was he crazy enough to propose. No way. They'd only really known each other properly for three days. She couldn't say yes. But she also couldn't say no in front of all these people either.

But he didn't get on one knee or anything. He opened the box and pulled out the ring, which was attached to a long chain. "I'm not crazy enough to think you want to marry me. But I'm giving you this ring to wear. And if you ever feel like wearing it on your finger, you can feel free to, and I promise you a tiny, private wedding somewhere with just Tammer, Jubilee, and my sisters. That's all. Is that a deal, soldier?"

A wave of warmth washed over her. Her shoulders unbunched and it was like all the suppressed feeling in her body evaporated into the air. She felt a ton lighter, and hell, did she love him. Her hand shook as she reached for the chain. "Deal."

Cheers erupted around them, feet stomped, silverware clanged against plastic glasses, and fists thumped tables, making dining trays jump. So much for flying under the radar and keeping a low profile.

She pointed to the door and he nodded, grinning. She followed him outside into the warm evening air. They stood apart. Hugging, kissing, and fraternization were strictly forbidden while deployed and she was glad, and pissed, that he obviously felt the same way as she did about the rules of engagement.

"I really want to kiss you right now," he said, his eyes tracing her features. She was so in tune to him that she could almost feel his touch on her face. He took the ring from her and placed the chain gently around her neck, so the ring rested between her breasts. He took the small opportunity to stroke the nape of her neck, lingering for a second. Beth closed her eyes at the touch and tucked the chain under her BDU blouse, so no one would see her flouting uniform regs.

"I...still can't believe you are here," she said softly, eyes still closed.

"I can't believe it either. Ever since you left, I've been thinking about you. Been faithful to you, even though you had no idea. So yes, I've been in a one-person relationship. I've said it. I have no pride left. I thought I'd give you a couple of weeks. I'd come back from the hospital and sweep you off your feet at your house. First your security guard wouldn't let me into the country club, then Tammer wouldn't see me. Then after a week, she told me you'd already deployed. I've been working for months on this. I've written you dozens of e-mails that I couldn't send. Eventually, I found a delivery that needed to be made and, well, let's just say that I'm going to be my Commander's bitch for the next few years."

She burst out laughing. "Oh no. That sounds like taking all the nightmare duties, speeches and meetings."

"For the next three years. You see what I sacrificed for you?"

She paused. "I'm sorry. I told you I heard you tell Harry you loved her..."

"And I told you that I do. I do love her. But not the way I feel about you. You know where she is right now? In Iraq. I begged her not to go, but she has something wrong with her. She always needs to be this close to trouble." He showed her two fingers an inch apart. "We broke up because I spent every day thinking I wouldn't see her again. I was young. I couldn't deal with it, and neither could she. I love her like I love Sadie." He paused. "I only want you. I want to see if this can be anything." He stepped closer and whispered, "Or everything. You get me?"

"I get you," she whispered back. She cleared her throat. "So I didn't see anything in the papers about William."

James looked at his feet. "I can't believe he's dead. Really." He sighed and lifted his head up again. "His startup was going belly-up, so he took foreign investments in return for a hacking job they had for him. By the time he'd taken the money and realized what the hacking job was, it was too late. Either he had to get into the CIA system or die. Despite his skills, he couldn't hack the system so he opted to crash the wedding and try to get in that way. He really did think he was working for the Russian government, but he wasn't. There was no diplomatic immunity for him; we found out they'd just said that to assure his cooperation. So sad, really."

"And the kidnapping attempt at the JibJab?" she asked.

"Just a fake-out. Along with the e-mails. William needed to create just enough of a security threat to have some of the high-profile guests, like the Vice President, cancel. The VP has way too much security. As soon as the wedding was reduced to family and close friends at the house, William had his in."

"So him blurting out that Sadie was planning to elope was his way of making sure the wedding happened at the house?"

"He manipulated us the whole way." Silence fell between them.

"I'm sorry you lost your friend. But at least that's all you lost," Beth said.

He nodded and held out his hand as if to shake hers. She put her hand in his and he gripped it, stroking his thumb over hers. "My transportation leaves in an hour, and check-in is right now." He slipped a card into her top jacket pocket, "For the love of God, please e-mail me and don't make me come back out here."

"I promise." She smiled.

"And I'll be waiting for you when you come home. I promise. Are you okay with that? Can you put aside your fears of a deployment relationship? I promise, if I do anything to piss you off, you can shoot me. Or sic Tammer on me." He grinned. "I'm not sure which I'd be more scared of."

"I think you've proved yourself crazy enough to take the risk, and if you can, I can." She squeezed his hand. "Besides which, I'm hoping this will be my last deployment."

He frowned. "Anything you want to share with me?"

She shook her head, smiling. That her CIA application was, so far, progressing through the stages was a secret she would hold until she got back.

"Walk with me?" he asked.

They slow-walked to the base terminal, not touching, just perfectly in pace with each other. Her heart was light and so filled with joy that she wanted to run a hundred miles an hour around the base. Was this what love felt like? She'd never felt this before, and she'd never been in love before.

As they got to the entrance of the hangar, he turned. "Hurry home, sweetheart. I'll be waiting."

Beth gripped his arm. "I'll be coming." She winked at him.

"Hell yes you will. Every day until you beg for mercy." He paused, looked around and gave her the briefest hug imaginable to mankind. But she felt every part of it. Every part of his body against hers, and hers screamed for more contact.

He turned to leave, but he'd only taken two steps away from her when she said, "James."

He turned back to her.

"I think I love you." She bit her lip, wondering if that was the right thing to say, if saying it would make him feel worse about leaving. But he smiled.

"I won. Tammer bet me a burrito that you wouldn't admit to that until you got back."

She waited for a second, but he didn't say it back. He smiled. "Look at the card," he said, nodding toward her top pocket. He turned and disappeared into the crowded hangar.

She whipped the card out of her pocket. It was his business card, with the TACP emblem on the front. She laughed. On the back it said, "I love you. And I said it first."

Epilogue

She'd been home from her deployment for nearly six months. James had practically moved in with her and Jubilee. He travelled quite a bit, at his Commander's beck and call as he had foreseen, and he was returning from one of those trips this afternoon.

An open letter lay on the countertop: an invitation to a final interview to be a Protection Officer at the CIA. No word from Director Walker, so she hoped that their shenanigans no longer mattered. The check he had written to "Beth Cojones" was framed and hanging in her bathroom.

Beth had got home early, showered, and dried her hair. Applied makeup, carefully put on the tiniest lace lingerie, with stockings and a lacy garter.

Now she sat on the edge of the bed, took the chain in her hand, and examined the ring. Very slowly, she pulled the chain over her head and unfastened it, removing the ring and putting it on her finger. It fit perfectly. He must have gotten it sized. It glinted in the light, flashing like a beacon. Excitement threaded through her veins.

Jubilee suddenly stood up and Beth followed his gaze. She

heard the garage door open and James pulling his car in. She fluffed the bed and lay down on it, propped up by pillows. She even allowed one leg to drop open, just so he would immediately see that she was going commando, and dropped one camisole strap halfway down her arm.

He came into the house and banged his bags down on the floor. He was already undoing his uniform when he rounded the corner and clocked her on the bed.

"Sweetheart," he drawled. "Are you happy to see me, or are you…" He hesitated. "Are you showing me how much you want to marry me?"

She gasped and sat up. "How could you possibly know?" She looked ruefully at her hand and wondered how he'd noticed it so quickly.

He sat next to her on the bed and let his fingers slide up her leg. The feel of his starched BDUs on her skin aroused her as much as his fingers. "You see, I have a secret," he said softly, moving his fingers so slowly toward the heat between her legs.

She whimpered as his fingers touched her. She opened her legs wider in wanton need. His finger lazily circled her clit as he continued. "Want to know what it is?"

She groaned and nodded, moving her hips along with his fingers, urging him to touch more, harder and faster.

"Ever since you got home from your deployment, your ring finger is the first thing I look at whenever I see you."

At his words, a flood of love, longing, and desire radiated through her. She whispered his name as he leaned down to kiss her. His tongue touched her lips, her teeth, and then her tongue, lightly sucking on it. With his other hand, he pulled down her camisole a fraction, so he could circle his cold fingers around her nipple. As he increased the pressure on her clit and dipped his head to taste her breast, she tensed under him.

He raised his head. "So the question is…" His touch between her legs increased in speed and force, making her pelvis jerk off the mattress to meet it.

She felt the beautiful warm wave of orgasm start building, and just as she reached the crest, he finally asked, "Will you marry me?"

Please turn the page for a preview of the next book
in the Alpha Ops series

Pushing the Limit

Available Winter 2014

Iraq, present day

Harry lightly fingered the artifact in her pocket as she watched her grad students at work. Okay, she was pretty sure it wasn't an important artifact, historically anyway. But it was still an unusual find.

About three inches square, it was a piece of metal with embossed numbers. When she'd taken a photo and sent it to her lab, they had discovered the numbers were a code for an aircraft part. A military aircraft part.

She wondered if the piece had fallen from the sky, or if there had been a plane crash, or if it was just incidental detritus. As an archaeologist, she was very aware that the discovery of one artifact didn't necessarily mean the rest of it was close by. Someone could have dropped it. Or sold it to someone who'd dropped it.

But to be safe, she'd e-mailed her friend Sadie at the Department of Defense, and passed on word of her discovery. It was out of her hands now, but she couldn't help rubbing the piece of metal. It had become a touchstone. A talisman.

She pressed a button on her walkie-talkie. "That's the farthest north side of our site, so mark that, please." Molly and Jason pulled small red flags from their backpacks and placed them at intervals along the line of sight.

Harry checked the laptop and stopped them. "That's the western border, there." She did the same when they reached the other two sides of their site and then called them back. They hopped on their little ATV, and Harry smiled when she saw Molly wrap her arms firmly around Jason's waist. Molly had driven the ATV a hundred times before and definitely did not need to hold on to anyone. Maybe recruiting Jason was more than just a good thing for Harry's company.

She handed them bottles of water from the cooler when they got back to their small lab-trailer pop-up to the south of the site. Then she threw one at Mueen, who sat on top of the trailer. He was their armed security guard. Quiet, unassuming, with a slight American accent borne of study at U Penn, he was ever vigilant for problems, looters, or anyone that he deemed a threat to the team.

Harry had worked with him before, on her first visit to Iraq. He and his wife had been pillars of strength for her, coming for the first time to the country where her husband had died. And thanks to them, she'd felt almost at home here. She'd been delighted and excited when she'd heard she'd been chosen for this job, mostly because she could see her friends again.

"The site doesn't seem very big," Jason said.

Harry smiled at the newbie. "It's plenty big for the three of us, trust me."

"But we're not excavating or anything, are we?" he asked, sitting on the blue and white cooler and taking a hefty slug of water.

Harry pulled up an image on the laptop and swiveled the

screen so it faced them. "We will be working the site in a grid. In each square, we will take samples, survey for anomalies, and do a cursory check for surface artifacts. In places I've marked, here and here, we will auger boreholes to test the composition of the earth. At the end of the two weeks, we'll use geo-phys across the whole site. That's all we're here for this time. If we find something interesting, chances are we'll be invited back to investigate further before the team of university archaeologists takes over. And if we don't, we'll still have earned our money."

Her Blackberry pinged and she elected to check her e-mails inside the cool trailer. Harry left the students chatting outside about how to attack the grid in the most efficient way, and escaped inside. She was actually itching to get back to their hotel this evening. She hadn't slept well since she'd found the piece of aircraft part right where they had set up the trailer. Above all things, she wanted a long sleep.

The inbound e-mail was from Sadie, telling her that the Pentagon was sending an advance man from the JPAC team in Hawaii to look at the site. Sadie explained that the people at JPAC were in charge of finding the remains of U.S. military service members and bringing them back to their families.

Harry closed the e-mail and shivered. This was the last thing she needed. But as someone who had lost a husband to war, she couldn't begrudge the man access to the site. She hoped the artifact was just an anomaly. That a downed aircraft wasn't hiding in the dunes somewhere. Immediately shame flushed through her body, but her priority was to her client, a foundation that funded important archaeological digs for universities. The U.S. government definitely didn't have any authority over her work here, and she didn't want to be put in a position where she'd have to choose between her work and a grieving family.

She knew how slowly the military worked, so she hoped the advance man wouldn't be here until they had finished. She closed her e-mail when her eyes started blurring. Sleep. She really needed sleep. Time to wrap today up.

There was a knock at the door. Mueen. Jason and Molly would have just burst in. She grabbed her backpack and the padlock for the door, and opened it. Indeed, it was Mueen, and as always, he'd anticipated her every need.

"Are you ready to leave, madam?" he asked.

"We are." She turned to the others. "Let's load the truck and go back to the hotel. I, for one, need an early night."

They visibly brightened, and she wondered if they were planning on spending their personal time together. Her mind skipped back three months to Sadie's wedding. And Matt. The man she'd very nearly had sex with in a city restaurant's garden. He'd been outstanding. Really outstanding. Handsome, charming, a real player too, yet strangely he hadn't tried to have sex with her. But that night still lived on in her daydreams. She sighed. Maybe she'd dream about him tonight. Kill two birds with one stone: the need for sleep and the need for sex.

But by the time they got back, had eaten, and gone to their rooms, sleep evaded her yet again. If she believed in curses, she would have thought the metal on her bedside table was hexing her sleep abilities. The only other time sleep had evaded her for weeks was just after Danny had died. For weeks, every time she closed her eyes, all she saw was his smiling face and then an explosion as he evaporated into thin air. *The pretty pink mist as he evaporated.*

Gah. She sat up in the dark and pulled on a long-sleeved t-shirt and jeans, and quickly braided her hair. Maybe a brandy in the hotel bar would help.

* * *

Air Force Senior Master Sergeant Matt Stanning stretched as he got off the army transport he'd hitched a ride on. As the humidity of the night settled heavily on his body and the familiar smell of Iraq's dusty air assaulted his senses, he tensed. He hadn't been back since his last tour as part of an Explosive Ordinance Disposal team. His tour in the Iraq theater had ended the week after they'd gathered the pieces of his best friend Danny Markowitz and transported what parts of him they could find back to the U.S.

He'd been on his way back from a conference in Kuala Lumpur when they'd asked him to stop by here and check out something an archaeologist had found that suggested there may have been a downed military aircraft there. He doubted it strongly, since none of the records he'd looked at during his flight reported any unrecovered American plane crashes. Fucking checking the box; that's all he was here for. And he couldn't think of a worse place to come for a pointless exercise. He heaved his pack onto his back and tried to ignore the crush of people in the arrivals area, the constant clamor of noise that crept up his spine like a desert viper.

"Boomer! Boomer!" A voice penetrated the fog that was settling around his brain. He was slow to react to the old call sign, but not slow to react to the hand on his arm. In a second he'd dropped his bag, grabbed the hand with his, and spun out so the person attached to the hand was now facing away from him with his arm twisted halfway up his back.

"Damn it, Boomer. Let me go," the man hissed, trying to look behind him.

In a flash Matt recognized David Church and let him go. "Sweet hell, Nitro. You don't grab someone like that."

David rubbed his shoulder. "Yeah, sorry. I've been out of uniform too long, apparently."

"Jesus." Matt dragged his hand over his face, unwilling to admit his fight instinct was still front and center. "What are you doing here?" Matt asked, grabbing his pack and then steering them through the throng of passengers and greeters who were now very definitely interested in the two men.

When they reached the relative calm of the taxi rank, Church filled him in. "I went private, man. I'm in MGL Security. We're contracted to look after you guys in-country."

"Well, it's good to see you, brother, but I don't need a security detail. I'm my own security detail."

"You don't say," Nitro said, rubbing his shoulder again. "I'm going to fuck you up if you damaged a nerve."

There was a pause and then the two men laughed and briefly hugged, thumping fists on each other's backs. "It's good to see you, too," Church said. "It's been too long. What was it? 2005?" He shook his head. "That was some fucked up shit. Danny, man. What the fuck." He sighed.

This was absolutely, one hundred percent not the conversation he wanted to have here and now. "Hey. Everything was fucked up. It was a long time ago. Things change."

Church pointed to a black Suburban. "This is my ride. It's bulletproof," he reassured as he got in the driver's seat.

Shit on a stick. Talk about sticking out like a frigging sore thumb. He'd planned on getting an average, beat up, barely running cab to the hotel. And this? This was not subtle.

"Too fucking right it's bulletproof. You're like a moving target. Nothing says invading American quite like a big American car. Jesus, Nitro. What happened to you?"

Church put on a pair of aviators, pulled a toothpick from

behind his ear and stuck it in his mouth, all the while grinning at Matt's discomfort. "I'll tell you what happened. I sold out for the big bucks. You'll never get rich sticking it out as an enlisted troop."

Matt watched the street scene as they left the airport complex. As soon as they got outside, arid desert stretched as far as he could see. His fists clenched. It was along roads like these that insurgents set bombs in cars, old deflated soccer balls, children's toys…or just barely buried by the blowing sand. It was the ball that had got Danny.

"I have some gear for you in the back." Church said.

Matt turned in his seat and looked at the large sports bag. "Any booze?"

"Two Glocks, fifteen clips, a rifle and mags, a Canadian ID, just in case you get taken, a bottle of Jack Daniel's best and a satellite phone. Hold down the pound key to get a direct line to me."

"You're not going to babysit me?"

"Nah. I was told to hold back, come when needed. I guess they figured you could take care of yourself."

"God bless you, Nitro."

"For the phone?"

"For the JD."

Church grinned back at him and offered a fist to bump. Matt hesitated and then complied. They both laughed again. Man, he wished his whole team could be back together, but they'd never had so much as a reunion after Danny had died. Would have been weird.

"I already checked you into your room at the hotel, and we swept the room. Everything looked fine."

"Thanks, but my mission here isn't covert, or even important. Just liaising on a rumor. You know I'm with JPAC now, right?"

"They briefed me. When did you leave EOD?"

"A few years back. You know how it goes. A man my age can't live on adrenaline alone."

"I definitely get that, brother. So what do you live on now?" he asked as he pulled into the hotel's dusty driveway.

"Women. JD. A satisfying job." It sounded weak even to him. But as he thought briefly about women, Henrietta came to mind—in the rain, sitting on top of him and leaning back to feel the rain on her body. She was an archaeologist. Maybe he could use that as an excuse to call her. Get her number from Simon and Sadie, and say he needed her professional advice.

Food for thought.

Church handed him his room key. "Number thirteen. Figured fewer people would have been in it."

Matt took the key with a low laugh. No one was more superstitious than an EOD technician. He stood in the doorway of the Suburban and hesitated before he closed it. "Let's get together for a drink before I head off again."

"Hit the pound key, baby!" Nitro said as he revved the engine.

He slammed the door and watched Church roar off, sunglasses still on despite the onset of dusk.

A gust of wind followed in his wake. Strong enough to make Matt wince and turn away from the splatter of sand against his face. When it abated, he looked at the sky and saw the telltale fast-moving clouds across the moon.

A storm was brewing.

* * *

Harry sat in the corner of the bar sipping a glass of red wine, face to the wall. The hotel only really catered to foreign workers and she had no wish to attract anyone's attention. She flipped over her black Megellin Foundation folder and reexamined the briefing she'd been given on their project requirements for her and her team. Now that they'd staked their area, she rethought the plan she'd given Jason and Molly. Their first whole day there tomorrow would now be geo-phys, instead of leaving that until last. She hoped that the results from the ground-penetrating radar that scanned three feet under the surface would head the military off at the pass, and they could get on with their work.

She turned her attention back to the briefing pack. It was a slightly unusual remit. They weren't asking her to age any artifacts, just to scan the area and report back. It was a little strange, but their money was good. Less work for more money...well, it didn't happen often.

Recrossing her legs under the table, she drained the last of the wine. It was nearly midnight. God only knew why she couldn't sleep. She was too used to travelling to be bothered by jetlag. She was so sleepy, yet unable to sleep.

"Can I buy you a cocktail...Henrietta?"

She jumped and turned around. She blinked in disbelief. "Matt?"

"You are a sight for sore eyes, darlin', and I mean that literally." He slid into the booth next to her, making her shift around to face him. His eyes were so red they looked like they'd been sandblasted.

"What are you doing here?" Briefly she wondered if she was hallucinating, or dreaming. But no. He leaned in and kissed her cheek and she could smell his skin, all soapy musk. Definitely not an apparition. Her heart rate made a definite uptick.

"I could say the same of you. I was literally thinking about you as I arrived here, and an hour later, here you are. It's like I picked up a genie on my travels."

"I don't understand…" Harry shook her head, almost in a daze.

He took a swallow of his beer. "I want to make a comment about all the gin joints in all the world, but I guess I stumbled into yours, not the other way around."

Harry bit back a smile. "You know you didn't have to come here. If you'd wanted to take me out for a drink you could have just asked."

"But this is so much more fun than just asking Simon for your number, isn't it." Crazy. Surely this was too much of a coincidence.

"Seriously, what do you do that would bring you here?" she asked, still wondering about being asleep, or dreaming…or hallucinating, come to that.

He looked serious for a second. "I can't really tell you." He looked at her as if he were trying to gauge her reaction to his non-response.

"Do you work for the government?" She frowned, trying to make sense of the whole situation. "Wait. You must do something like that. Didn't you help with the attack at Sadie and Simon's aborted wedding? I was stuck in the bathroom most of the time, but I think I heard…that *was* you, wasn't it?" Sadie and Simon's wedding, the day after the rehearsal dinner where they'd met, hadn't exactly gone off smoothly. In the end it didn't happen at all. Armed gunmen had stormed the house and that kind of put an end to any thoughts of a romantic wedding. Not to mention the bride's brother had been shot.

"Funny." He nodded slowly, taking a deliberate pause. "I was there, all right. Just in time to see you running off with the brother of the bride."

Urgh. She cringed. "Yes. That wasn't my finest moment. It really wasn't what it looked like."

"So you weren't completely devastated at the thought that you might lose him?"

She paused. "I wasn't devastated. James being shot…shocked me. But I realize now that it was just that: shock. I thought it was something else, but it wasn't." Hell. She looked at her glass. *In vino veritas.* She wanted to admit that she hadn't really felt anything after the initial shock dissipated. But she also didn't want him to think of her as that…cold. She changed the subject. "So *are* you with the government?"

"I am. Do you trust me now?" He gave that player smile that had so intrigued her at the rehearsal dinner.

She relaxed into the corner between the vinyl cushion of her booth seat and the wall. "Not even slightly," she said. "And you can get me another red wine, if you're up." She looked at him, still seated.

A split second later he realized what she meant and he jumped up. "I'm up. I'm up."

Harry felt a frisson of pleasure rush through her as she watched him at the bar. Of all the gin joints, indeed. Maybe this would mean they could actually seal the deal this time. And she was only in Iraq for two weeks, so she wouldn't have to declare everlasting love or anything unsavory like that. No awkward conversations explaining that she'd already met, and lost the love of her life, that she wasn't looking for love or commitment, white picket fences or happy families. For a second she remembered the feel of his hands and eyes on her, being practically naked for him in the garden, in the rain.

He returned with her wine and this time sat opposite her. He jumped straight in. "You told me you're an archaeologist, right? What are you excavating here?"

"Nothing. We're just doing some forward prep work for a

foundation that finances student archaeological digs. Obviously the students have a finite time in which they can work and get credits outside of the classroom, so occasionally my company takes the job of surveying and prepping a site for them." Slowly, she swirled her wine about the glass, thinking about the shard of metal that they'd found just setting up the trailer on the site.

He cleared his throat. "Have you found anything interesting? Anything to report?" The question was breezy, casual even, but she immediately knew who he was and why he was there.

Ah-ha. "What kind of thing do you mean?" she asked, probing. He leaned back in his chair and smiled.

"You're my liaison?"

* * *

Bingo. And boy was he up for a bit of liaising. "I guess I am. You haven't told anyone about your discovery, have you?" Instinctively his eyes flickered from one barfly to the next, checking their level of interest in either Henrietta or him.

"God, no. My assistants and our security guard know, but they know better than to tell anyone. Anything we find, be it ancient or modern, is kept secret until it can be secured from looters or other...interested people. It's an absolutely normal protocol in my line of work." She frowned.

"That's good. That's the same SOP as we have. No one talks about anything until we can secure it." He drank some beer.

"I thought maybe I'd have a couple of weeks before someone came," she said.

"Normally it would take that long, maybe longer. Usually there is a whole process to go through before we set boots on the ground. But I have an Iraqi visa, and I was in Kuala Lumpur at a conference, so they just diverted me here on the way back."

"You've been to Iraq before?" Her fingers slid around the glass, barely touching it, and he felt it as if she was tracing those designs on his skin. His dick twitched in his pants. *Really?* Shit, he hadn't slept for thirty hours and he was still interested?

"Of course. We had a war here not so long ago. You?"

"Once before. I was part of a dig close to Ur, southeast of here."

"I know Ur. The ziggurat, right?" He remembered the huge, stepped, pyramid-like building outside town.

She grinned. "Wow, a soldier who knows the ziggurat. Beautiful, isn't it?"

"I'm an airman," he said, "And yes, it was. Agatha Christie wrote some of her books there, right? While her husband excavated?" He could swear her face fell a little when he said he was an airman. Strange. Most women heard that and thought "fighter pilot." He'd gotten a lot of ass because of *Top Gun*.

"Yes, she did," she replied absently.

He steadied her hand that was now tapping on the table by placing his on top of it. "Are you okay?" Her skin was velvet under his fingers. He wanted to relive that night in the garden, her wet body driving him crazy. He thanked God he'd been given this second chance to possess her, to close the deal once and for all. The opportunity to get her out of his system, because hell had she been in his system since he'd met her.

"I'm fine. Just tired." She looked up and smiled. "I am happy to see you, though. How long are you planning on staying?"

"Depends. Maybe just tonight. I need to send details of the"— he looked around—"apple, back to HQ."

"Apple?"

"First thing that came to mind. Maybe something to do with

how tempting you look to me." Did he just say that? Well, she was tempting, looking like she'd just got out of bed, with her messily braided blond hair, and a sweatshirt with a neck just baggy enough to allow him sight of a pristine white bra strap. *So she did wear a bra sometimes.* She looked innocent, and he knew she was anything but. Still, he wanted to corrupt her in the worst way. Her angelic looks just made him want her more.

Her eyelids lowered a fraction as she held his gaze. He loved that she didn't demur, or deny his attraction. Try to negate the complement the way women sometimes did.

"Do you want to...come up and see my apple?" she asked with a barely perceptible wink. Her mouth twitched as if she was hiding a smile.

"Yes. Yes I really would."

"I'm in room twenty-three. Give me a few minutes, okay?"

About the Author

Emmy Curtis is an editor and a romance writer. An ex-pat Brit, she quells her homesickness with Cadbury Flakes and Fray Bentos pies. She's lived in London, Paris, and New York, and has settled, for the time being, in North Carolina. When not writing, Emmy loves to travel with her military husband and take long walks with their Lab. All things considered, her life is chock-full of hoot, just a little bit of nanny. And if you get that reference... well, she already considers you kin.

Learn more at:
EmmyCurtis.com
Twitter, @EmmyCurtis19
Facebook.com/EmmyCurtisAuthor

CPSIA information can be obtained at www.ICGtesting.com
Printed in the USA
LVOW08s2130031214

417066LV00001B/40/P

9 781455 530946